FADED PORTRAITS
Library of the Indies
E. M. Beekman, General Editor

Faded Portraits

E. Breton de Nijs

Translated by Donald and Elsje Sturtevant

The University of Massachusetts Press
Amherst, 1982

The publisher and the editor gratefully
acknowledge the support of the Translations and
Publications Programs of the National Endowment
for the Humanities, the Foundation for the
Promotion of the Translation of Dutch Literary Works,
and the Prince Bernhard Fund,
in making this publication possible.

Copyright © 1982 by
The University of Massachusetts Press
Printed in the United States of America
Library of Congress Cataloging in Publication Data
Nieuwenhuys, Robert, 1908–
Faded portraits.
(Library of the Indies)
Translation of: Vergeelde portretten.
I. Title. II. Series.
PT5860.N485V413   839.3'1364   81–19653
ISBN 0–87023–363–7   AACR2

Two sisters keep this little shop:
Jane Memory and Ann Reminder.
When Jane's asleep or not yet up,
or out or absent, Ann must find her.

Contents

Preface

THIS VOLUME is one of a series of literary works written by the
Dutch about their lives in the former colony of the Dutch East Indies,
now the Republic of Indonesia. This realm of more than three thousand
islands is roughly one quarter the size of the continental United States. It
consists of the four Greater Sunda Islands—Sumatra, larger than Cal-
ifornia; Java, about the size of New York State; Borneo, about the size of
France (presently called Kalimantan); and Celebes, about the size of
North Dakota (now called Sulawesi). East from Java is a string of smaller
islands called the Lesser Sunda Islands, which includes Bali, Lombok,
Sumba, Sumbawa, Flores, and Timor. Further east from the Lesser
Sunda Islands lies New Guinea, now called Irian Barat, which is the
second largest island in the world. Between New Guinea and Celebes
there is a host of smaller islands, often known as the Moluccas, that
includes a group once celebrated as the Spice Islands.

One of the most volcanic regions in the world, the Malay archipelago is tropical in climate and has a diverse population. Some 250
languages are spoken in Indonesia and it is remarkable that a population
of such widely differing cultural and ethnic backgrounds adopted the
Malay language as its *lingua franca* from about the fifteenth century,
although that language was spoken at first only in parts of Sumatra and
the Malay peninsula (now Malaysia).

Though the smallest of the Greater Sunda Islands, Java has always
been the most densely populated, with about two-thirds of all Indonesians living there. In many ways a history of Indonesia is, first and foremost, the history of Java.

But in some ways Java's prominence is misleading because it belies
the great diversity of this island realm. For instance, the destination of
the first Europeans who sailed to Southeast Asia was not Java but the

Moluccas. It was that "odoriferous pistil" (as Motley called the clove), as well as nutmeg and mace, that drew the Portuguese to a group of small islands in the Ceram and Banda Seas in the early part of the sixteenth century. Pepper was another profitable commodity and attempts to obtain it brought the Portuguese into conflict with Atjeh, an Islamic sultanate in northern Sumatra, and with Javanese traders who, along with merchants from India, had been the traditional middlemen of the spice trade. The precedent of European intervention had been set, and was to continue for nearly four centuries.

Although subsequent history is complicated in its causes and effects, one may propose certain generalities. The Malay realm was essentially a littoral one. Even in Java, the interior was sparsely populated and virtually unknown to the foreign intruders coming from China, India, and Europe. Whoever ruled the seas controlled the archipelago, and for the next three centuries the key needed to unlock the riches of Indonesia was mastery of the Indian Ocean. The nations who thus succeeded were, in turn, Portugal, Holland, and England, and one can trace the shifting of power in the prominence and decline of their major cities in the Orient. Goa, Portugal's stronghold in India, gave way to Batavia in the Dutch East Indies, while Batavia was overshadowed by Singapore by the end of the nineteenth century. Although all three were relatively small nations, they were maritime giants. Their success was partly due to the internecine warfare between the countless city-states, principalities, and native autocrats. The Dutch were masters at playing one against the other.

Religion was a major factor in the fortunes of Indonesia. The Portuguese expansion was in part a result of Portugal's crusade against Islam, which was quite as ferocious and intransigent as the holy war of the Mohammedans. Islam may be considered a unifying force in the archipelago; it cut across all levels of society and provided a rallying point for resistance to foreign intrusion. Just as the Malay language had done linguistically, Islam proved to be a syncretizing force when there was no united front. One of the causes of Portugal's demise was its inflexible antagonism to Islam, and later the Dutch found resistance to their rule fueled by religious fervor as well as political dissatisfaction.

Holland ventured to reach the tropical antipodes not only because their nemesis, Philip II of Spain, annexed Portugal and forbade the Dutch entry to Lisbon. The United Netherlands was a nation of merchants, a

brokerage house for northern Europe, and it wanted to get to the source
of tropical wealth itself. Dutch navigators and traders knew the location
of the fabled Indies, they were well acquainted with Portuguese achieve-
ments at sea, and counted among their members individuals who had
worked for the Portuguese. Philip II simply accelerated a process that
was inevitable.

At first, various individual enterprises outfitted ships and sent
them to the Far East in a far from lucrative display of free enterprise. Nor
was the first arrival of the Dutch in the archipelago auspicious, though it
may have been symbolic of subsequent developments. In June 1596 a
Dutch fleet of four ships anchored off the coast of Java. Senseless violence
and a total disregard for local customs made the Dutch unwelcome on
those shores.

During the seventeenth century the Dutch extended their influence
in the archipelago by means of superior naval strength, use of armed
intervention which was often ruthless, by shrewd politicking and exploitation of local differences. Their cause was helped by the lack of a cohe-
sive force to withstand them. Yet the seventeenth century also saw a
number of men who were eager to know the new realm, who investigated
the language and the mores of the people they encountered, and who
studied the flora and fauna. These were men who not only put the Indies
on the map of trade routes, but who also charted riches of other than
commercial value.

It soon became apparent to the Dutch that these separate ventures
did little to promote welfare. In 1602 Johan van Oldenbarneveldt, the
Advocate of the United Provinces, managed to negotiate a contract
which in effect merged all these individual enterprises into one United
East India Company, better known under its Dutch acronym as the VOC.
The merger ensured a monopoly at home, and the Company set out to
obtain a similar insurance in the Indies. This desire for exclusive rights
to the production and marketing of spices and other commodities proved
to be a double-edged sword.

The VOC succeeded because of its unrelenting naval vigilance in
discouraging European competition, and because the Indies were a polit-
ically unstable region. And even though the Company was only interested in its balance sheet, it soon found itself burdened with an expanding empire and an indolent bureaucracy which, in the eighteenth
century, became not only unwieldy but tolerant of graft and extortion.
Furthermore, even though its profits were far below what they were
rumored to be, the Company kept its dividends artificially high and was

soon forced to borrow money to pay the interest on previous loans. When Holland's naval supremacy was seriously challenged by the British in 1780, a blockade kept the Company's ships from reaching Holland, and the discrepancy between capital and expenditures increased dramatically until the Company's deficit was so large it had to request state aid. In 1798, after nearly two centuries, the Company ceased to exist. Its debt of 140 million guilders was assumed by the state, and the commercial enterprise became a colonial empire.

At the beginning of the nineteenth century, Dutch influence was still determined by the littoral character of the region. Dutch presence in the archipelago can be said to have lasted three and a half centuries, but if one defines colonialism as the subjugation of an *entire* area, and dates it from the time when the last independent domain was conquered—in this case Atjeh in northern Sumatra—then the Dutch colonial empire lasted less than half a century. Effective government could only be claimed for the Moluccas, certain portions of Java (by no means the entire island), a southern portion of Celebes, and some coastal regions of Sumatra and Borneo. Yet it is also true that precisely because Indonesia was an insular realm, Holland never needed to muster a substantial army such as the one the British had to maintain in the large subcontinent of India. The extensive interiors of islands such as Sumatra, Borneo, or Celebes were not penetrated because, for the seaborne empire of commercial interests, exploration of such regions was unprofitable, hence not desirable.

The nature of Holland's involvement changed with the tenure of Herman Willem Daendels as Governor General, just after the French revolution. Holland declared itself a democratic nation in 1795, allied itself with France—which meant a direct confrontation with England—and was practically a vassal state of France until 1810. Though reform, liberal programs, and the mandate of human rights were loudly proclaimed in Europe, they did not seem to apply to the Asian branch of the family of man. Daendels exemplified this double standard. He evinced reforms, either in fact or on paper, but did so in an imperious manner and with total disregard for native customs and law (known as *adat*). Stamford Raffles, who was the chief administrator of the British interim government from 1811 to 1816, expanded Daendels's innovations, which included tax reform and the introduction of the land-rent system, which was based on the assumption that all the land belonged to the colonial administration. By the time Holland regained its colonies in 1816, any resemblance to the erstwhile Company had vanished. In its place was a firmly established, paternalistic, colonial government which ruled by edict and regulation, supported a huge bureaucracy, and sought to make the colonies turn a profit as well as legislate its inhabitants' manner of living.

It is not surprising that for the remainder of the nineteenth century, a centralized authority instituted changes from above that were often in direct conflict with Javanese life and welfare. One such change, which was supposed to increase revenues and improve the life of the Javanese peasant, was the infamous "Cultivation System" (*Cultuurstelsel*). This system required the Javanese to grow cash crops, such as sugar cane or indigo, which, although profitable on the world market, were of little practical use to the Javanese. In effect it meant compulsory labor and the exploitation of the entire island as if it were a feudal estate. The system proved profitable for the Dutch, and because it introduced varied crops such as tea and tobacco to local agriculture, it indirectly improved the living standard of some of the people. It also fostered distrust of colonial authority, caused uprisings, and provided the impetus for liberal reform on the part of Dutch politicians in The Netherlands.

Along with the increased demand in the latter half of the nineteenth century for liberal reform came an expansion of direct control over other areas of the archipelago. One of the reasons for this was an unprecedented influx of private citizens from Holland. Expansion of trade required expansion of territory that was under direct control of Batavia to insure stability. Colonial policy improved education, agriculture, public hygiene, and expanded the transportation network. In Java a paternalistic policy was not offensive because its ruling class (the *prijaji*) had governed that way for centuries, but progressive politicians in The Hague demanded that the Indies be administered on a moral basis which favored the interests of the Indonesians rather than those of the Dutch government in Europe. This "ethical policy" became doctrine from about the turn of this century and followed on the heels of a renascence of scientific study of the Indies quite as enthusiastic as the one in the seventeenth century.

The first three decades of the present century were probably the most stable and prosperous in colonial history. This period was also the beginning of an emerging Indonesian national consciousness. Various nationalistic parties were formed, and the Indonesians demanded a far more representative role in the administration of their country. The example of Japan indicated to the Indonesians that European rulers were not invincible. The rapidity with which the Japanese conquered Southeast Asia during the Second World War only accelerated the process of decolonization. In 1945 Indonesia declared its independence, naming Sukarno the republic's first president. The Dutch did not accept this declaration and between 1945 and 1949 they conducted several unsuccessful military campaigns to re-establish control. In 1950, with a new constitution, Indonesia became a sovereign state.

I offer here only a cursory outline. The historical reality is far more complex and infinitely richer, but this sketch must suffice as a backdrop for the particular type of literature that is presented in this series.

This is a literature written by or about European colonialists in Southeast Asia prior to the Second World War. Though the literary techniques may be Western, the subject matter is unique. This genre is also a self-contained unit that cannot develop further because there are no new voices and because what was voiced no longer exists. Yet it is a literature that can still instruct because it delineates the historical and psychological confrontation of East and West, it depicts the uneasy alliance of these antithetical forces, and it shows by prior example the demise of Western imperialism.

These are political issues, but there is another aspect of this kind of literature that is of equal importance. It is a literature of lost causes, of a past irrevocably gone, of an era that today seems so utterly alien that it is novel once again.

Tempo dulu it was once called—time past. But now, after two world wars and several Asian wars, after the passage of nearly half a century, this phrase presents more than a wistful longing for the prerogatives of imperialism; it gives as well a poignant realization that an epoch is past that will never return. At its worst the documentation of this perception is sentimental indulgence, but at its best it is the poetry of a vanished era, of the fall of an empire, of the passing of an age when issues moral and political were firmer and clearer, and when the drama of the East was still palpable and not yet reduced to a topic for sociologists.

In many ways, this literature of Asian colonialism reminds one of the literature of the American South; of Faulkner, O'Connor, John Crowe Ransom, and Robert Penn Warren. For that too was a "colonial" literature that was quite as much aware of its own demise and yet, not defiantly but wistfully, determined to record its own passing. One finds in both the peculiar hybrid of antithetical cultures, the inevitable defeat of the more recent masters, a faith in more traditional virtues, and that peculiar offbeat detail often called "gothic" or "grotesque." In both literatures loneliness is a central theme. There were very few who knew how to turn their mordant isolation into a dispassionate awareness that all things must pass and fail.

E. M. BEEKMAN

Introduction

E. BRETON DE NIJS is the pseudonym of Rob Nieuwenhuys, a chronicler of that literature written by the Dutch about their lives in their former colony in southeast Asia. To be such a chronicler one must be of two worlds: of the colonial Indies and of the small northern European nation. The latter provided the intellectual stimulus which gave form to the peculiar experience of the former. Inevitably, the most honest expression for this contradiction would be one of ambivalence because, quite literally, one was forced to be of two minds. Nieuwenhuys has this ambivalent voice and it has served him well when mapping out the literary territory of the colonial period. But it has also left him with a quandary that is so characteristic of this kind of writing and that has provided the impetus for his own fiction and essays.

Nieuwenhuys was born in 1908 in Semarang, a large port on the northern coast of Java. His father was a Dutchman, a *totok*, and his mother was of mixed blood, a descendant of a matrilineal line of Javanese from the city of Solo in central Java. In 1909 the Nieuwenhuys family moved to Batavia, where in 1912 the father advanced to the prestigious position of manager of the most famous and, at the time, largest hotel in the Indies: Hôtel des Indes. Nieuwenhuys received his secondary education in Surabaya and did not go to Holland for an extended period of time until he was nineteen. At the University of Leyden he first studied the particular law of the Indies under Cornelis van Vollenhoven (1874–1933)—an expert on *adat* (native) law, whose writings are still authoritative sources—but then switched to the study of literature.

In 1935 Nieuwenhuys returned to Java where he taught in Semarang from 1935 to 1940. From 1940 to 1942 he was a lecturer in literature at the University of Batavia and was active in literary circles. He spent the next three years (until 1945) in Japanese concentration camps, separated from his wife and child. He did not report on these harrowing experiences until 1979.

After a year's furlough in Holland, Nieuwenhuys returned to the Indies in 1947, where he worked for the ministry of education until 1952. In that year, when Indonesia's independence had become an unalterable fact, he repatriated to The Netherlands where, contrary to custom, he did not settle in The Hague which was the city most old Indies hands retired to, but chose to live in Amsterdam and returned to teaching until 1963. From 1963 to 1973 he was employed by the Royal Ethnological Society in Leyden where he established a documentation center for Indonesian history. In his retirement Nieuwenhuys has continued to produce works of distinction which, with the exception of a study of a nineteenth-century Dutch poet, deal with the colonial Indies in one way or another.

Nieuwenhuys is ideally suited for the task of fostering that particular genre of literature that deals with the colonial experience. As a child, young man, and adult he spent nearly four decades in the Indies. It was part of his life from the very beginning, not as something extraordinary, but as a daily fact of life. His mother used native expertise and lore without the embarrassed self-consciousness of Europeans who considered such things superstition. For instance, the *dukun* (Javanese medicineman) was consulted in case of illness; certain native rituals were observed for funerals and, as in *Faded Portraits*, the house was purified with incense once a week. He learned Javanese as a child from his *babu* (*ayah* in British India), Nènè Tidjah, who cared for him for the first seven years of his life. She imbued him with a sense of awe for tropical nature, an environment the Javanese consider to be spirited, (*angker* in Javanese), and made him party to an existence where nothing is static or barren but alive with a fertile magic that maintains no barrier between the natural and the supernatural worlds. Her importance can be assessed by the fact that, even as a man in his seventies, Nieuwenhuys could recollect her smell as clearly as when he was a child.

This background provided Nieuwenhuys with a sympathetic perspective on Indonesian life, something that was by no means a matter of course for the Dutch colonialists. For example, he could be persuaded of the rightfulness of the Indonesian independence movement when, as a student in Leyden, he was confronted by the passionate arguments of Setijadjit (who appears here as Sudarpo). This exposure was a formative experience in his life, and was important enough to be included in this, his only novel.

Though Nieuwenhuys was a product of both worlds, he was always partial to his mother's homeland. In his father's country he acquired knowledge, and it was there that his intellect was formed. But this was a superstructure; below the surface lingered the Java of his *babu* and his mother, which nurtured his imagination, his emotions, and his passion. As was true of others from that era, Nieuwenhuys remained intellectually and emotionally a displaced person, a liminal man because he could never call himself a native of either region. In the Indies he would always remain an outsider to the Javanese community but—to echo what Kipling said of England—Holland could only be "the most wonderful foreign land I have ever been in." And if we consider those mutually exclusive regions metaphorically—the Indies as summer and Holland as winter—Henry Adam's characterization in his youth in New England provides an apt corollary. "Winter was always the effort to live; summer was tropical license . . . summer and country were always sensual living, while winter was compulsory learning. Summer was the multiplicity of nature; winter was school."

There really can be no synthesis of these antipodes, and one will always live on the margin of both. But such a paradoxical situation may turn out to be one of strength, because the vision is different, refracted, perceiving elements of either place that would otherwise go unnoticed. Theory will speculate about one or the other, and scholarship will codify, but that disjointed existence is really fit only for literature. And then it can turn out to be a benefit for a writer like Nieuwenhuys who may well join in the praise of Kipling's "Two-sided Man" [from *Kim*] who feels that he owes the "most to Allah Who gave me two / Separate sides to my head."

Faded Portraits (*Vergeelde portretten uit een Indisch familiealbum*, 1954), Nieuwenhuys' only novel, was begun when he was in his thirties and interned in a Japanese concentration camp. The greater part of it was scribbled in pencil on Japanese wartime toilet paper. The extremity of his situation appears to have triggered the desire to know where his existence was rooted, and *Faded Portraits* is to some extent the imaginative record of that search.

The novel is typical of colonial Dutch literature in several ways. It is, for instance, the evocation of a place with its tactile and olfactory peculiarities. T. S. Eliot correctly noted in his essay on Kipling that "the first condition of understanding a foreign country is to smell it, as you smell India in *Kim*." Although this seems obvious, it is often the snare that trips up authors who are either not gifted with a chameleon imagination or lack the unreflected familiarity with a place that a child has. One form of proof was the author's surprise when he discovered how many Malay and Javanese expressions had surfaced in his prose without his ever being aware of them until the book was finished. Anyone familiar with the Indies will recognize the authenticity of physical details—the floral profusion, the overbearing climate, the smells of incense and Indonesian cooking. There is a genuineness in the description of quotidian existence of that time, with the evenings' relaxation on the veranda, when, at ease in long chairs or rocking chairs one was entertained and informed by gossip after the long daily grind in a climate that was never accommodating. One will also find the familiar negative aspects: the bickering, the preoccupation with the color of a person's skin, the obsession with one's place in the social hierarchy, the snobbism, and, despite the fear of it, the daily involvement with native life. It was a feudal society, paternalistic, overbearing, conservative, but it was also so much imbued with the Indies that it could never be excised from the lives of those who experienced it, even after repatriation.

But one should not read *Faded Portraits* only as a metaphor for the colonial Indies. It is, first and foremost, the portrait of a family and, within that context, especially a representation of Aunt Sophie. Despite claims to the contrary, *Faded Portraits* is a crafted narration. It is enclosed by the frame of Aunt Sophie's death, and is unified by the voice of the narrator. One could consider the "argument" or impetus for the novel the desire to know why the three girls are so insensitive to Aunt Sophie's death, what form her "meddling" took, and why the house on Salemba Avenue was *sial* (unlucky).

At the time this novel was written no Dutch author writing about his youth in the Indies could escape the influence of one of the most influential figures of Dutch colonial literature in the first half of this century, E. Du Perron. His novel, *Country of Origin* (1935; published in this series), is a fictionalized autobiography of a childhood and youth in the Indies written from the point of view of an adult living in Europe. Nieuwenhuys was well aware of the inevitable comparison critics would make with Du Perron, a man Nieuwenhuys knew personally and whose work he applauded. But there is little resemblance, except for the inevitable similarity of place and time.

In *Country of Origin* the narration of events is solipsistic, for Arthur Ducroo is only interested in determining what effect his life's history has had on him; everything else is ancillary to his attempt to understand what kinds of influences molded the adult who is living in Europe in the 1930s. In contrast, Nieuwenhuys is not interested in how the De Pauly past shaped the present narrator. In fact, he could echo Henry Adams who noted about his own family that it "was rather an atmosphere than an influence." *Faded Portraits* is the depiction of such an "atmosphere." Although Du Perron's novel has been shown to be an almost exact replica of his own chronology, enriched by meditations on his experience, Nieuwenhuys' book reveals very little about its author. Such reticence makes, I would assume, for better novels.

The actuality of past events is less important to Nieuwenhuys than the quality of remembrance. The De Pauly history is felt too deeply to be recorded in any way other than by feeling and imagination. Perhaps in general terms, some of the events in the book may have happened as they are presented, yet it also seems clear that much did not and that a great deal of material may have come from other sources, from stories about other people, or even from inaccurate and partisan versions of these same events reported by people with a personal axe to grind. As an example of this fictionalization of so-called real events one may consider the portrait of Geraerdt Knol, who is said to have been the patriarch of the De Paulys. Nieuwenhuys calmly offers proof of this by referring to a famous work of scholarship about Java from 1600 to 1800. Actually, Geraerdt Knol did not exist. He is a fiction assembled from descriptions of several historical figures which can be found in De Haan's *Priangan*. In other words, facts are subservient to fiction, veracity subservient to mendacity. There is, then, the touchstone of reality, but only to the extent that all writers employ it. For there can be no such thing as perfect fabulation; it is impossible to invent fiction in a vacuum.

Nieuwenhuys has stated repeatedly that he is not truly a creative writer because he cannot invent. This is, of course, disingenuous, for he is not a writer of memoirs either. In *Faded Portraits* he calls himself a "memorialist" which, if I understand him correctly, means that he commemorates a past, perhaps celebrates it. But one can only commemorate by recollection and it is the quality and tone of the memory that is important, not its truth quotient. Nieuwenhuys makes the point quite clear in his book about his experience in the Japanese concentration camps. Although the subject prevents this work from consideration here (because the present series considers the beginning of the Second World War beyond the termination point for this genre of colonial literature), the manner in which it is written is instructive. Called *Een beetje oorlog* in Dutch, the very title is ironic, because to typify these horrible events as "a bit of war" is an understatement, to say the least. The title may be a direct quote from Kipling who, after his first visit as a journalist to the Boer War in South Africa, wrote to a friend that "there happened to be a bit of a war on, and I had the time of my life." Nieuwenhuys' conscious defusing of the horror of the events he went through is both an act of piety (because he felt that compared to other people's suffering, his was far less excruciating) and a method of preventing the writer from emotional and stylistic hyperbole which, ironically, would do injustice to the terror. The style of the book is appropriately sober and unadorned. But the very sobriety of the style intimates that what is told is true, and this turns out not to be the case. "My memories have become stories which, of course, closely resemble real events but which at the same time are no longer authentic truth." He confesses that he has "manipulated the truth" because "as a story teller or writer you can never escape the lie." "The truth" Nieuwenhuys concludes "lies not in reality but in the story." He then refers with approval to the epigraph of his book, which is a quote from a novel by John P. Marquand: "A writer must be an untrustworthy, mendacious fellow who can tell a good falsehood and make it stick."

This perennial (and fascinating) question of where fiction begins and truth leaves off is still vital. Since Goethe's designation of his autobiography as a mixture of *Dichtung und Wahrheit* (1811), most writers would concede that their work, no matter how much based on fact, has little to do with actual reality. Especially if the text is narrated in the first-person singular and professes to be autobiographical. In his most recent novel, *Earthly Powers* (1980), Anthony Burgess has his narrator, Kenneth Toomey, ponder this question in terms very similar to Marquand's. "But the real question for me was: how far could I claim a true knowledge of the factuality of my own past, as opposed to pointing to an artistic enhancing of it, meaning a crafty falsification? In two ways my memory was not to be trusted: I was an old man, I was a writer. Writers in time transfer the mendacity of their craft to the other areas of their lives. In that trivial area of barroom biographical anecdotage, it is so much easier and so much more gratifying to shape, reorder, impose climax and denouement, augment here, diminish there, play for applause and laughter than to recount the bald treadmill facts as they happened." Marguerite Yourcenar who is particularly known for her novels set in the distant past, such as the autobiographical meditation called *The Memoirs of Hadrian* (1951), insists that "you must believe in reality. You can only write what really happens. I do not imagine." Even the work of that supreme fabulist in English literature, Kipling—a work that seems to draw from unlimited supplies of imagination—always began with something very concrete, although he "described imagination as a form of imperfect memory." Such problems of form and the demarcations of fiction are apposite for a discussion of Dutch colonial literature because a great deal of it is a commemoration of the past, of childhoods, and of an emotional reckoning, if not a moral one.

Nieuwenhuys' acquaintance with Marquand's novel *Wickford Point* dates from the beginning of the Second World War. Published in 1939, it was Marquand's most autobiographical novel. It describes the life of the Brill family in the homestead that gave the novel its title. In reality this was Curzon's Mill near Newburyport, on the northern shore of Massachusetts. "Wickford Point" is quite as lovingly considered by Jim Calder, the protagonist, as is the house on Salemba Avenue by Ed in *Faded Portraits*. And even though the Brills are very much an old family of Yankee Puritans, one has the curious feeling that one is reading about a New England version of Faulkner's Sartoris family, or the Compsons and Sutpens. The Brills are also a good family that has gone to seed. They are people not only incapable of dealing with present reality but also loath to do so because they feel that their present eccentricities and their past glory make them unique and somehow worthy of being supported by others. The picture of this indolent and genteel family living in and off the past, who has dismissed modern society and hankers after an agrarian past, as well as Marquand's evocation of place—an erstwhile Eden of hunting, dogs, fishing, and the indulgent camaraderie of the servants—gives the book its distinctly Southern flavor. If we disregard a substantial part of the novel that deals with Jim Calder's career as a writer, one can understand why *Wickford Point* struck a chord with Nieuwenhuys.

For instance Ed, the narrator of the Dutch novel, must deliver himself from the bondage of the De Pauly family just as Jim Calder must extricate himself from the alluring lassitude of the Brills. In that sense, both books are novels of a struggle for deliverance, of the desire to be set free from stifling families. It is also a wry irony—although it may be that such singular families are alike no matter what hemisphere they chose to brood in—that the New England host of aunts, uncles, and cousins could be so readily transplanted to the tropics and the colonial experience. It would seem that Marquand's Aunt Clothilde was the understudy for Aunt Sophie because the former also "wants to manage someone. She'd like to manage everyone because it means that she's doing something." Aunt Sophie is also kin to the Brills in her ferocious concern with the purity of the family's bloodline, which is a holding action to stave off change, reality, and the future. She hopes that her efforts will maintain the past glories of the De Paulys and the colonial Indies, even while Ed and his family are trying to accommodate to an unpleasant reality of the here and now. And the following passage from Marquand's novel not only hints at the title of Nieuwenhuys' novel, pinpoints an era as irrevocably vanished in New England as it is in Indonesia, but also echoes the earnest bewilderment of Nieuwenhuys' narrator trying to comprehend the peculiar distortion which time gives to individuals from another era who, though they might be kin, are also alien.

> It was always hard to think of my forebears as people with thoughts and desires like my own. Even the pictures in the family albums— and there were a number of those albums, fastened with heavy brass catches, placed upon the third shelf of the whatnot in the small parlor at Wickford Point—even those pictures were unreal. The subjects sat in constricted positions, staring at nothing with cold grimaces that did not indicate either ease or pleasure. Some of the likenesses were tintypes and others were the faded brown of my father's well-colored meerschaum pipe.

There are other parallels between these geographically dissimilar novels. There is, for instance, a ferocious kind of love that is called upon by the respective families to help them withstand hostile reality. For however virulent Aunt Sophie's actions may be, they have their genesis in the law that legislates that the affairs of the De Paulys come before affairs of the heart. It is this sense of obligation and of duty that does not allow either novel, especially *Faded Portraits*, to become morbid. There is a sense of sadness, of loss, of missed opportunities, and of the folly of contiguous misapprehensions between family members. But overriding any potential tragedy is the hope for the continuation of the line, and the preservation of what these people consider the best in them, though, inevitably, the hope must fail. And it is only in the final chapters that describe the disintegration of the De Pauly family when they succumb to the danger without, that the novel suggests—but never overtly—a parallel with the demise of the colonies. The disbanding, repatriation and deaths parallel the crumbling of an empire. And this is right, for the most persistent theme of this literature is decay, the spoilage of a fond dream which, as is true for Faulkner's Yoknapatawpha saga, is no match for change whatever shapes it takes, be it a Snopes or the "ethical" liberalism of the Dutch government. And again we will recognize an unwonted similarity between the Dutch colonial Indies, the American South, and a vanished New England when Marquand observes that few writers not native to New England have really understood the area because "there was something which they did not see, an inexorable sort of gentleness, a vanity of effort, a sadness of predestined failure."

The sensuality that Marquand concentrates in his portrait of the volatile Bella who, like a hazardous essence when unstoppered by a man will asphyxiate him, is divided in Nieuwenhuys' novel between Kitty and Aunt Sophie. Kitty acts like a younger version of Couperus' Leonie van Oudijck in *The Hidden Force* (forthcoming in this series). She embodies the easy sexuality that one has come to expect from tropical literature almost with the inevitability of a cliché. It is a powerful attraction, a languid seductiveness that lures the untried European male, but it will not last in marriage.

Kitty does not move the reader. Even in the tropics, a Nabokovian nymphet is far less interesting in herself than are the reactions she stirs in her admirer. In *Faded Portraits* it is, paradoxically, Aunt Sophie who embodies a tragic sexuality. Uncle Tjen is lost to her as a man because he will never relinquish Winny, the girl whom he should have married but who died before he could. Aunt Sophie misreads her caring for a person as reciprocal love, which it can never be. When she takes care of Uncle Tjen she makes him (as well as others) beholden to her, but a dutiful response of gratitude can hardly masquerade as passion. She is a woman unfulfilled despite her frantic activity, and her apparent hysteria is more likely a barely controlled anger and despair. Her pathetic rivalry with Kitty for the affections of John, a callow *totok* realistically drawn, betrays an untapped emotional force that must spend itself by proxy because it does not partake of a sexual reality. It is Nieuwenhuys' carefully understated prose that makes her plight so poignant, for it could have been a sentimental portrait bordering on the ridiculous, if the description had been more flamboyant. As it stands, with its oblique hints and indirections, it is a touching portrait of a woman who will never have what that era and that society ascribed as her due.

Aunt Sophie will manage to take care of everyone with a bitter efficiency that is most likely hatred denied expression. Her sister Christien bears her children for her, dead Winny holds her husband, Kitty wins what seems to be Aunt Sophie's adolescent love delayed to middle age, and she can indulge in motherhood only by practically kidnapping Uncle Alex's illegitimate offspring. The almost frightening convolutions of her sexuality are only intimated when it is mentioned that she might have followed the example of native women and straddled the erotic fetish of the holy cannon in Batavia, acceding in her desperation to the very life she consciously despises. Aunt Sophie, and not the narrator, is the center of *Faded Portraits*, and hers is a fine characterization because it seethes with unfulfilled longings and unutterable despair.

Marquand might have provided Nieuwenhuys with a literary credo, but there should be little doubt that his most influential model was Willem Walraven (1887–1943; see the anthology in this series), a writer Nieuwenhuys admired and knew personally when he was still living in Java. Walraven died in a Japanese concentration camp in 1943. Nieuwenhuys was instrumental in getting Walraven's stories and sketches collected and printed, and he supervised the printing of a substantial collection of letters that reveal Walraven as a superb craftsman and master of Dutch prose.

It must be emphasized that a direct, forceful, and plain style of prose was by no means the norm in Dutch literature. Romantic effusion and stylistic excess had been the hallmark, and the genius of Couperus' baroque style only confirms the artificiality of the norm. Multatuli had been the great innovator and cast a long shadow, for it was Du Perron, Multatuli's apostle and gray eminence, who made a more natural prose a virtue, calling it a "parlando" style. This is an Italian musical direction to indicate that a passage is to be sung or played as if speaking or reciting. Walraven is, arguably, the finest example of "parlando" style in colonial literature and Nieuwenhuys did well to heed his example. Not only was this a literary counterrevolution but it can also be proven that a finely tempered prose is far better suited to convey the excessive reality of the tropics, because the latter does not need amplification. Plain facts will be remarkable enough. Such prudent control, offset by the baroque or grotesque details that are inherent in the setting itself, energized, for instance, the genius of Kipling's prose. In any case, it would seem that it is certainly far better to err on the side of control than on the side of license. This problem of excess in Dutch literature is no longer so great, but when Nieuwenhuys was developing as a writer it was still very much an issue and it benefited him a great deal. It made it possible, for instance, for him to write a readable literary history of Dutch colonial literature (published in this series), and made his countless introductions in various anthologies palatable.

In 1941 Nieuwenhuys sent Walraven the story ("One of the Family") that was the embryo of *Faded Portraits*. After a diatribe against the kind of people Nieuwenhuys was describing, Walraven took the trouble of providing the budding author with practical comments on craft and style, and encouraged Nieuwenhuys to expand the story because it was "a peach which tastes like more." It took Nieuwenhuys more than a decade to comply. Walraven may also have influenced Nieuwenhuys' reliance on actual experiences, because everything Walraven wrote (except for the end of his story "Borderline") was, as he stated in a letter, "mere copying of daily life."

Although Nieuwenhuys knew personally and admired both Du Perron and Walraven, it is clear that, as a writer, he chose wisely in following Walraven's example rather than Du Perron's, because Walraven was the superior stylist. One may also wonder if Nieuwenhuys was encouraged by Walraven to read English and American literature, because his letters make clear that Walraven, who had been in the United States and Canada, liked reading Dickens, Kipling, and Conrad in the original. It is possible that in choosing Walraven over Du Perron (a Francophile), Nieuwenhuys was consciously choosing the second language—English—more compatible for a Dutch writer.

Nieuwenhuys had found his "voice" and adhered to it throughout his career. In fact, it suits his personality, for seeing and hearing him talk seems like an echo of his prose; a "parlando" style indeed, where the written word is molded by the spoken one. It is also perfectly suited to the subject of colonial literature and forms a link with the literature of the American South where, for instance, one finds the well-known example of Faulkner's use and adaptation of the rhythms and style of oral storytelling for his great fictions. The same is true for Kipling in India. It is interesting to note how one's style reflects a person because Nieuwenhuys championed the cause of writers who, though at odds with each other in terms of content, are stylistically related. There is the neglected Van der Tuuk whom Nieuwenhuys "discovered" as a writer of superb letters quite apart from his being a linguist of genius; or Daum, whose novels "combined everything he encountered in his life into a unit and then phantasized a few additional things around it." And, though he had no place in colonial literature, there is the nineteenth-century poet and preacher François Haverschmidt (1835–1894), better known in Dutch literature under his pseudonym Piet Paaltjens.

Nieuwenhuys has maintained a lifelong admiration for this tragic figure, for reasons other than merely a personal elective affinity. This appealing, tormented minister from Friesland (a most inhospitable province of Holland, certainly in the nineteenth century) committed suicide. He was a gentle man, sensitive and brittle, and not suited at all for the horrendous task of trying to practice what he preached in the stultifying parishes of northern Holland, or in the bleak industrialized cities further south, below the Rhine. Nieuwenhuys discovered that

Haverschmidt was not only a fine poet, but also a writer of impressive prose. In his book about Haverschmidt, Nieuwenhuys quotes a contemporary who characterizes Haverschmidt's delivery and style as follows:

> If one has not heard Haverschmidt one has not known him. He made everything come alive with his voice, his eyes, his smile, with his gestures. And one thought that the way he read them, was the way those sketches and stories must have come to be. What was written or printed seemed like a copy of what had been voiced or told. It was popular, artless, spoken, and had little so-called literary value. For wasn't it a literature by itself, one that was particularly suited for the human voice, such as a play for instance, which, after all, has to be clear and distinct above all else, and which demands vivacity and naturalness rather than style? Haverschmidt . . . did not write the way one writes but the way one talks. His voice can be heard between the lines.

It was that "parlando effect" of Haverschmidt's work that was—among other things to be sure—so attractive to Nieuwenhuys. For it can also be applied to his own work, be it creative or discursive. This style, of course, is not a natural function but becomes polished and perfected only with practice, but it is this "artlessness" that suits Nieuwenhuys' personality and is therefore fitting for his work. And I doubt that it is coincidence that—mutatis mutandis—the best of colonial literature comes across with a similar delivery.

E. M. BEEKMAN

I

AUNT SOPHIE HORTENSE CÉCILE DOBLIJN, née De Pauly, passed away in 1940 in Batavia. Though she was nearly sixty, she was still very agile. She still walked through the spacious verandas and rooms of the family house on Salemba Avenue in high-heeled slippers: red velvet ones, stitched with gold thread. Click-clack, click-clack, click-clack. Very quickly. You heard the clicking sound approach, heard it echo under the high ceilings, and then it died away again. That click-clack on the shining marble floors will forever be connected to my image of Aunt Sophie.

She was like that right to the end, just as busy, energetic, and attentive, and always on the go. Nothing really indicated the approaching end. She had, however, complained a lot in the previous few weeks about pain in her left shoulder, stitches in her side, tightness in her chest, and of being afraid at night. She didn't look too well in fact, but no one in the family had been worried. We were used to her complaining—and complaining passionately—about her many aches and pains. Nervous, excited, jumpy, with heart murmurs, rheumatism, bladder infection, and especially headaches—always headaches. It had been that way for years. This time, however, it was serious, although no one noticed. And how could we have known? The eternal complaints had obscured the seriousness of her condition.

The previous evening Aunt Sophie had said at dinner that she was already "dead tired," and had gone to bed around eight or eight-thirty. According to the servants she had gotten up later to check if the windows were bolted—something she did every night. At the same time she had sent the girls to bed: "Auntie doesn't feel well. Why don't you go to bed too?"

"The girls." They were the three children of her brother Alex, dark girls, aged thirteen to sixteen, with big black eyes and timid gestures.

They lived with Aunt Sophie, who had raised them, fed them, clothed them, and taken care of their physical well-being. Uncle Alex lived in the country, near Sukabumi, on a family estate, though it was the smallest of the properties. Although he grew mostly fruit—*djeruk* and *papaja*—he also grew rice which he sold to Chinese middlemen. For years he lived an independent, monotonous planter's life. Uncle Alex was not married to the native woman with whom he lived and who was the mother of his children. Her name was Titi. The whole family knew that he had fathered more children with "that woman," as Aunt Sophie referred to her, but he acknowledged only the first three. Subsequent ones he must have allowed to disappear in the *kampong*. The money he spent on them was obviously less than would have been needed for a European education, and, above all, there was less *susa*, less trouble. And he already had enough trouble with his sisters: Aunt Sophie and Aunt Christien. Always about "the girls." As far as he was concerned it was all right if they stayed at home with Titi, but he had to yield to family pressure, and Titi had to give them up. They had to have a European upbringing; after all, they were De Paulys! And that was the reason why the three oldest girls went to Batavia and found in Aunt Sophie, if not a parent, at least a caretaker, who guarded their well-being with a sharp eye.

It was Fonnie, the oldest, who, sleeping with her sisters in the room next to Aunt Sophie, was up at four-thirty that morning and who felt that something had been going on throughout the night, though at that moment it was dark and quiet. When she came out of the bathroom in her robe ten minutes later, there was a light on in Aunt Sophie's room. Old, sleepy-eyed Midin was already warming some milk. It would not be long now before the entire house would wake up. Everything indicated a normal day. But when Fonnie was drying herself in her room (that child had the nasty habit of never doing it in the bathroom), she heard the door of the next room open, heard Aunt Sophie take several steps, then stumble, fall, and bang against the wall. A choking and a stammering could be heard, but this didn't seem to hurry Fonnie either. Unbelievable really, such an indifferent child. And when something was said about it later, she had the audacity to snap: "I can't very well stand naked in front of the servants, can I?" She certainly had a real native temper.

Midin and the two *babus* carried Aunt Sophie to the bedroom and laid her on the big iron bed "which already had been in the family for three generations." She lay there pale, with eyes closed, and moaned when she tried to sit up.

Midin had awakened Aunt Christien and her husband immedi-

ately. His name was Dubekart and we never called him anything else—
just his last name, Dubekart. They lived in the cottage, and when they
heard the noise, they came right away, still dressed in their night
clothes. It was all very frightening. Dubekart immediately called the
doctor. He came soon, with just a coat thrown over his pajamas. This
time he said little, felt the pulse, and silently went about his business.
He gave Aunt Sophie an injection in the arm, watching her intently.
After some time he shook his head and shortly thereafter informed the
family of the seriousness of the situation.

The doors and blinds had to be closed and the lamp dimmed. Aunt
Christien and Dubekart stayed in the room to wait for the end. It took a
long time. Outside, the night faded and slowly a new day dawned. The
gray light filtered through the cracks of the blinds while the first birds
began to sing. The waiting was torture. The labored breathing, and later
the death rattle: oh, it was "a terrible death struggle." For the next of kin
it was an ordeal. It was a relief when, at seven o'clock, the end came.
Aunt Christien was the first to tell the servants. Their quarters were
deadly silent. The dejected family had sat together while they drank
strong coffee. Then Dubekart had gotten up and gone into action. He
called the undertaker and asked him to come as soon as possible, "to
arrange a few details."

Aunt Sophie would be buried in the Tanah Abang cemetery, of
course. For that is where the De Paulys had a large tomb with handsome
marble pillars and a zinc roof. Even the living had already been assigned
their places there. Aunt Sophie had also known where she would be
buried one day. She had selected her own place while she was still alive.
It was she, in fact, who had been the actual caretaker of the family
mausoleum; she visited it regularly, and she was the one who paid for
most of the maintenance. And it was quite a bit of money she had to
spend. A part of the roof had to be replaced, or a precious vase seemed to
be broken again—each incident leading to endless wrangling, accusa-
tions, and reproaches aimed at the undertaker, who was also responsible
for the maintenance. Nevertheless, these perpetual problems must have
made the grave familiar to her because it—like everything else she was
involved with—was embroiled in bickering and financial problems.

By four in the afternoon numerous wreaths were already lying on
the front veranda of the family home, the big old house with its four
white columns and marble floors. The scent of the flowers and greenery
was penetrating. White and purple flowers, with ribbons which had
printed on them in beautiful letters: "Rest in Peace," "Sleep Gently,"
and once even "Till We Meet Again." The middle of the five window

shades had been pulled up to a man's height. It was as if one stepped out of the glaring sunlight into a dark cave. A servant received the flowers and brought each note to Dubekart, who signed for them. He did this in his own way: slowly and deliberately. At the same time he acted as a master of ceremonies and paced pensively up and down, hands behind his back, head down, as if he were looking for a fallen object. When guests arrived he turned around, went up to meet them, shook their hands gravely and silently, and directed them to the veranda in the rear, where others were sitting together in a large circle. Not much was said, however. They whispered and mumbled a little but avoided anything noisy because they knew that the veranda adjoined Aunt Sophie's bedroom and that the corpse was lying there.

My parents were already present. Mother greeted me with a quick look and father nodded encouragingly, almost joyfully. Otherwise he smoked, silent as always, deeply ensconced in his chair. Because I knew that my mother expected me to, I went straight to Aunt Christien and embraced her. Aunt Christien. In one day she had become thinner and smaller, emphasizing her little pointed chin. Sitting there in her chair, she was a picture of sadness and grief. Her tiny hands lay helplessly in her lap and she kept on shaking her head with its upswept hair as if she still could not believe it. "Poor child," and then more to herself, "she had so little happiness in her life."

After a moment of awkward silence, other, more shocking details were mentioned. About the death struggle. How purple the nails had become and how distorted the features, although these had softened into a "peaceful repose" when death had come, which was consoling of course. Aunt Sophie had also whispered Uncle Tjen's name a few times, and had looked at his portrait on the wall. Uncle Tjen had passed away in Davos in '32. *Kassian*, they wouldn't rest together in the same cemetery, but of course—Aunt Christien had no doubt—"their souls" as she said, would "be united in heaven." Again silence fell: this time a calm before the storm, because shortly thereafter Aunt Christien burst out vehemently against "the girls" with a ferocity and bitterness that was frightening. How grieved the servants had been, how praiseworthy they had behaved in other respects too, but the behavior of the girls had been, to say the least, peculiar—very peculiar. They had coolly continued to sit around the radio, while the sound of the dying woman could be heard all the way to the rear veranda. They would even have found some music if Dubekart had not snapped at them to turn the radio off. Even the middle girl, the most sensitive one, had been unmoved. Aunt Sophie had certainly deserved better from these children! Aunt Sophie, who had been everything to them, to whom they owed their European upbringing! After she had died, they were called in, and they had looked blankly at the body of the woman who had taken care of them for years, but who had also scolded and hurt them. Aunt Christien kissed them by way of condolence ("God, what will become of these poor lambs!").

Only then did she think she saw tears in Fonnie's eyes, otherwise "those eyes were so cool and so cold." But the youngest ones, Joyce and Deetje, neither shed a tear nor showed any sorrow; they merely stood there rigidly and were noticeably relieved when they were allowed to leave the room again.

"Poor Fie." Then out came the handkerchief.

In the meantime more guests arrived, family and friends, who had traveled from Buitenzorg and Sukabumi. Among them were the strange, brown faces of people who were accustomed to long hours in the sun: a yellowish brown that stays, even after years in Europe.

There was Uncle Alex. He was the most striking of all. He had the enormous physical bulk of someone who is not accustomed to much exercise, although Aunt Sophie always said that he never left anything to his supervisors, but checked his plantation himself every day.

He had come immediately after the summons from his sister, because she was his sister, but God only knows how much he dreaded it, and how little he could contribute to all of this. There he sat in his ill-fitting, open jacket amidst the family, lost in his own thoughts. Sometimes he joined in the conversation, about the war in Europe of course, about the quick German offensive (which had their scarcely concealed admiration), about the treason of the Dutch Nazi Party which was discussed with horror and condemned by those who, only recently had sympathized with the same movement. "This we could not have foreseen," they declared unanimously. It was incomprehensible!

It seemed that all the wreaths had finally arrived. The cars were more or less lined up and the hearse waited next to the house, in front of the door of Aunt Sophie's room. The bearers, dressed in black shorts and *baadjes*, crouched behind and next to the car while smoking their last cigarette. It was after four-thirty and it seemed as if the climax would soon be reached.

Dubekart was still quickly leading small groups of three or four volunteers into the room of the deceased.

I was prepared to smell camphor, but the scent of flowers and greenery prevailed. The coffin was of handsome *djati* wood, stained dark and then varnished, with little adornment and simple fittings. The light in the room was subdued, streaming in only through the cracks between the blinds. The eye sockets were in the shadow; the features were sunken. I hardly recognized her the way she was lying there. A typical death mask, taut and glassy, without a trace of previous physical suffering, but also without the "serene peace" that had granted Aunt Christien the needed consolation. The first signs of decay and the total immobility of the body: a state more earthy than earth itself, but also without even a single observable sign from higher regions. In any case, an irrevocable farewell to life.

My mother walked on tiptoe when she entered the room. She had some flowers in her hand, which she put in the coffin with Aunt Sophie. She adjusted the arrangement and then stepped back, apparently, as is said, to linger in thought for a moment with the deceased. Then she started to cry and turned away.

My father did little else but look, although I could see that the sight of death—even "good death"—also affected him, as in fact it did all of us.

Fortunately a gentleman in black soon entered. He consulted briefly with Dubekart who then set the example by slowly leaving the room. We understood that the crucial moment had come. Dubekart led all of us by way of the rear veranda to where we could witness Aunt Sophie's final departure. We still had to wait awhile before the same gentleman in black stepped outside, followed by the six bearers, who carried the coffin on their shoulders. Walking precisely in step they went down the stairs. They slid the coffin into the car quickly and quietly. A matter of practice and routine of course.

There was no noise and no unnecessary delay with the departure. The whole funeral procession paused for a moment to prepare itself, then, without a signal, we moved slowly and smoothly but inexorably toward our goal. It was still warm and bright outside, and at first it wasn't unpleasant to have the curtains lowered discreetly, but it was so unusual for all of us not to know where we were that, one by one, we started to peek through the cracks.

We rode through a strange street. I knew that this was Kramat and that Senen began there, yet everything was different. In the glaring afternoon light the town seemed unfamiliar, separated from reality by its emptiness. It was as if the heat emphasized the shabbiness even more. The few passing Europeans took off their hats. The first time this happened I had to restrain myself from nodding back. We rode through poor streets. It became stifling, and only one wish dominated us: that it would all be over, especially this agonizingly slow ride.

At last Museum Avenue. Across the trolley tracks and to the right, then past the driveway lined with rustling *tjemaras* and we were there. At the entrance the darkly dressed pallbearers were again quietly active. I saw one of them bump himself, but he was too disciplined to do anything but make a hissing sound. We had all left the cars and while waiting for what was to come, we could be absorbed by looking at the old gravestones forcing themselves upon us from all sides. Born in 1709, passed away in Batavia in 1730. Twenty-one years old, thirty, twenty-three, some in their forties, but none older. They offered us ample opportunity to understand eighteenth-century misery. We didn't have much time to think about tropical misery, however, because the procession started to move as soon as the coffin, covered by a black cloth, had been placed on a bier. The time had come.

First Aunt Christien and her husband, and next to them Uncle Alex. It struck me again how enormously fat he was, with how much difficulty he walked and how his arms had to swing. For a moment I saw his close-cropped head and the folds in his neck before others came between us. Sometimes there was a gap, but this was soon filled by other people, who were all forced to walk slowly and solemnly. Together they formed an undulating mass, a swaying body, a kind of reptile, which moved along the paths of the cemetery, the head turning suddenly to the left or right before slowly drawing along the shapeless tail. But soon the reptile broke down into people again, individuals who became aunts and uncles, family and nonfamily, acquaintances and strangers. I saw them; they actually passed me, these funeral goers: white and black, brown and purple, light and dark.

From time to time I again saw the unknown man in black, who now walked in front. He turned around and indicated a direction with his hand. Now I saw the pallbearers with the coffin, and then nothing but backs under bent heads. Everybody glanced stealthily at the touching inscriptions on the headstones. It was remarkable how many young children were buried here and how neglected some of the tombs were. A vine had gripped a small grave in its tentacles, loosened the stones and damaged the plaster. Elsewhere a small Christ figure was lying under a weathered shelter. It was being slowly pulverized to white powder. There was no one to care for it anymore.

We didn't have far to walk. The De Pauly mausoleum with its numerous arches and marble slabs was in sight.

Mechanically we gathered around the opened vault. The last phase of the ceremony had started. Noiselessly the pallbearers carried out the orders that were indicated by a few gestures. In the meantime one of them had disappeared into the grave, but fortunately he climbed out again later. He did this quickly without drawing much attention. His footprint on the dry cement suggested water or moisture inside.

The sun, which had bothered us so much during the ride, had disappeared behind some high trees when Dubekart started his eulogy. Although he was not a De Pauly, he was the closest male relative. We would have been embarrassed by Uncle Alex who, as far as he was concerned, was thankful that we had left him alone. Dubekart lowered his voice, and we could barely understand him because flocks of constantly twittering birds circled around us. As one would have expected, he started solemnly. At first he said something about life and death in general, and after that he wove in a few words about the war in Europe that was "mowing down so many." He spoke as if he read from notes. Only toward the end did he address his remarks more personally to the deceased, but the last sentence was like a formal flourish at the end of a farewell letter.

Head bowed, he stood for a moment at the edge of the grave as if noticing something. Abruptly he raised his head, looked behind him—fortunately there were no obstacles—and took a step back. Everyone was undeniably touched. Apparently he had satisfied the wishes of the family: "beautifully done" as they said.

There was an awkward pause until those in the rear started to leave, signaling the general departure. When we were finally settled back into the car seats, a feeling of both relief and weariness came over us.

Once underway we said very little and looked outside. There is something sad when daylight fades and the shadows lengthen, and on this day it was perhaps sadder than ever. It seemed as if this dying, fading light shamelessly betrayed the slow decay of the long day.

Back the same way we had come, but now fortunately much faster. As we turned in at the gate of Aunt Sophie's house and heard the stones pop under the tires, the long shadows were dissolving into a uniform light. The tropical twilight had begun.

We walked up the marble steps and along the stout pillars through the front to the rear veranda. There was now a smell of carbolic acid in the house. The girls were huddled together in a corner like three sick little birds. They got up slowly and stood uncertainly until Uncle Alex took pity on them. Maybe he was, in his way, moved by the thought of his children losing something like a second mother. He stroked their hair, pinched their cheeks and, apparently feeling the need to say something, spoke to them, but much too loudly.

"Well, Fon. How's your stomach?"

"Still a little trouble, Pa."

"What trouble? Stomach ache?"

"Yes, Pa."

"Ah, they should make *saté* out of you! And you Deetje?"

"Fine, Pa."

"Sure, you're a strong girl, aren't you?"

He shuffled a little further and collapsed in a rattan chair, his fat arms hanging down limply. He first asked for a glass of ice water and emptied it noisily, but then he just sat there, staring straight ahead. His eyes were old and had a film over them. Through the window I saw the green of the trees darkening; I waited for the last bird to call and the first chirp of the crickets: sounds forever bound to that hour of the day someone from Batavia calls "menggirip."

I saw Uncle Alex call a maid. She carried a chair over and put it next to his. He said something in Sundanese and she answered him in the same language with a smile and a hint of conspiracy. Then he beckoned me; I was to sit beside him. After a few preliminaries he launched into the only thing that ever really interested him even in moments like this: his *kebonan* and everything related to it. Did I still remember it from several years ago? Well, at such and such a place he had made a small test field. Through cross pollination he had discovered an excellent variation, and now it was only a small thing, a "perkara ketjil" as he said, to preserve this variety and develop enough for cultivation by increasing the seed stock. Just a few weeks ago he had been able to buy another piece of land, though this had cost him a lot more *susa* than ever before.

How immense he was, sitting there in his chair, occasionally drawing himself up with great difficulty. A real *orang udik* in his wrinkled white cotton suit. I saw how his thighs resembled tightly stuffed sausages, and that the sleeves of his jacket had crept up over the cuffs and the back of the jacket had bunched up over the collar. And above that his tanned face, though it did not give an impression of health; there was something pale, discolored, and weatherworn about it. A curiously formed head that ended in a pair of heavy jowls. The family said that this especially made him resemble his father, but the life-size portrait hanging in the inner veranda showed enormous muttonchops, thus eliminating any certainty. But I did recognize the same light-colored eyes which, when talking excitedly as he was now, showed some life.

Poor Uncle Alex. How delightedly but artlessly he could talk about his land, unaware of the embarrassment he caused the rest of us. His deep voice, which sometimes seemed no more than a low rumble in his body, gradually filled the whole room. Finally he was the only one speaking. There even followed some precise calculations which were supposed to prove a guaranteed profit, but this was too much for Aunt Christien. It distressed her that he seemed so little upset by the events of the day, and especially that he seemed to lack precisely that which both sisters had to such a high degree: the sense of kinship and of the need to unite family members at celebrations and ceremonies, christenings and marriages, births and deaths. It was a bond that lasted into the grave, that sacred family grave in which Aunt Sophie had just been left. It was more than just annoyance that made Aunt Christien suddenly snap: "Now Lex, stop all that babbling, we really do have something else to think about."

Startled by the sharp edge in her voice, he looked at his sister like a big child who knows that he has been caught. The disappointment could be read on his face, but he remained silent. Maybe he understood his mistake; in any case he must have known he no longer belonged in this family gathering. Perhaps in that moment he was overcome by a longing for his home where his position was totally different from what it was here, where he could walk around all day in his pajama pants and a *badju kaos*, where he was free to say and do what he wanted, in short, where he could be himself. Here he had to dance to their tune in a suit that constricted him and only emphasized his pitiable position; back there he could lie for hours in his *krossie males* and look at the leaves of the trees with the dull boredom that had gradually become a habit. Here he had to speak about things that had been removed one by one from his life; there he could be silent and make do with few words because things required little more than a hint. Here he had to express himself in a language that he had sometimes not spoken in months and that lagged behind his thoughts; there he simply spoke Sundanese.

In any case, not long after this somewhat embarrassing incident, he let us know that he wanted to return home that very evening. And it did not matter when they reminded him that the guest bed had already been made, nor when they implored him to stay. He was bound and determined to leave. The chauffeur was called and ordered to fill the car and bring it around.

Was this his revenge? Or did he merely act on an impulse? I still believe the latter. We were all quiet for awhile until Aunt Christien resolutely began to speak. What else would she talk about but the deceased?

And she began: "*Kassian*, Sophie didn't have much fun in her life, only worry. . . ." First as a girl, then as a young woman caring for a helpless and demanding mother, and after that living with a man who was "eternally ill." Tjen had always been kind and good to her, but—oh, she didn't say so, she merely hinted at it—Sophie had never known real married life, and after Tjen's death she had to worry about bringing up "the girls," who—more often than not—had showed no gratitude. Of course this would affect anyone, she understood that, and she also understood that sometimes it had all been too much for her sister. But it was also understandable that the other members of the family and acquaintances had found it difficult to put up with her irritability.

Of course it was different for her—and raising her voice slightly— as her sister she had never "blamed" Sophie for anything. She had always been able to keep in mind that Sophie was "mentally ill." These were the redeeming words which, when used in the right place, could "explain" much and even provide the opportunity to adopt a forgiving attitude. As we listened in silence we felt the change in Aunt Christien's monologue: the emphasis had been unnoticeably shifted to herself. She talked and talked, no longer about the deceased, but about how *she* did this and how *she* did that, all interspersed with many "oh's" and "ah's."

She alternated between calling heaven to witness her own exemplary behavior and then burdening herself with self-reproach. In this way she rattled on for quite a while until, as expected, she burst into tears. Not one of us was very startled; so many tears had already flowed that day and there had already been so much emotion. It was impossible to offer any more sympathy; we were just too tired. Only one of the women got up and put an arm around Aunt Christien, but the others, including her husband, sat waiting quietly for the tears to stop. When this didn't happen too quickly, Uncle Alex signaled to one of the servants with his fat hand, pointed at his sister, and made drinking motions. For a second it seemed as if he would speak, but apparently he realized immediately how superfluous any further instruction would be. His arm fell again over the back of the chair and his face resumed its former docile, wait-and-see expression.

By the time her personal maid knelt down in front of Aunt Christien with a glass of water, she had already calmed down. She sniffled a little more, took a few sips and blew her nose quietly. Finally, after a sigh, there was the long-awaited silence. Only then did we notice the first swarms of buzzing mosquitoes floating into the house with the gentle and familiar scent of burned leaves. It had slowly grown dark on the large veranda in the back but no one felt the need to turn on the light. And suddenly there came over us that special mood brought on by the slowly falling evening and by seeing the colors of nature slowly fade.

Outside the tall wide window the trees stood black against a lighter sky, as they had the day before, as they had months and years ago, as they had always stood there, as if there were no death or war.

A car drove up to the front. A crunch of tires on gravel, then for a moment the noise of the engine, and again quiet. The chauffeur could come any moment now. There he was on the veranda steps.

Dubekart was the first to understand and get up. Uncle Alex followed. First he slid his chair forward, and then pushed himself up from the arm rests. He stood there, hesitating for a moment. The three girls, who had remained quiet as mice all the time, came forward, one after the other, to be kissed on the forehead by their father. He did it in the native fashion: he sniffed rather than kissed. And he no longer made any jokes.

"Goodbye girls, all the best," was the only thing he knew how to say. He also said goodbye to the others and padded slowly to the front of the house. Aunt Christien walked along with him and put her arm through his. She was of course "sans rancune." Dubekart followed a few steps behind.

When the engine started, the others went also to the front, taking advantage of the opportunity to end the gathering. Yet there was still some hesitation. "You must keep on coming here," mumbled Aunt Christien, softened by all the emotion. In one day her face had become smaller.

Dubekart kept it short. He was tired. Anyway, he wished to avoid new crying spells, and therefore encouraged the departure of the guests by acting resolutely.

"Well, see you again soon, all the best," he said in a determined tone of voice. "Good luck."

It was nearly dark outside when we walked across the veranda. A few hours ago the wreaths and ribbons had been still lying here: now everything had been cleared away and the space seemed deserted and bare. Yet the smell of flowers lingered somewhere. But where? When we walked down the marble steps, everything seemed suddenly more spacious and less permeated by the death and dying of inside. Behind the house the sky was a dark blue. The moon had risen. A little breeze brought a feeling of relief. Finally.

2

U N C L E T J E N. A thought so obvious, and perhaps therefore surprising because without him I would never be able to write about Aunt Sophie, not a word, not one single letter. Not because her life was bound to his for so many years, nor that his happiness and misfortune—in short his fate—determined hers: no, not that, but because their marriage formed the link between her family and ours. It was this bond that connected Aunt Sophie to my parents, especially to my mother, and it was by way of my mother that I could reach back to Aunt Sophie.

If it is true that I would never have been able to return to Aunt Sophie without Uncle Tjen, then it is also true that I couldn't have understood her without my mother. And if in the end I have an image of Uncle Tjen and Aunt Sophie, it does not derive from my personal experiences only, but also from the numerous details I gathered from my mother. I heard her stories so often. I devoured them and cast them back transformed, or perhaps deformed. And in this way they did indeed become mine, and yet something about her resounds throughout this family chronicle. At any rate, I cannot separate her from my story, and this makes it necessary for me to clarify the family relationships. Strictly speaking, Uncle Tjen—his name was Etienne of course—was not my uncle at all; he was a first cousin of my mother, but since in the Indies almost every friendly man or woman is addressed as "uncle" or "aunt," it seemed natural to me to call him "Uncle." What's more, I considered him our closest relative, probably because my mother always regarded him as her younger brother, and she was always an older sister to him. The explanation is obvious: when my mother was fifteen she lost both parents within two weeks, and a short time later became a member of Uncle Tjen's family. Tjen, who at that time was four or five, was the youngest. For a few months she had stayed with a grandmother, who ran a boardinghouse, but for a girl her age it had been unbearable to accept this kind of charity. One of many run-ins with that grandmother ended in a nighttime flight to "aunt" and "uncle" who, though far from rich themselves, took my mother in, and fed her and took care of her as if she were their own child. Especially "Auntie"—who was "Grandma" to me—was beyond praise, and my mother always spoke about her with respect and gratitude. Their two children, Charles and Tjen, had also been very close to her, perhaps even more than her only brother, though she always had a soft spot for him.

I never knew Uncle Tjen's father. My mother always spoke about "Uncle" and I have no alternative but to call him "Uncle" too, even at the risk of causing confusion. At that time Uncle had a job with the Credit Bank. Salaries weren't very high, especially not for the position he held at the time. Occasionally there was some extra income, though the money never rolled in; it was a struggle to make ends meet. Nonetheless they managed. The children were always fed and well clothed, and when my mother arrived on that memorable night, they also managed to find a place for her. They immediately cleared a room for her in the house that she was to consider her second home from then on.

Of course, I never knew it in its original state, though later on I did see it more than once when—usually at dusk—we were out riding in Batavia. Every time we passed it, my mother would show it to us. I can still see her lean forward, point to it, and say: "Look, over there, that's where the veranda was in the back, and that's where the small bench stood where Mommie [as she always called herself] read and wrote her first stories." I still hear her say it exactly like that.

The house was on Pasar-Baru-East, and was one of the smaller European dwellings, built close to the street, longer than it was wide, and with a small compound. Even now I can find it easily again among all the similar houses on that road. A tree (I can no longer remember what kind) with shiny, yellowish-green leaves, would have to serve as a guide. If one stood in front of it, one saw first two low, outwardly curving walls which seemed to lead into the garden path; and then there was the entrance which, as was so common in older houses in the Indies, was flanked by a pair of heavy, six-sided pillars: stuccoed stone masses supporting a solid pediment on top. Next came a shallow front yard. In addition to the tree with the yellow leaves there were also two *djeruk* shrubs and one of them, according to my mother, must have been there when she lived there, though the white-washed pots and kerosene cans filled with all kinds of flowers and plants no longer existed, of course. No *melatti* to scent the closet or the bath water, and no pungent *daun mijana* to treat boils and wounds. Everything that contributed to a typical Old Indies garden had

already disappeared by then. Only the house remained. It was already
badly in need of repair when I knew it. Inside it probably smelled damp,
but it was still the same house, with the same veranda in front, the same
row of rooms with a gallery running along them, another veranda in back
and, of course, the traditional outbuildings with their many storage
rooms and servants' quarters. What would have been on the front veranda? A table with a round marble top and the famous rocking chairs
around it. And what else could have hung on the wall but blue plates
with fish and flower patterns, and wooden or bamboo shelves with fleshy
hanging plants in porcelain flower pots. My mother could have re-
produced every detail of the interior from memory. She often told us
about this house, though never more than a few things at a time, and
now when I'm trying to write this down I can no longer make them fit
into a mosaic. All I have left are images, images of what is itself already a
memory. I see big stone tiles, white walls, tarred edges, doors painted
gray, white porcelain knobs and, strangely enough, always the rear veranda, and always at evening: an old fashioned sideboard with some
gendihs on it, chests with thin legs in cups filled with kerosene against
ants, and, in the middle, the dining table with chairs around it. An
ornate, bronze gas lamp that had curved tubing, sprays of flowers and
leaves in relief, and a bluish light that shone far into the garden. And on
this brightly lit veranda, which was open on two sides, are three figures I
never really saw like that in real life. And I can hardly say that I see them
before me, or that I would recognize them. They are merely figures in the
reconstructed setting of an Old Indies room: Aunt, Uncle, and my
mother, a young girl in a *bébé*, her hair in a long thick braid, Aunt in a
sarong kabaja, and Uncle wearing a pair of batik pants and a *kabaja tjina*.
He lay there stretched out in his *krossie males*, his legs over the worn arm
rests, with Aunt sitting beside him. She couldn't have had a book in her
hands because she hardly ever read; perhaps she and my mother were
mending clothes. After both boys had gone to bed the family spent many
evenings together like this: never on the front veranda, but always here,
where they could walk around freely in their night clothes. Usually they
didn't say much. Uncle was taciturn by nature. Occasionally he said
something about the boys, or a few words about his work, but most often
he read the paper until he suddenly got up and by saying "shall we" to his
wife, indicated he wanted to go to bed. He'd close the windows and turn
down the light. Aunt would also get up and follow her husband, as
usual. And my mother had no other choice but to put her sewing away
and go to her little room, where she sometimes read by the light of a
small kerosene lamp.

Uncle is typified by this apparently indisputable right to decide daily when to go to bed, without regard for the wishes of his wife, or anyone else for that matter. That Aunt always obeyed him says something about their relationship, and also about her character, which was gentle and accommodating, always prepared to keep the peace. So little seemed to her worth the trouble of an argument. She had complied as a matter of course with the smaller and sometimes also with the larger wishes of her husband from the day she was married. It never occurred to her to oppose him, especially where trifles were concerned. Here she let him have his way. Only when the children were involved did she sometimes resist. She would especially protect the youngest one, Tjen, with what was for her a surprising obstinacy. And he needed her protection the most, much more than did his brother Charles who was two years older, had never been sick, and, though still a little boy, had inherited his father's broad and robust build. Tjen was small and somewhat delicate, and remained so when he was older; even when a full-grown man he was still slender and boyish. The two brothers were very different. It was amazing that one looked so much like his father while the other resembled his mother. The similarity between Tjen and his mother was especially remarkable. Although she was much shorter—Tjen was a head taller by the time he was twelve—they had the same slightly darker complexion, the same black and wavy hair, and the same oval-shaped face. But it was the similarity of the eyes and mouth that especially made friends and acquaintances speak with a knowing smile of a "mother's boy," for they knew only too well how much the small and timid Tjen was attached to his mother. These two had much more in common than mere physical appearance; they shared the somewhat bashful, quiet, and even tender quality that characterized so many of their expressions. It was as if he grew naturally closer to his mother, who had indeed a scarcely concealed preference for her younger child, the one needing so much of her care. The story of Uncle Tjen's childhood includes long periods of illness and slow recovery. My mother remembers the many days and nights when he was in bed with high fever, his arms lying so helplessly limp beside his body that more than once she was afraid for his life. The image of a sick room must always have occurred to her whenever she spoke about Uncle Tjen: ice bags, medicine, Hoffmann drops, and a small boy in a big bed. She probably sat for hours beside his bed, either reading to him, or telling long stories about the *kantjil*, the turtle, and the monkey. But perhaps even more vivid than these bouts of illness were her memories of the fights at home between Aunt and Uncle, though they were never ferocious because Aunt said little and endured much.

Once my mother found her crying in her room, which must have impressed her greatly because, as she told us, she had never been able to forgive Uncle for having caused her unhappiness. But the most frequent and most severe conflicts were those between father and sons, which sometimes became quite dramatic. As was generally known in the family, Uncle was "very strict," which meant that he didn't tolerate negligence, and backtalk even less. He punished the boys mercilessly, whipping them and locking them up in the *gudang*. Most of the time Charles withstood such punishment with courage and pent-up fury, perhaps even with some admiration for the forceful figure his father still seemed to be at the time. Tjen, however, stammered excuses very quickly and would humiliate himself, behavior his father could only despise. Childhood fears and cowardice had to be overcome by Spartan upbringing, and he called upon his own youth and upbringing which had "in no way bred gutless cowards, but people with courage, daring and persistence." He wanted to make his sons into big and strong men, men who might be silent and rough perhaps, but who were always honorable and who were always ready for action. He wanted them to fit the Doblijn mold, and in order to do so he found it necessary to invoke the image of the grandfather the boys had never known. He showed them the almost life-size portrait that hung in the bedroom, and tried to instill respect and admiration for the forbidding face, although all they could feel was fear or, at best, awe for the eyes that had been retouched and, like bright coals, followed them everywhere in the room. It never occurred to Uncle that it was possible and justifiable to have an attitude toward life other than the one he had in mind for his sons. As far as he was concerned, he lived stubbornly according to a code he had inherited from his father. He probably never realized that in fact this code had provided him with nothing more than the means with which to conquer his own sensitive nature.

As his father had done before him, he also taught his sons to swim, shoot, and hunt at a very early age. In front of the house flowed a brownish *kali* that had *pisang* trunks, pieces of wood, and sometimes even a body floating in it. When it was quiet in the shimmering afternoon heat, he would order his sons to follow him. Naked to the waist in his pajama pants, he would swim to the middle of the stream and then call for the boys to follow his example. Here again the big difference between the children became evident. Charles, who enjoyed this adventure, plunged into the water, while Tjen, who couldn't summon up the courage, stood on the bank of the river unable to make up his mind, knowing that there was no escape and that his father would come and get him and simply throw him into the middle of the muddy *kali*. Uncle would hardly have understood the fears Tjen experienced, but he did have the satisfaction of rescuing him each time, thereby confirming his own power. He also set up a large target in the yard and gave each of them a rifle loaded with live cartridges, which later made several holes in the wall behind it. After only a few instructions they had to manage for themselves.

Every few weeks preparations were made to go hunting; they usually hunted pigs, but Uncle also shot at deer sometimes. He cleaned his double-barrel shotgun days ahead. The boys watched him and were allowed to help, and while he was taking the weapon apart, he tried to teach them how to use it as best he could. Later, when they were old enough. . . . It also went without saying that both had to go along with him.

He always bought the cartridges from a Chinese *sobat* in the lower part of town. He would be driven to him in a *sado*, preferably in the afternoon; there he met his hunting companions, real *Indos*, but also some Chinese. They exchanged information, made their arrangements, and discussed over and over again each rifle standing in the cabinet. They talked for hours about Sauers and Bayards, double-barrel shotguns, "spread," and caliber (always expressed in inches). Not until late in the afternoon would Uncle return home, hot and sweaty. He was usually more talkative then, and less abrupt. Most of the time that great day, the day of the hunt, had been arranged beforehand. Only Charles would be happy and exuberant; Tjen, though sensing some of the excitement, always felt a vague fear. He shuddered when the guns fired and could tell from the hoarse sound that the animal had been hit. The sight of the dying animal, the labored breathing, the trickle of blood, and the glazed eyes made him cringe. And then knowing that he had been an accomplice! Back home, exhausted from the strenuous walking, he lay awake for hours or in that state between dreaming and waking, and he would again relive those terrible events. And because his father had conveyed the notion of retribution, he silently prayed for forgiveness. The first few times the feeling of remorse had been so bad that he had called for his mother in the dark. He heard her answer softly and start to get up, but as soon as a deep commanding voice told her not to, he knew that the door would remain closed, not only this time, but for any other time as well. And all he could do was pull the sheet over him, hoping to escape the threatening unknown. In the morning he'd get up with a headache and sometimes even a fever, but his father didn't need to know that; it was enough to find a sympathetic audience in his mother. No matter how many times he was forced to go, he always had an aversion to hunting and killing an animal. I remember one day when, as children, he caught us shooting sparrows with a BB gun. The way he lectured us and his simple appeal for the right of all life to exist made such an impression on me, that to this day I don't dare so much as aim a gun at animals.

The touching story my mother once told, and that I've always remembered, also fits my image of Uncle Tjen. On his sixth or seventh birthday Tjen had asked for a rooster instead of toys or something else. He chose a young one, barely full grown, and took care of it with patience and devotion, fed it himself, sat for hours with the bird near him, and would have taken it to bed with him if it hadn't been forbidden. After a while it followed him everywhere, even after it had grown into a big and majestic rooster. One day, in some sort of game, Tjen hit the bird with a stone from his slingshot. It died instantly. The uncontrollable sobbing that followed—at first everyone thought that something had happened to him—the plaintive self-reproach, and the very solemn funeral, all were part of a terrible drama. According to my mother, the rooster's body was kept in an old Devoes petroleum can in the *gudang* and, despite the snickering servants, there had to be native flowers: *tjempaka*, *kenanga*, *melatti* and *ramping*. A burial service was organized and after Charles came home from school (but before his father's return), the impressive funeral took place in a quiet spot in the garden, close to the well, opposite the wall. Whether she wanted to or not, my mother had to read from the Bible and lead in prayer. She also delivered the eulogy and in it she mentioned that God, who knows all and sees everything, would therefore know about Tjen's grief, and not condemn his act, and would certainly forgive him. Later ivy grew along the wall, and on the grave an irregularly shaped marble slab appeared, apparently a broken piece of a table top. Coming up with an inscription caused a lot of trouble, because until then no one had noticed that the lamented rooster did not have a name. Everyone simply called him "the rooster," even the servants. Something suitable had to be found in a hurry to be put under the indispensable "Here Rests." My mother suggested the appropriate name "Chérie," though the pronunciation and spelling caused Uncle Tjen embarrassment. He said slowly *Tjéérie* and tried to carve the letters, which had been outlined in pencil by someone else, into the marble. The work was really too much for him and took a long time, but Tjen persisted and one afternoon a kind of dedication took place. Aunt, my mother, Charles, and all the servants had to parade to the grave where the stone was unveiled. The letters were rather crooked and irregularly shaped, but this only made the gesture more touching.

Later I often wondered which story, which children's book had inspired this act. Was it all Charles's idea? This sense of drama and these theatrics seem completely unlike Uncle Tjen. When I was about ten I saw him shortly after the death of his fiancée. He was grief-stricken, but nothing that I remember seemed exaggerated or anything but genuine emotion. I must postpone this event from his life—Uncle Tjen would then have been twenty-eight or twenty-nine—in order to return to his childhood. I could tell about other events like this, but by themselves they are not important and add little to the picture of the child that became Uncle Tjen. However, I do want to record one more story that he told us later on, and that made him blush with pleasure. It is too nice to omit.

Although the two brothers differed in so many things, in one respect they showed a touching unity: both opposed increasing the family with a sister, something Aunt must have threatened occasionally.

One day a rattan cradle was brought into the house and Aunt and my mother decorated it with mosquito netting and pink ribbons. It was probably meant for one of Aunt's friends. Both women must have looked forward to the boys' reaction to the sudden presence of the cradle. It was priceless! Charles became furious, raged at such a betrayal, and withdrew sulking. For several days he managed to say only a few words. Tjen had tears in his eyes, felt wronged and sad, but for the time being he didn't take any countermeasures. My mother did see him kick the cradle in an unguarded moment. At night he added to the simple prayer he rattled off—"Now I lay me down to sleep / I pray the Lord my soul to keep"—something else, a plea to the Almighty not to send a sister. Wet with tears he fell into bed and immediately turned his face to the wall.

Here my mother's story ends; the sequel is Uncle Tjen's account of the "stork hunt." It so happened that in those days many *blekoks* lived in the *asem* trees along School Road, on the opposite bank of the *kali*. They fouled the road and forced people to walk on the other side. One of these storks would be the deliverer of the unwelcome sister. He had to be found and killed before that would happen—naturally the right one could be distinguished from the others in one way or another. One afternoon the boys stole out of the house in their pajamas, armed with Charles's new BB gun. Uncle had taken the pellets away as a security measure, but Charles thought it would work just as well if he dropped *katjang-idju* pits into the barrel. The expedition ended in a great fiasco. Neither the sound of the shots nor the *katjang-idju* pits could scare the *blekoks* away. They simply sat there and continued their dirty business, showing a true contempt for death because the pits probably fell back down without getting even close to them. To compensate for this Charles began to shoot at the women who were bathing and doing their laundry at the edge of the *kali*. They complained to Aunt and Uncle. Knowing their father, the boys tried to hide under the bed, but they were dragged out and given a merciless beating of course.

There is one final story from this time that shows an unexpected side of Uncle Tjen's character, a side that turns up later again: his persistence in maintaining an accepted attitude, stubbornly keeping to an intention. Perhaps this also explains his strong sense of duty.

The "old man" had the strange habit of interrogating his children once a week. This was meant as a kind of confession, "the only good thing in the Catholic church," as he used to say. He was probably guided by the wish to get closer to his sons in this alternative way, but his searching and authoritative manner intimidated them and made them conceal precisely what would have led to intimacy.

No matter how often Tjen submitted to that piercing gaze, by keeping what he felt to himself he began to show his character, his stubbornness, and his perseverance. He would never admit his father to his intimate world, not for a moment, because that world belonged to his mother, and he guarded it scrupulously; even a single word would have been a betrayal of her. He gave of himself recklessly, yet at the same time maintained a cool reserve. This combination of trust and fear, of intimacy and inaccessibility, confused him and made him insecure, with the result that in time he became the quiet, shy boy people were familiar with. In school he was an inconspicuous student who sat at the back of the class, and tried to hide behind the pupil in front of him. At first it was thought that he was trying to escape notice of the teacher, but no one had ever been able to catch him in any mischief or inattention.

The principal said that he was generally well liked for his impeccable behavior, his neatness, and his sense of duty; if one took his high absenteeism into account, the results were "not unsatisfactory." Tjen was no genius and had to make the most of his mental capabilities, which he certainly did. Whatever he may have lacked, it wasn't diligence or dedication. All this made him well liked by his teachers, perhaps even more so because one was led to believe that his perennial sad face hid "a great sensitivity." The principal even tried to find an explanation in the family situation, but found instead a taciturn person who had only the best intentions for his children. The mother who briefly joined the conference was graciousness and gentleness itself. Maybe part of the answer lay in her supposed leniency, although, on the other hand. . . . The principal must have left burdened with a problem that remained unresolved for the time being. They parted at the gate.

When he was twelve Tjen took his entrance examination for the King William III Gymnasium in Batavia. As expected he passed with satisfactory grades; this time he was even several points above the required minimum. But on the day when the results were to be announced and the principal was to address the successful candidates in the large school *pendopo*, there was another disappointment. Uncle thought it necessary to make an appearance for the teachers, but his father's presence was enough to spoil Tjen's joy. He had looked forward to talking with his friends, perhaps even talking with some "big boys" about grades and other things to be anticipated, such as the blue cap with thick gold bands and a gold star above them, the coveted symbol of a H.B.S. student. But the knowledge that he was under those sharp eyes made him incapable of letting himself go, even for a moment. He would have been ashamed to show how proud he was.

Shortly after Tjen started the H.B.S. my mother left Aunt and Uncle to take an administrative job with a broker in Semarang, where her sister and brother-in-law lived. It was at that time in the Indies still unusual for a girl to go to work. At first Aunt and Uncle, especially Uncle, were opposed, and said that there was nothing to prevent her from staying with them. She was a great help in the household, an older sister for the boys, and if she wanted to argue about money, well, she was certainly worth her room and board, perhaps even more, because nothing could equal the help she gave Aunt, they would miss her, and so on. But my mother, who perhaps simply wanted to leave the nest, and needed a different environment and a more independent existence, left and headed for a new life. In Semarang she met my father. He was no longer young, nearly forty, and a real *totok* with blond hair and blue eyes. It caused some surprise in the family, perhaps even displeasure; in any case certainly some uneasiness, though they wouldn't have shown it. But my father, ignorant of such things, ignored the distrust and never realized that he had solved a sticky problem. His cheerfulness, his simplicity, and his helpfulness did the rest.

I can still hear Grandma say shortly before she died, in a whispering voice, and with the face of someone entrusting a deep secret: "You know—your father—is a—noble man."

On the wedding day came a sloppily written letter from Uncle Tjen along with all the other congratulations. He was then in the third year of the H.B.S. His health was better than ever, so he could keep his grades up without too much trouble. Yet throughout his school years he couldn't escape the presence of his father. He must have felt that the final examination was a gate leading to freedom. Once he had his diploma, he would find a job, leave home, and preferably live in another town. Though he couldn't bear the thought of leaving his mother, the idea of being able to escape the defenseless and indecisive little boy in himself was the incentive to make him work harder and harder.

But he stayed home after graduation. When he wanted to talk to his father about his plans, he found that his future had already been decided. He was to take a post office course in Batavia. No one even talked about freedom anymore. There was hardly any change in his life, but after a year he was finally transferred to the outlying districts, to Mokko Mokko in Benkulen.

He sent my mother a detailed account of the preparations and of the conflicting feelings that held him captive. Written a few days before he left, this letter was in more than one sense a recollection as well as a summary, including what she had meant to him. The letter itself is lost, either burned or thrown away, as one was wont to do in the Indies. The tone was "very sweet." With the abrupt candor so typical of his age, he wrote that he would only marry a girl like my mother. "It will be diffi-cult to find a girl like you," he wrote, "and yet she must be, otherwise I'd rather not marry." Years later, when Uncle Tjen and Aunt Sophie were visiting us after their engagement, the letter was brought up again. Enough time had passed to talk about it safely. Everyone laughed, Uncle Tjen too, but at the same time he turned bright red, and he was for the rest of the evening the helpless victim of Aunt Sophie's teasing. What vanity—what else could it be?—moved my mother to dredge up this memory at that moment in the presence of Aunt Sophie? It was easy for her to be superior about it, but for Uncle Tjen it stirred contradictory and conflicting emotions. My mother was certainly too much of a woman not to know this.

From the moment that Uncle Tjen left for Mokko Mokko, my story has to speed up, because Uncle Tjen's life is only known to me from what my mother told me, and she knows little about this particular time, presumably because written contact was difficult to maintain. But per-haps it is due to Uncle Tjen's distancing from his childhood, and conse-quently from my mother as well, who in turn had her own life now and was wrapped up in her husband and child. The little I know—and I must have heard it from Uncle Tjen himself—is that from Benkulen he traveled in an old-fashioned *pedati*, that he owned a horse in Mokko Mokko, and that he sometimes accompanied the district officer on his inspection tours. They were the only Europeans but their circle included the doctor *djawa*, "a noble and loyal man" as Uncle Tjen would say. I don't know how long he stayed in Mokko Mokko. He later turned up in Painan, but I wonder if he worked somewhere else in between. He must have, because there are many years between Mokko Mokko and Painan. In Painan he got a bad case of *malaria tropica* and had to go to Java on sick leave. I must have seen Uncle Tjen for the first time then but, strangely enough, I don't remember anything about this meeting. Yet he stayed with us several days before leaving for Sindanglaja to recuperate in a sanatorium. My mother gave him several bottles of salty *kètjap*, and he was supposed to take a tablespoon of it every morning on an empty stomach. I remember this detail very well—though I only learned it much later, of course—because its "fantastic result" for Uncle Tjen was the trump my mother played against my distaste for this revolting medicine. During the years between Mokko Mokko and Painan—I can't be more exact—his father died. He had a stroke, remained an invalid for several months, and died after another attack. My mother always said that Uncle's illness was "terrible," that he often had fits of crying, and sometimes raged like a madman. Sensing that his death was near, he asked for his two sons, but Tjen was somewhere in Sumatra and Charles lived with his family in Ambon, and it was impossible for them to come. I don't know how Uncle Tjen reacted to his father's death, but he never said a word about it.

When Uncle Tjen returned from Sindanglaja his mother, who lived with Charles, also came to visit. Of course she stayed with us, and even remained several weeks after Uncle Tjen had left for his new assignment, somewhere in Java this time. Again my own memory, or my mother's information, fails me. There are gaps, and when I pick up the thread again Uncle Tjen is staying with us once more: this time in the "new house." From that time on the images assume a separate existence and have their own decor. I can see him arrive and get out of the car we had sent to the station. I remember how anxious I was: Uncle Tjen, about whom I had heard so much, was coming; I had high expectations, though I no longer remember why. He wore a duster over his *djas tutup*. My father went to greet him but Uncle Tjen, holding his hands up in front of him, walked past him, and I still remember that he went to the washbasin first before embracing my mother and shaking hands with my father. I was totally forgotten in all the excitement, but I enjoyed the role of spectator so much that the pleasure of the visit was in no way spoiled by this. That afternoon when he sat in his pajama pants on the side veranda with my parents, I completely monopolized his attention by boasting about my marble-shooting ability and by challenging him to a game of checkers. There was already a holiday atmosphere even before I went to school the next morning. The first few days were great: to be allowed to sit with the adults after school and tell a story from time to time; but the longer Uncle Tjen stayed the more the novelty wore off and the more he became part of the family.

Suddenly one day the news came that Uncle Tjen was leaving. Fortunately he was not leaving Batavia, but he was going to live by himself. My mother had already shopped around with him for several days to look for a suitable cottage. They found one in Kramat, close to Salemba Avenue. It was a good location, because Uncle Tjen could use the steam trolley to go to the office. My parents furnished his new home as a matter of course, and my mother took care of the servants. Later on we often visited there. Usually I played in the garden or talked with Karto and his wife. To this very day I can describe them in detail: he was small, thin, and wizened ("Si Kriput," as he was also called), and she was tall and fat. "Mah" I always called her. She knew some Dutch songs, and while singing them she did a strange kind of dance. I thought that it was all a lot of fun and clapped my hands with the beat. I also remember how my mother would sometimes bring along a gray-brown earthenware kettle with *obat seriawan*. I say this because I now realize that it was the first sign of Uncle Tjen's illness. About this same time Winny appeared, whom I only knew as "Uncle Tjen's girlfriend." I neither knew her for very long, nor did I see her very often, yet my image of her is one of intense feeling rather than exact description. Her appearance was, literally, unforgettable to me. My mother spoke about her to family and friends as a "doll." She was small and blond. I still remember that she had a high hairdo, and I will always see her the way she came to visit us for the first time: in a white lace dress with a light blue velvet ribbon around her waist. Uncle Tjen wanted to introduce her to us and had apparently announced her visit. My father had come home early to be on hand and I had to get dressed; this meant no pajamas. I found this event so important that I chose to wear my lucky suit, the one I had worn to school when, quite by accident, I got a passing grade for arithmetic. While waiting for the arrival and inspection of "Uncle Tjen's girl" I practiced shooting marbles. My father had just come to watch me, when their carriage came into the yard. From where I was standing, next to the house, I had a good view of the meeting. My mother waited for them on the side veranda. Uncle Tjen came first, with Winny just behind him. I noticed that Winny hid behind Uncle Tjen; she had to stand on tiptoe in order to see my mother over his shoulder. Then she suddenly darted out and both women simply embraced each other.

When the initial greetings were over, I was called. I had been watching for quite a while, presumably open-mouthed, but at that moment I acted as if I was very busy and walked slowly, pretending not to be interested. "This is Edu," my mother said, and then to me, "Look, this is Uncle Tjen's friend." When I made no move to shake her hand my mother said: "Shouldn't you say hello to Winny?" I said, "Hello Winny," and that's the way it stayed, never "Aunt Winny." During the visit I stayed close to my mother and even syrup over crushed ice couldn't lure me to the back of the house. Winny remained shy for a long time. She was ill at ease and said little.

I myself was deeply impressed by someone so fragile and soft. I found her blond hair very beautiful, the way it was combed up high, with small curls in her neck. And although I can't picture them, her eyes were light blue, almost translucent. She wore a discreet perfume that reminded me of my mother's scented closet where she kept her clothes.

The relationship between Uncle Tjen and Winny didn't last long, only several months, I think. She died of typhus. I had known for some time that Winny was ill. One day my mother came home with Uncle Tjen, and whispered to me that Winny had become "worse," and that she was in the hospital now. Uncle Tjen would stay with us, because he found being alone at home "so unpleasant." I should act normally, and especially not bother him. He had enough to worry about. I thought the mere idea of his sorrow so awful that I didn't even dare to look at him.

Several days later when I came home from school, it appeared that my mother wasn't home yet. Hour after hour came and went. I must have been worried; in any case, I felt terribly wronged and threatened to retaliate by running away from home, and so on. Just when the *djongos*, at wits' end, was going to warm up some food, I saw the car arrive. It was only my father, who said that I should go ahead and eat. I could see that he looked gloomy. I stood on the front veranda, while he was several steps below me to avoid the fierce light that came in from between the lowered blinds. "Your mother will come later; she and Uncle Tjen are at the hospital with Winny." Remarkable that, though a boy, I understood immediately. I asked: "Is Winny dead?" My father nodded.

But the turmoil and depressing atmosphere of that entire day escaped me; I can't remember a thing of it anymore. Toward evening Uncle Tjen came home with my mother. At that age I was so afraid of grief-

stricken people that I withdrew to my room, and was easily persuaded to
eat before the others did, and to go to bed.

But I couldn't sleep, and when I was sure that Uncle Tjen had gone
to his room I called my mother. I was allowed to get out of bed, and
could stay for a long time with my parents, who were sitting outside in
the dark. My mother wore a *sarong kabaja*. She leaned back, her long hair
hanging loose over the back of the chair. My father had also changed, and
wore pajama pants. His cigar was an ember in the dark, every now and
then flaring up to become a fiery dot. I went up to him and stood between
his knees and, as he had done often, he pointed the stars out to me, while
whispering: "That's Venus, there's the Southern Cross, over there is the
Great Bear," and I had to trace the outlines of the constellations.

I can easily recall that beautiful night, because I have known others
like it. An enormous starry sky and around us ever-present nature: a bird
singing, rustling in the bushes and, especially, crickets chirping. There
was an atmosphere of calm and peace, yet there was always something
astir. That was precisely what my parents must have wanted. I can understand their feelings well: they were bruised by the events of the day,
but were now slowly recovering again. And when my mother put me in
her lap, smiling because I was already too big for that, everything that
had happened that day had been redeemed. I must have fallen asleep after
that, because my memory of the night ends there, and only begins again
with the next morning.

I awoke with an unpleasant feeling. After a moment I knew what it
was: Uncle Tjen had stayed with us after Winny had died. I tried to
imagine her dying and her being dead. She wasn't gone of course, but
was still with us. But how? Was it as a spirit or a ghost, as in the stories
I had heard so often? I became more and more afraid. Any minute now I
could be surprised by a figure or a voice, especially when, from my bed, I
stared into the dark hall that had already seemed sinister enough. When
it was fully light my mother came into my room as usual and opened the
windows. Cool morning air poured in with the light, and all anxiety
seemed swept away again. She sat down on the edge of my bed and told
me that Winny would be buried that morning. I found it hard to understand: the body under the ground and the soul in heaven. I wondered if
we would ever see Winny again, even as a ghost, but my mother shook
her head slowly and then smiled, but she did so too mysteriously to
remove my doubts. I could choose between staying home and going to
school. For the first time I found the choice difficult, but the idea of
going to school when I didn't have to seemed so ridiculous to me that I

chose to stay home. I don't remember too much about that day, but my curiosity must have been greater than my fear of seeing Uncle Tjen cry. That's why I'll remember forever the image of his infinite sorrow: back bowed and, when he turned around for a moment, a look of such sadness that I fled. Depression and sorrow had abruptly entered the house and it stayed like that for days, without diminishing. At the time I didn't know anything about the small drama, so typical of the Indies, that had taken place against the backdrop of this death. Later on I heard my parents speak casually, though carefully, about it; but even then I was not in a position to interpret the facts. For years I never wondered about it, only later did I begin to suspect something.

We were in Holland and got talking about Uncle Tjen who was already in Davos. Suddenly Winny's name came up and the conversation turned to what had taken place between her and Uncle Tjen. I told them that I could still remember her death and the image of Uncle Tjen's sorrow, which I had never lost. Not until then did I get to hear the whole story though my mother couldn't, or wouldn't, remember all the details. She didn't know exactly where to begin, often confused the facts, and each time seemed to have to overcome a certain shyness. To her I was still a child, with whom one doesn't discuss a family tragedy.

Winny had been—she got the words out with great difficulty—"an illegitimate child" who had a past when she met Uncle Tjen. She had been the victim of circumstances although, in my mother's romantic terminology, she had "remained pure in soul and spirit." She was the daughter of a well-known Padang notary at the time, whom I'll call Gravenhorst. He was an aristocrat from head to toe, but to the small European community who had next to nothing to talk about, he was "an eccentric," especially because he remained unmarried. He seems to have led a romantic life, even for the Indies. As a youth he had an affair with a "woman from the dregs of society," as my mother expressed it with a certain distaste. I immediately knew of course, that Winny had come from this relationship. Forced by his family, Gravenhorst left for the Indies before the child was born. Each month he sent some money to the mother, increasing it as the cost of her upbringing went up, or when his income grew. Every now and then the mother sent him some sort of financial statement, and in those same letters she also wrote that Winny went to the H.B.S., and so on, but a friend of his who was on leave in Holland—Gravenhorst never went back himself—revealed the real environment the girl was brought up in. They corresponded back and forth, until Gravenhorst cut the Gordian knot and gave the mother a choice: either the money would stop or the child came to the Indies. And that was how Winny arrived in Padang where Uncle Tjen met her at a party. It was love at first sight. When Uncle Tjen was permanently assigned to Java, she followed him and even my mother knew nothing about this. When he first talked to my parents about Winny and his engagement plans, they were surprised, perhaps even a little hurt. They didn't understand how and why he had kept all of this a secret. He laughed, but never answered their questions. For it is likely that Uncle Tjen himself guessed about, rather than really knew of Winny's past in Holland. Shortly before her death, part of the mystery of her life was revealed. She told him about a number of letters (or were they pages from her diary?) which—as my mother always added—were held together with a red ribbon. No one ever knew their exact contents, neither my mother nor Uncle Tjen. Winny took them with her into her grave. And Uncle Tjen felt that her image had to remain as lovely as it always had been.

Less than a year after Winny's death, Uncle Tjen visited us with Aunt Sophie, his new fiancée. This time my parents were sufficiently prepared. One day when my mother went to Uncle Tjen's house, she found a small jar of *obat seriawan* on the sideboard, and *she* hadn't brought it. Knowing my mother, I'm sure that she called Karto and Minah immediately to account for it.

"*Apaitu?*" ("What is that?") she probably asked.

"*Dari njonja muda.*" ("From the young lady.")

"*Njonja muda jang siapa?*" ("What young lady?")

And so it must have gone on, with her sitting in a chair, and the servants standing in front of her. And I'm sure that it was a thorough interrogation.

It turned out to be one of the De Pauly girls. My mother knew them by name, of course. They were known to be wealthy, but they were no longer young, especially by tropical standards. They even had something of the old maid about them, though it is difficult to be precise about it, perhaps something polished, a neatness and smoothness that struck me even as a child. According to my mother I had said that they also smelled clean, like starched clothes or a linen closet. It became a family anecdote.

They lived together in a big house, surrounded by a host of servants who had been with them for a long time. Many people came and went, but always family—aunts and uncles, cousins, sisters- and brothers-in-law—and they only discussed family matters. One seldom heard a strange voice in the big house, which scared me a little when I was still a small child. It seemed as if everything merely vegetated: the plants, the animals, the people. A house asleep.

Yet it must have been strange for Uncle Tjen, perhaps even embarrassing, to have to present Aunt Sophie in almost exactly the same way as he had introduced Winny not that long before. Maybe that's why he came unannounced: to prevent this second visit from being a repetition of the first one.

My mother was somewhat agitated. When the *babu* announced the visit she disappeared for a moment into her room, put on a new *kabaja* and *sarong*, powdered and sprinkled some perfume on herself. In the meantime the *djongos* was hastily sent to get my father from the office. I wasn't present at the first meeting this time. I missed it because I was totally preoccupied with their car. It was an impressive Mercedes with a marvelous brass snout on its horn. Naturally this caught my interest first, and Aunt Sophie came second. Yet I must really have scrutinized her later on, because I can still remember how she was dressed: in a skirt and blouse, as she always was—a white skirt with large fancy buttons, and with a formidable cameo on her chest. She also had a silk Japanese fan hanging from a long golden chain around her neck. From time to time she fanned herself. She was very friendly to me and kept on laughing. And each time she did so she squeezed her eyes shut. I'll never forget it.

But how different from Winny! I was by no means prepared to like her just like that and, especially at first, I could only see her as Winny's rival. For quite a while I behaved uncertainly toward her, always on the defensive. And only because of this comparison does what I am about to relate make any sense.

Aunt Sophie and Uncle Tjen were staying with us. For a few days? A weekend? Shortly before or after their wedding? I no longer remember, but in any case it happened in our pale pink dining room early in the morning. I had just gotten out of bed and was probably still a little groggy. While I was standing in the dining room that was higher than the rest of the house I saw Aunt Sophie and Uncle Tjen walking together on the walkway that led to the outbuildings. Both were still in night clothes. This in itself was nothing special, but I saw that Uncle Tjen had put his arm around her waist and, what I thought especially "funny," Aunt Sophie's hair hung loose down her back.

She must have been proud of this treasure, and perhaps that was the reason she had it down like that—I can hear my mother saying: "Oh, you have such beautiful hair, Fie." Or maybe she hoped to affect Uncle

Tjen with her "flowing hair" that must have been dark and lustrous. Or it may simply have been her habit to walk around like that early in the morning. No one seemed to find anything unusual about this, yet for me something wasn't quite right. I had never seen Uncle Tjen act "in love" before, not even with Winny, and now he suddenly behaved differently. This human attentiveness he showed Aunt Sophie made him lose something of the inaccessibility of the adult. It was only natural that I reacted negatively toward her. I had more or less accepted Aunt Sophie as "Uncle Tjen's new girl friend" who was "very nice" to him, but this was the first time I refused to accept her as Winny's substitute. I can still see how Aunt Sophie squatted in front of me with her face close to mine, and how I pushed her away from me with both hands and pulled myself free from her grasp. Heaven knows what I said, or if I cried, but it became part of family lore. Yet I'm sure that I would have accepted it if Uncle Tjen had paid that kind of attention to Winny. I am sure that Uncle Tjen would have been no less attractive if only it could have been Winny that had replaced Aunt Sophie. What an unconscious world of identifications and transferences, of shifts and exchanges, must have been behind all this!

I don't know what explanation they gave for my outburst; a child is always easily forgiven. My mother spoke of *betinka* but she must have suspected, if not entirely understood, a deeper cause. What could she, an adult, have known of the feelings that touched a child; what could she know of my relationship to Winny? I concealed my innermost feelings even from her. I've never told her that as an eight-year-old boy I too was in love with Winny.

I remember all too well how once I suddenly kissed Winny's hair very softly, when her head accidentally came close to mine. I don't know what made me do it, but in a split second something happened that was so shocking that whenever I remember my childhood, I'm condemned to bump into it again and again.

And it is always this image that returns, vague, faded, and transformed by many rememberings: the blond, scented hair bending down toward me, then the brief moment of dizziness, and then the slow—yes, especially *slow*—surrendering to an impulse that welled up from deep inside of me.

Amazement followed, and not only mine. She looked at me with a strange expression, but she didn't act startled, nor did she say anything, or walk away, or laugh. I only see that thoughtful look in those soft eyes; then everything was over.

No one has ever hinted at what had happened, neither she, nor Uncle Tjen, nor my mother. Perhaps Winny's shyness saved me from disclosing my deepest feeling, but it is also very possible that she kept quiet because of a feeling of either loyalty or pity for the little boy who had surrendered himself so defenselessly to her. If so, I have every reason to be grateful to her.

This event meant an awakening, the realization of a hidden depth I had never plumbed before. At first I experienced astonishment and consternation, then confusion, and later fear and rapture; they all belonged to a state of mind that had a dark side to it. This event, the most important one of my childhood, fostered a silent agreement between me and Winny; we were partners in a common alliance. The remarkable thing was that I could easily sign my partnership over to Uncle Tjen. I could be in love with Winny through Uncle Tjen, therefore I never needed to feel any jealousy toward him, but at the same time I could just as easily become the lover again. Only in this way can I understand my urgent opposition to Aunt Sophie. And I am writing this deliberately, convinced that that must be the way it was.

The first visit of Aunt Sophie and Uncle Tjen must have been equally embarrassing for them both. He guessed what my parents would think, while she knew that she would lose if compared to Winny. I often heard my mother praise Aunt Sophie's attitude during this first visit. She behaved with dignity and didn't pretend to be younger or more in love than she really was, which made her sympathetic from the very beginning. In fact it was my mother who had the most trouble deciding on the right attitude. She was excessively friendly, but in a forced manner, and laughed a lot—that nervous little laugh I know so well, which indicated when she felt unsure of herself. Instead of Winny—who was still a teenager really—she was now confronted with a woman who was only a few years younger than herself. Didn't she have the reputation of being a "business woman," who took excellent care of the family interests, who was a capable administrator, and so on. This must have impressed my mother, if only because she herself was no more than a mother and housewife. And this woman was going to marry Uncle Tjen? For her Uncle Tjen was still something of the little boy she had taken care of when he was sick, and whom she had helped with his homework. This lopsided relationship must have caused some difficulty at first, and yet I remember nothing but an intimate friendship between Aunt Sophie and my mother, even before the wedding. I only need to remember our daily trips to Salemba Avenue, for the wedding preparations, to know that those two really clicked.

"I'm so glad for Tjen that you two are getting married. You know, Fie, I feel like a sister to him, and I'm so happy that he'll have a woman who will take good care of him, and who loves him. He can't be alone, that boy. . . ."

Then Aunt Sophie smiled, partially flattered and moved a little, and answered: "I'm glad that I can be something to him, Lien. That dear man, he's so kind, you know, so gentle. . . ."

And then my mother could agree with her by telling stories that were meant to demonstrate Uncle Tjen's accommodating nature.

"Just like his mother, Fie. You don't know her yet, but she's such a sweet old dear; I'm sure you'll love her."

After that, the feeling of mutual understanding was perfect. Think what you will about these conversations now, but at the time they established the close tie that now exists between the two families. And it stayed this way until Aunt Sophie's death. It must have been satisfying for Aunt Sophie to hear from *his* side of the family that her care was recognized and appreciated, and I'm sure that on that very same day she doubled her efforts in preparing the *obat seriawan* and the *nassi tim*. And I'm also sure that Uncle Tjen enjoyed extra attention that day, and that he was questioned about his stomach even more than usual. At the time he must have condoned this overwhelming care as tenderness, but it changed later on. I once heard Aunt Sophie say, with tears in her eyes, that Uncle Tjen was becoming "cantankerous," and she was particularly hurt when he said: "Why can't you leave me alone for a moment. You're always all over me. . . ."

But during their engagement which, as was customary in the Indies, didn't last longer than the time it took to prepare for the wedding, Uncle Tjen must have basked in that feeling of security.

What must he have felt during the time when he got to know Aunt Sophie but still had Winny on his mind? It's hard to say. After Winny's death, the desolation of the first weeks, and the loss of his dreams, he must have been in a state of "malleability," similar to the aftermath of a long and serious illness: a longing for sympathy, if not pity, and the need to have someone around to relieve his loneliness. Aunt Sophie provided all this. She "drew him out," she invited him for dinner, she changed the atmosphere. Through her care she soon came to possess the young man who had roused her compassion from the very beginning because, as she once said, he could "look so terribly sad." Choosing her was for Uncle Tjen totally different from choosing Winny; it was a choice that was adumbrated, stripped of all romanticism, and that he could only justify as the result of a feeling of affection, without any reference to love.

His voice was soft and dull when he came to talk with my mother about these things the day after his visit with Aunt Sophie. My mother was standing in front of her petroleum stove when he came in. She was taken by surprise, although she knew of course what he would ask: "And Lien, what did the two of you think of Sophie?"

She didn't answer, but took him along to the side veranda where we always sat "en famille" and where formal guests were never allowed, the same veranda where I had seen Uncle Tjen cry. Again I see the ribbed tiles with green, reptilian figures shining in the sunlight that came through all the cracks and darted across the floor. That's how I know that the blinds were lowered. In fact, when I recollect the side veranda, I can sense once again the atmosphere of subdued light and coolness, perhaps because everything was green. My mother made Uncle Tjen sit in one of our Raffles chairs, walked past the back of his chair, suddenly kissed him, and sat down right in front of him. She answered with a question:

"Tjen, do you really love Sophie?"

And while looking at his hands Uncle Tjen said: "I understand Lien. You two can't understand how I can think of getting married again so soon after Winny. It's difficult to explain, in fact, I can't even explain it to myself."

And then after a pause:

"It's a good thing that I don't have to tell you anything about my feelings for Winny, you know about those . . . and as for Sophie, well Lien, I know that she loves me. She'll take good care of me." And then he added while looking at her with a smile: "You can hand me over to her, Lien, without worrying about it."

3

AUNT SOPHIE ENTERED our lives at a time I can just barely remember. Part of my childhood did not include her, so it isn't too difficult to recall memories of events that happened before she arrived, for example the relationship between Winny and Uncle Tjen, or the events connected with Winny's death. And then there is, of course, the image of Winny herself—the way I have described her and remembered her a thousand times—which made such a lasting impression that any memory of Aunt Sophie must pale by comparison.

But everything considered, there isn't all that much. The oldest memories have faded so that they've become mere "atmosphere," and it is hard for me to give them shape. Then there are those memories that do not need to recall Aunt Sophie because she's part of them as a matter of course. She was part of our lives for many years; in fact, she was there from the very beginning until the end, an end marked by her death. But even after she died her image remained, because time and again we talked about her within our family, as well as with her own. I have never really been able to escape her, not because I feel strongly attached to her, but because she is involved with almost all the family events I know of— love and divorce, inheritances and quarrels, jealousy and devotion—and with all the dramas, be they large or small, that every family in the Indies is heir to, especially such a large one as ours.

Now that I hope, after so many years, to have put enough distance between me and my family—and hence from myself—it is Aunt Sophie who steps immediately forward to serve as the main character of this family chronicle. Through her I can meet the others: introduce my mother, see my father again, and then all those countless aunts, uncles, and in-laws. I can hear them talk and see them act in a manner that was derived from, what is to me now, a frightening awareness of clan and class. Taken together they represent not only "one big family" but also a dying class, even when they were alive: plants without sap or soil.

They were a ruling class accustomed to giving orders, administering justice, and, if necessary, deciding the freedom of others. At the beginning of this century they were still landed gentry, businessmen, civil servants sometimes, but always wielding power. This family branched out and fell apart, "mixed," as it is called, with native blood. Some are light blond with blue eyes, but others are obviously darker, with light, gray, or yellow eyes. Yet they are sometimes not to be distinguished from the type of native who has broad cheek bones, though almost always with a light skin because this family comes from the Sunda region, around Buitenzorg and Bantam, where the people are noted for light skin color. The younger members of this family, particularly the women and especially where there's some evidence of mixed blood, are often beauties with their soft *kulit langsep*, their white teeth, and their lightly swaying way of walking. I have seen photos of "aunts" ("Aunt Jozien," "Aunt Dorina") when they were girls, real beauties with their dark hair piled up high. Yet there was something cool and hard in their gaze. Perhaps it wasn't a question of being just hard, because they were often quickly moved, melodramatic, even kindhearted, but there was a tendency toward calculation, coquetry, domination and vanity. They are curious figures to us, a mixture of contradictory characteristics. They are often just as endearing as they are forbidding. Our clever psychiatrists would have difficulty classifying them, yet it would be a real injustice if they were seen by even cleverer sociologists as mere products of the "colonial patriarchy" in order to tacitly condemn them.

This family always had style, the men as well as the women. They had something of the grand seigneur even if they were impoverished or reduced to living in a *kampong*. They were hospitable and generous, even when they had nothing left, and kindhearted, with a sincere need to do good. They were willing to give you everything, to feed you generously and well, and even let you marry their daughters, but with the condition that you behaved as they did, since they acknowledged no behavior other than their own.

If one comes from this kind of family, even if one has "drifted away" as I did, then one can play along with their way of life unnoticed for a while, because they tend to see you as one of them. But if the time comes when the distance is too great, then you become an "eccentric," and they will refuse you their daughter, or she will do so herself. They will slowly lock you out and you become an outsider beyond recall. But when you come right down to it, this is the best position to be in if you want to write about these people, write without hatred and without love but rather with a great ambivalence that, unfortunately, also causes confusion sometimes. For instance, where do I stand in relation to these people? Where do I stand in relation to Aunt Sophie? I want to make her the center of my story now, not only because of her family relationship, but also because she represents an individual variation within a type, this type of Indies people. Where do I stand in relation to her? I can't make up my mind. Again I have "mixed feelings." I find her ridiculous, despicable, and at the same time tragic, for it is true that they were all really tragic, especially if situated in the present. I also find her tyrannical and at the same time pitiful, narrow-minded, silly and prejudiced, but then again tolerant, accommodating, if not self-sacrificing.

Recalling Aunt Sophie is easy enough; I only have to close my eyes for a moment and she appears. When one memory fades another appears, followed by yet another. Together they form a series of situations that are different each time, but the images telescope into each other and prevent a true portrait from forming. I'm well aware how unsatisfactory it is to work with memories.

Yet there is a photograph, taken shortly before her wedding, by Charles & Van Es on Rijswijk Street. She stands against a background that leaves everything to the imagination: is it a park, wilderness, or a mountain landscape? She is wearing a spotless white skirt and blouse, which is not very original nor very fancy, holds a fan in her left hand, and leans with her right on a delicate little table. She looks small rather than tall, and stiff. Her gaze is serious and she looks straight at the camera. Her dark hair, which she apparently parted in the middle even then, must have been long and full, and confirms my memory of Aunt Sophie in the garden with Uncle Tjen, with her hair hanging loose. The large chignon is clearly visible. This is no longer a girl, though still a young woman: not unattractive, and without the tired features and the worried mien of her last years.

Although Aunt Sophie appears to me in images that surface voluntarily from my memory, I am still obliged to shape them if I want to maintain the fiction of creating a true likeness. I have to establish a connection between the image and reality, develop it, and create a background. I cannot separate Aunt Sophie from her house or her garden, and certainly not from her family, especially such a closely knit one. But I must go back even further, not only to my own first meeting with her—that time with the Mercedes, when Uncle Tjen brought her into our lives—but even before that. I also have to ask myself what I know about her life before we met her, and about her own family. For even the dead family forms a background, especially with someone like Aunt Sophie.

First the house. Here she grew up as a girl, got married, and eventually died. I can only think of Aunt Sophie as being part of her family's home on Salemba Avenue.

The house was quite a ways back from the main road, on the side that had a double row of *kanari* trees. The trolley tracks were between the high trees. The unforgettable old steam trolley clanged between them as if going through a green tunnel, the same way the more inland train sometimes went very close by the houses and *kampongs*. This pastoral atmosphere was enhanced by a rough path and a ditch with brown water that ran along the front yard.

The house was pure Indies. It was built in typical nineteenth-century fashion like those that are still left in the Kramat section and on Salemba Avenue. They were apparently built as country houses with big yards around them. In the last century the nouveau-riche merchants lived there, those who could do what they wanted and who knew how to spend money lavishly. Because there were few diversions, they put all their money into their houses, which were big, tall, wide, deep, and cool. They could only have been built by people who had neither taste nor originality. Their stereotyped construction always included thick walls and stout pillars, and they were always stuccoed and whitewashed. They had to be big and impressive. These houses inherited something from their inhabitants: even if they didn't have style, at least they were in the grand manner.

It started with a veranda across the whole front and a white, gray-veined marble floor, which reflected the massive pillars, the furniture, and all other objects—the rocking chairs and the potted palm trees, the end tables and the chandeliers. Floor maintenance was always a matter of deep concern for Aunt Sophie. She washed it, soaped it, *kramassed* it, and, from time to time, oiled it with grated coconut to make it shine. "You should be able to eat off it," was her standard remark.

Inside it was always cool, even when the sun was at its highest. Aunt Sophie explained that she kept the heat out by letting the bamboo curtains down and closing the blinds before it could get in. Perhaps that is why I remember the house as being always in semidarkness, which could either be somber or pleasant.

The inner veranda especially was always rather dim: a mysterious clair-obscur. The big carved sideboards were there and antique Chinese porcelain, "rose famille" and "bleu royale," hung on the wall as ornaments. There were also large and small vases in the corners on the floor, and on top of closets. They sometimes depicted complete life stories, of Chinese hermits for instance, with a few sparse hairs on their chin. Aunt Sophie was accustomed to act as a great expert on antique porcelain. In reality she depended exclusively on her intuition, and on that basis, she readily separated "antique" from "imitation." Occasionally she waved in the direction of a few plates and mumbled "Ming period," or "Kiang period," or something like that. No one contradicted her, not even Hap Hoo, the antique dealer who lived in Krèkot. He only smiled courteously. On the inner veranda were also some chairs, a couch, and a cupboard from the time of the East Indies Company. The cupboard, however, was not old. Aunt Sophie had the copy made at a later date. I can still see her stand in front of it and point with her bejewelled fingers at a silver rice bowl or a cut-glass carafe, quoting its estimated value: "I was recently offered so much for it. . . ." But she would never sell any of these *pusakas*; she only needed to express the significance of her possessions in fictitious and ever changing amounts. "We're also entitled to the silver dish that goes with this," but—as always—it had gone to another branch of the family. It always ended with the things *her* family had been deprived of and then we were right back to the eternal bickering.

Among the important pieces—the expensive china, the gold plates, the silver fruit bowls and jardinières—were many large and small medallions. There was one Aunt Sophie guarded very carefully. It was a miniature from the late eighteenth or the beginning of the nineteenth century, depicting the patriarch of the De Paulys. Although their name was French, the French blood must have come later into the family— just as the native blood had, for that matter—because this man with his thin face and small piercing eyes had the plain Dutch name of Geraerdt Knol. Knol must have been a man of distinction. Originally a surveyor (a very lucrative job by the way) he later became the prefect (something like the resident) of Cheribon, and in the end he even became a member of the Council of the Indies. He served under Raffles, Van Muntinghe, and Daendels, which only goes to prove his political flexibility. He was the founder of the large family wealth that consisted mainly of real estate. In addition to the vast estate in Tjidané, he owned other estates around Tangerang and Buitenzorg. Among them was Tjiluwur, where he preferred to stay.

Sometimes he behaved rather strangely. This is verified by the regent of Sumedang who stayed with Knol in the *pasanggrahan* in Gawok for several days. He said that Knol "behaved completely different from other Dutchmen." And we can believe it because in the original reports it says that "sometimes it seemed as if he was startled. Then he clasped his head or beat his chest. That was his manner when thinking about something. When one saw him like that, it seemed that he was insane, though he wasn't." In Tjiluwur he had some *sawas* dug out and sometimes sailed a small boat in them, so that from a distance he seemed to be taking a pleasure cruise in those fields. It must have been a strange sight. There were also other things that showed he was unbalanced. In any case, he was different from the man Aunt Sophie described. One can read more about this patriarch of the De Pauly family in *Priangan*, that superb historical study by De Haan. He quotes a certain Engelenburg "who never tires of talking about Knol's villainy." It is true that another contemporary refers to him as a "noble friend of mankind," which he certainly was not because Engelenburg's documentation of his villainy is far too convincing. Besides, one only needed to look at the portrait Aunt Sophie had of a bony, long face with a hawk's nose, a low forehead that seemed even lower because of his curly bangs, and beneath them, dark, sharp, and sly little eyes.

The evidence concerning his intellect is also contradictory. "A man with many ideas," someone said about him. But a later governor general, Jean Chrétien Baud, who was a competent man, simply called Knol "scatterbrained." One thing is certain: all this information and contemporary evidence would have been dismissed by Aunt Sophie as gossip and lies. I wonder if she ever read De Haan. She never gave any evidence that she had. Either it was part of her tactics to ignore the book, or she really had not read it. In any case she told us the story of the family patriarch as if we weren't familiar with it. It was her own version, just as if there were no historical documents, and no spoilsport named De Haan. She simply told us her own legend, allowed no distractions, and invoked the image of a powerful man who was happily married, lived amidst his family, and was "puissantly rich." In Aunt Sophie's imagination he was a man of great talent and one who, above all, had a "heart of gold," as she put it.

This man, who had three children from a liaison with a woman from central Java, was at the top of the family tree. These children were the beginning of the "Indies branch," which grew very strong indeed. As usual, after two or three generations, its members had completely disappeared in the *kampong*, nameless, left with only the mannerisms of a grand seigneur. After a rather odd life, with very odd pleasures (De Haan also informs us of these) Knol, at the age of forty-seven, married the eighteen-year-old daughter of a family from Medemblik. He had her come to the Indies by steamship, first class. A painting shows a strong, heavy, farmer's daughter with red cheeks wearing a light blue silk dress and a red coral necklace. A dark slave in pink knee britches stands behind her holding a huge fan on a long pole which was less for practical use than an attribute of dignity and power.

Seven children came from the marriage to this healthy farmer's daughter, though only three reached maturity. The other four died. Family letters say that the cause was a dangerous "bloody flux." The three surviving children began the series of marriages and births, illegitimate children and mistresses, beautiful French names and housekeepers, but all the while the bloodlines and material possessions gradually merged until no one could distinguish them anymore. There were families with such well-known Dutch names as Palm and Ament, Van Vollenhoven and Motman, but also families named Brétancourt, De Sablonnière, Jut de Bourgelles, De Lizer de Morsain, or De Pauly.

Numerous family photographs hung in Aunt Sophie's bedroom. They dated from the time when photography still resembled a stage production, when they worked in studios with heavy drapery, console tables, and tripods, with vases and fake backgrounds, with shawls and artificial flowers. No snapshots but real portraits of cabinet format, six by four inches or even smaller, always with the photographer's name in silver or gold script at the bottom. I can remember Koene, and Woodbury & Page. Despite the large number of photos hanging in Aunt Sophie's bedroom, many more were collected in the heavy family album with its gilt edges and brass ornamental lock. On the light green linen cover the word "Photos" was printed in gold and there were small purple flowers, violets I believe. It seemed a massive book, a kind of richly illustrated Holy Bible. Aunt Sophie had turned looking through this album into a rite. There was something sacerdotal in her actions. She turned the pages with her finger tips, which made the binding crackle, and when each page fell, one smelled age and naphthalene. There were old stains from dampness on the passe partouts. They resembled brown clouds drifting between the faded portraits.

What was it that made these photographs so important to Aunt Sophie? She could not have known many of these people. Perhaps a feeling of piety, or a memory? That may be. But there must have been more to it: a belief that souls live on in objects and images. An inheritance of many generations! That is why she took care of the family graves and collected brooches and photographs, locks of hair, rings, buttons, earrings, and necklaces, including those braided from human hair, both blond and dark. But especially many rings, with diamonds or sometimes with only a single red stone. There were some that brought luck, but

others were not allowed to be worn anymore because they were *"sial."*
She kept them in cans and old soap dishes as *pusakas* and amulets. Both
the living and the dead were always present in these objects and portraits. They surrounded her day and night. Sometimes they even
haunted her dreams, or appeared as spirits among the outbuildings.
Then incense would be burned the next day in order to appease the
ancestors.

She knew all of them by name. "This is Aunt Dorina," she said
tapping her nail against the smooth pasteboard, "and this is Uncle
Léon." Sometimes she was lost in thought while looking at them and
would wake only gradually as if from a dream. "God," she said, becoming herself again, "if they were still alive they would have been married
seventy years today." Or: "Look, that's Aunt Eugénie. A beauty, isn't
she?" And then in a low whisper, "she was very unhappy; she couldn't
have any children and she suffered terribly later on . . . breast cancer,
you know."

For everyone else these photographs were merely a series of lifeless
portraits of men with mustaches in black shining jackets and women
with hair either piled high or hanging loose. They gazed thoughtfully in
front of them, as softly as in dreams. Some were in costume: one as a
geisha (Madame Butterfly), another as an Oriental dancer (Lakmé by
Delibes), and yet another as a dark-eyed Amazon. It was during the time
that French and Italian operas were extremely popular in the Indies.
Among all those portraits of smiling and coquettish women there suddenly was a photo of a girl with an unforgettable face, a sixteen-year-old
child who had died young. The dates of birth and death were written on
the back in the delicate handwriting of a woman. For me as a boy, this
girl was long the standard of all that was lovely and desirable in a
woman. She came into my life after Winny did, and the more I identified
her with Winny, the more I loved her. Perhaps I transferred my feelings
for Winny to her and that is why she slowly acquired Winny's soft gaze,
and why, in the end, she could hardly be distinguished from her. Both
Winny and this unknown girl died young—such pure romanticism
shaped these details—and when combined into one image, they were
my great love. Only years later did they give way to darker, more realistic figures.

I will never forget this photograph. I can even picture the album
itself. At the moment I could tell you exactly how thick it was, and if I
make myself think about it long enough, the memory becomes so alive
that I can almost smell the naphthalene and the moisture and feel the
nearly crumbling leather of the binding under my fingers. Looking at

the photos as a child was already a big event; how much more could I have done with them now. But during the Japanese occupation the album was irretrievably lost. Hence the only thing left is to rely entirely on my memory. And it can happen that what was lost appears again, and gradually takes on a shape. But the familiar engagement photo of Aunt Sophie's parents has become too clear to be entirely authentic. Memory even falsifies photographs. Strangely enough, though the image is clear, I can no longer remember if it was big or small. I have completely forgotten its dimensions, but I do know that it was a touching, almost romantic photograph made by the English photographer from Woodbury & Page, whom I mentioned already, and who lived in Rijswijk when the horse trolley still went there. This man, whose work always had a romantic touch, must have possessed the bountiful fantasy that his profession demanded at the time. He was an "artist" and must have paid close attention to the appropriate poses for his characters. He took great care to find the correct stance that always resulted in an artificial naturalness. So too in this case: *he* is placed on a chair at an angle, and stares with his bewhiskered face up at *her*, his wife-to-be, who returns his gaze from a standing position. Her left hand is intertwined with his, and his right supports his head. This portrait could have been subtitled "Proverbial Fidelity." At least this is the impression the photographer managed to create, and more power to him. But we all knew that it was not a happy marriage. If Aunt Sophie—who was the oldest—was seven when her father died, then in the photograph he must have been twenty-four or five. And she? Even younger. How old could she have been? Sixteen, seventeen, perhaps even twenty. We would say now that she was a "pretty Indies girl" with dark hair and a remarkable small waist, the much-desired wasp waist. Were they really in love? Was this marriage their own choice, or was it prearranged by the parents? She was the daughter of a colonel who was not very rich, but of a social level distinguished enough to make her quite an acceptable match for the eldest son of the wealthy *Tuan tanah* of Tjidané. People congratulated her parents on the good marriage their daughter was about to make, and joked about a "golden wedding." It turned out otherwise.

At the time no one could foresee that, because of the death of old De Pauly, she would become the *njonja besar* so soon after her wedding, and before she was really prepared for it. She had been used to a different life: musical evenings at home, balls in Concordia, seats of honor at parades, and rides around in her own carriage. She took voice and piano lessons, was an active member of the musical society, Aurora, and sang in the Opera Club. In "La Navarraise" she had been very successful as the passionate Anita. In short, she was seen everywhere in the Batavian high society of uniforms, officials, and rich merchants. From this world that seemed so beautiful, so richly entertaining, and so full of light and music, she went to one where each day resembled the last. The quiet estate was indeed a drastic change for her. The stillness and peacefulness became boring, a boredom that quickly became oppressive.

Aunt Sophie told us little about her father, but wasn't that natural? After all, she was only seven when he died. The stories she told about him and her characterization of him must have come secondhand, yet this much is certain: he was a quiet, blond man with a gentle nature, but without much will power. He loved the countryside where he was born, was familiar with nature around him, with the silence, with the ever-present view of the mountains. It had become a part of him. His wife always wanted to return to town and to her family, and he had neither the will nor the authority to stop her. For weeks he was alone in the quiet country manor, and it seemed at times that the woman who was staying somewhere in Batavia never existed.

They had children, because, of course, a marriage must be blessed with children, but only the oldest, Aunt Sophie, was born in the country. For the births of the other three children she went to her parents' home in Batavia months before they were due. It was clear from the beginning that they were living at cross purposes. The expectations they might have had of each other were never fulfilled, and their incompatibility became, as usual, apparent only after the wedding, when it was already too late. The strong ties to the family and the prevalent standards of behavior made divorce unthinkable. They stayed together, but there is no doubt that she dominated the relationship. Not that Aunt Sophie ever said this, quite the contrary; it is remarkable how sacrosanct her parents' marriage seemed to her. And, as before, she created a legend, this time of the woman who complemented her husband so well. Where he lacked the will to act, she would do so for him, and she must have done so often, with coldness, scorn, and disdain. One only needs to imagine this type of spoiled Indies woman in order to know her.

I am sometimes struck by my need to use portraits in order to find support for my interpretations which, I fully realize, contain a strong element of imagination. And writing about Aunt Sophie's mother now, I think of another photograph, taken of her alone, that hung in Aunt Sophie's bedroom. She looks straight at us with two dark piercing eyes in a rather broad face. There was some native blood here. A handsome woman with compressed lips and a broad mouth. Reserved and inscrutable. The shining hair, parted in the middle, has been smoothed over her temples and is pulled back to form a bun. She wears a striped taffeta dress with the same cameo brooch that Aunt Sophie wore on her wedding day. Naturally, it was meant to bring her happiness. I remember clearly that Aunt Sophie said that this woman had never shed a tear when her husband died; she had only stared straight ahead and not said a word. What went through her mind? I must say that this question intrigues me once more, although I already know that any answer or supposition will be unsatisfactory. Did she somehow feel responsible for the death of her husband who killed himself at the age of thirty-three? Aunt Sophie spoke about the financial problems caused by the well-known crisis of '83 and the following years. He was so convinced that he would never recover the loss of his property, and so possessed by the fear of bankruptcy, that one afternoon he hanged himself from the heavy, mirrored wardrobe in the bedroom. The financial catastrophe constituted enough of an explanation for Aunt Sophie. She never mentioned or even hinted at the possibility that something else might have contributed to it.

He was given a funeral and a grave in the countryside that suited him and to which he had a certain right. It had been his last wish. He was buried late one afternoon without many flowers or much interest, several hundred yards from the house, although not too close to the residence of the living.

He was carried to his grave by country people in a funeral as simple as it was rural. Yet to us it would have been a strange cortège that strode down the winding path of reddish soil to the burial site. Its location was visible from the high rear veranda as a dark button in an irregular pattern of greenish yellow: a growth of bamboo and foliage amidst sloping fields. One can imagine these people walking in their ordinary clothes, no black and nothing formal. The women in their "normal" *sarong* and *kabaja*, and the men in white with only a black crepe band around one arm. It would have been senseless to dress up in these quiet, rural, and quotidian surroundings. The house servants and representatives from the villages were also part of the cortège. They must have been dressed Sundanese fashion, in colored *kabajas* and light *sarongs*. Aunt Sophie said that she still remembered one thing very well: the slanting sunlight that kept on bothering her eyes.

Aunt Sophie never said more than this, but her father's death always brought her to her mother, and that was only one step away from talking about herself. She always said that Mama was not one to display her feelings. She could not help alleviating her sorrows differently than most other women, without unnecessary demonstrativeness. Yet the family had accused her—not directly of course—of being cool, unfeeling, and hard. But that was completely out of the question, Aunt Sophie would say emphatically, and then she began again about her mother's character, inevitably recognizing herself in that energetic, resolute, and cool woman who had always kept her emotions so much under control. Aunt Sophie did not refer to her mother's furious attacks that at times resembled frenzy; she had mentioned them once in passing. Again it was characteristic of Aunt Sophie to simply ignore those traits that did not fit her conception of her mother at that particular time. She simply abstracted certain characteristics, and put them aside as if they were the cogs of a clock. But it was unfortunate for her that outsiders like us could easily fit them back into a living counterpart. And so it was precisely those silences that allowed us to form a different opinion of the person she had drawn for us. More than once Aunt Sophie emphasized that she felt herself to be her mother's child, and yet her stories made it clear that there never was any intimacy or affection. Remarkable for such a strong identification.

"Oh," she sometimes murmured, "you know, I'm really just like Ma." True, even in her inability to love. That's what we always added in our minds, but what she meant was being capable, energetic, and self-controlled. She asked and thirsted for recognition, but who could give her that? None of us. Of course this must have either disappointed or bothered her, depending on her mood, but it never went further than a silent game of knowing and not-knowing, or of attracting attention and playing hide-and-seek. But at times this game became tiresome for the players, especially for my mother. My father was really the only one to find the right response to this continual self-affirmation. Once, while deeply ensconced in his chair as Aunt Sophie talked on and on in the twilight, I saw him suddenly yawn so much that he needed both hands to hide his lack of interest.

Aunt Sophie talked endlessly and much too much. When we sat at night in the dark on the veranda, it seemed as if the words began to lose their meaning and became mere sound, a stream of vowels and consonants. For my father this sound induced sleep, although it was merely tiring for my mother. As for me, I know that I also often had to shut myself off from the flood of sound breaking over us. But at times now, I regret having used this defense, because it made me lose a lot that I could have used in the writing of this story. Unfortunately I can no longer ask her anything, nor my mother or father either. They have been unreachable for years.

In trying to follow a chronology of events in this short account of Aunt Sophie's life, there are parts missing, whole periods of time remain foggy, and years have been wiped away. Sometimes it may have been no more than a few weeks, but even such a lack can be a hindrance. And it is so here, for what followed the funeral in the country? Where did this woman, who was still young, go with her children? She would not have stayed in Tjidané a minute longer than was necessary. It seems obvious that she moved back to her parents' home where she had already stayed so often during her marriage. But strangely enough, Aunt Sophie never mentioned her grandparents' house. I don't even know where it was. I remember nothing about it, nor did she ever speak about those old people or about the rest of the family on her mother's side.

From the time immediately after her father's death, it is Salemba Avenue rather than Tjidané that appears in her stories, though not the main house, only the cottage. Should I presume that they were offered shelter and hospitality there? Who were those people in the main house? Family, of course, but who? And why did they later disappear from Salemba to make room for this young widow and her children who came from the outlying districts after all, and who did not even belong to the immediate family? Why did they clear out the house for her? Perhaps these people simply died, but I already note another family problem, about the inheritance. Yet there may also have been another reason for the rift.

Aunt Sophie told us about an incident that she could never forget, though she was only a child when it happened. Shortly after her father's death, while her mother was still in mourning, she slept with her mother in the same bed. So this must have been on Salemba Avenue. One night—Aunt Sophie said she could still recall precisely how the moonlight shone through the blinds of the door—she was awakened by a sound as if someone were fumbling at the door. There was a shadow on the other side and a whispering, pleading voice. While her heart pounded she pretended to be asleep as best she could. Then she heard her mother slip out of bed and say slowly: "Not that Albert, never." The rest was whispered and then again: "For God's sake, Albert, go away." First there was silence, then the sound of bare feet on the gravel and she knew that it was over. Aunt Sophie heard her mother take a deep breath and saw her loosen her braids and comb her hair in the dark. Not until then did she dare to ask:

"What's the matter, Ma?"

"Nothing, child." And that was all.

I must say that I see this small, incomplete drama like a scene from a movie that is set in an old-fashioned Indies bedroom. I believe that one must have known such rooms in order to be able to sense their sinister atmosphere at night: the cement floor, a *sampiran*, a big iron bed with white mosquito netting, a rickety cabinet, and, of course, the inevitable commode. All of this under the weak light of a kerosene lamp and, on that particular night, the additional moonlight falling in white stripes through the blinds to the floor. And outside mighty nature with its tall black trees against a lighter sky.

If it is indeed possible to associate this event with Salemba Avenue, then identifying the family becomes easier because I can connect the name Albert to one of Aunt Sophie's uncles: her father's brother. Then it also becomes easier to understand why the family grew apart from then on.

But how should I continue now? Again there is a piece missing and because of it time shrinks and the years flow into each other. A remarkable illusion of chronology occurs that can only be discerned as an illusion through this act of writing. But like all illusions it is susceptible to the imagination. I could fill the gap any way I want to, keeping track of what came before and taking into account other available information, indications, and expressions. But this time there isn't enough material for the "memorialist," which is what I am instead of a writer of fiction.

More than a quarter century lies between the seven-year-old girl who that night witnessed an event that was, for her, incomprehensible yet unforgettable, and the young woman who, as Uncle Tjen's fiancée, sat on the front veranda with us one morning. What happened in the meantime? A quiet childhood spent on Salemba Avenue. A mother who was still young—"I was proud of her when I was still a child," Aunt Sophie said—a sister, two younger brothers, the servants and, not to forget, the servants' children. Aunt Sophie must have had a normal Indies childhood because, even when she was older, she still showed all the signs of one. As a small child she would have ordered the cook around, but also spent many hours on the walkway to the servants' quarters with the daughter of that cook, stringing *djali* pits into necklaces, playing *tjongklak*, or jacks. It is not hard to imagine the sheltered life these children led. They were brought up in prosperity, but always dependent on one another, as in a single family. Visiting this aunt or that uncle, playing with cousins, occasionally having a birthday party under Japanese lanterns, but always with family or family of family, never with outsiders. Things stayed that way for quite a long time, and it was this way of life that fostered the strong family bonds and the remarkable clannishness that withstood all the fights. The house was the symbol of this unity: a small world closed off from the big world outside; a miniature feudal community that only later—after the twenties—began to disintegrate through death, marriages, quarrels, and departures to Holland.

The carriage house was behind the cottage on the left, and the stables must have been behind that. The horse was called Kees (the driver would have said "Kis"). There were two carriages: a mylord and a bendy. The family went out riding or shopping in the first, and the bendy took the children to school. The two girls went to the Little Convent of the Ursuline Sisters, and Alex and Léon were in a Protestant school, the well-known Bible School. One can't imagine more indifference toward religion.

Because she had been a good student Aunt Sophie often told us smugly about her school days at the convent. According to her she had especially excelled in arithmetic. "Always nineties and hundreds." She had a teacher, Sister Brigitte—a nun Aunt Sophie always said—who "loved me very much." When no one else knew an answer she always said, "you my little one, why don't you tell us?" and Aunt Sophie always did. When she left school it also meant leaving Sister Brigitte, something that must have been heartbreaking. Aunt Sophie passed her entrance examination of course—again with nineties and hundreds—and went to say good-bye. Sister Brigitte took her to a kind of chapel and "cried a lot," and told her: "I wish you were my child." While telling this Aunt Sophie shook her head and whispered something about motherly instincts and the needs of childless women. That this instinct was also present in a nun made it all the more romantic. After the tears dried, they folded their hands and Sister Brigitte led in prayer. Aunt Sophie soon lost the need to pray, but her annual attendance at the early Mass in the Cathedral in Waterloo Square on December 25 can be considered a relic from this time, which she held on to until she died.

When Aunt Sophie was a child, it was not common for girls to continue their studies, especially in the Indies. Formal education ended after elementary school and then the training for real life began—that is, for society and marriage—with initiation into domestic and housekeeping activities, piano lessons, and French conversation. Every girl was supposed to show reasonable skill at the piano, not so much for her own musical development but rather to provide the music that was an inevitable part of the social game at all parties. Some girls also learned to sing, and a few even progressed enough to sing whole sections from operettas by Donizetti, Hervé, or Lecocq. I never heard Aunt Sophie hit a single note on the piano, there wasn't even one on Salemba Avenue, and as for singing, I did hear her hum a few times, but I never heard anything like the resounding songs with the delicious drawn-out notes that my mother sang. Yet she had sung as a girl, she said. She had even played in an operetta, in Lecocq's "La Fille de Madame Angot." With that my father's eyes would get hard and, having to fulfill a need for revenge, he would say as bluntly as possible: "She must have been outstanding in the tableaux vivants."

Aunt Sophie must have been more gifted in drawing and painting than in music and singing. In the veranda in the rear of the house hung a handsome, painted board depicting a mourning woman in a white pleated dress with a harp in her hand (pre-Raphaelite influences no doubt), but in the *gudang* there was a more realistic green doghouse. And every time Midin had to clean the *gudang* he was warned: "Awas andjing saja" ("Be careful with my dog").

With a little music, a little singing, a little French, and a better developed sense of proportion and perspective, she grew to be a teenager of sixteen or seventeen. That is when she started to wear her heavy hair up, although for a time she still wore a bow as a sign of her transition from a girl to a woman. A particular hairdo must have developed with the years.

Sometimes I suddenly imagine the two sisters, Aunt Sophie and Aunt Christien, walking together as young girls, two Indies girls, although Aunt Christien was perfectly white and Aunt Sophie only slightly darker. I imagine them from behind, walking with small, short steps—although I can never really have seen them like that—then they go down the marble stairs—as if I myself accompanied them to the front veranda—lift up their skirts, and step into the mylord. They were then going to attend the Wednesday evening concerts of the Military Band. And that music could already be heard at a distance because the band played on a bandstand in the garden of the Concor, and preferred triumphant marches or the blaring and pompous music of Hérold and Offenbach.

When presented this way, Aunt Sophie's youth seems to have been rather monotonous, though nearly without a cloud. But that's not the way it was. There were two sad events, two deaths: that of her youngest brother, Léon, and that of her mother. But I really know very little about those, certainly no details. I only heard that Léon drowned in the river behind the house, while playing with his friends.

And the mother? I don't know what ailed her, only that she was sick for a long time with a lingering disease. She certainly never got out of bed during the last months before her death, and she surely would have been lying in her own filth if Aunt Sophie had not taken care of her, washing her every day, combing her hair, and feeding her.

The sisters were left alone in the big house after the mother died. And Uncle Alex? When did he leave the nest? Again I don't know. There is nothing to go by, but when Aunt Sophie was getting to know Uncle Tjen in 1916 or 1917, he had already been living for some time on his property in the country. I don't know if Titi was with him then. In any case, Aunt Sophie and Aunt Christien must have lived alone together for years, with only the servants and the pets, such as the cockatoos, the birds, and the dogs.

To my knowledge there were no disasters in those years, no serious accidents or illnesses and no shocking events. It was the uneventful existence of two girls getting slowly older and more nervous. A life without ripples; though underneath the smooth surface, an undertow of impatience increased every day.

Then suddenly the waiting ended. Dubekart appeared. God knows where he came from, but he was a stranger, an outsider in every way: a *totok*, a bureaucrat, a man who acted important, solemn, formal, taciturn, and ambitious. He made the family slightly uneasy, but they came to understand. The sisters had been together for so long that for some time after her sister's marriage Aunt Sophie seemed to have been hurt. But Uncle Tjen appeared just in time, or more accurately, Aunt Sophie appeared to him.

The servants were responsible for their meeting. Karto, alias Pak Kriput, and Midin had met at the market and their common interests had brought them together. They exchanged visits and this was naturally noticed. One evening Karto walked into the yard just as Aunt Sophie was standing on the dark veranda in the front. As a matter of fact she had heard his steps on the gravel path. Pak Kriput approached and very politely, like a native who knew his place, asked permission to walk past the house to the outbuildings. It goes without saying that Midin was questioned the next day.

"Who was that?"

"Djongos Tuan muda dari Kramat," Midin said ("the *djongos* of the young man who lives in Kramat"), the same *Tuan muda* who walked every morning by the house on his way to the trolley stop.

I'm sure that Aunt Sophie stood guard the next morning.

"Kurus" ("He's so skinny") Aunt Sophie said, half disapprovingly and half compassionately, to Midin during their next conversation.

"Yes, the young man has trouble with his stomach."

"And who takes care of him?" Aunt Sophie asked.

"Minah and Pak Karto," Midin answered.

"Isn't there a wife to take care of him?"

"No, the young man doesn't have a wife. He was going to get married, but that *nonna* died last year."

Aunt Sophie must have been overcome by an immense and genuine pity. "Obat seriawan and nassi tim," flashed through her mind. For the time being she limited herself to *obat seriawan*, which is how the small jar landed on Uncle Tjen's sideboard: the same Chinese jar that had aroused my mother's suspicions.

And Uncle Tjen? He must have sent Karto to Salemba Avenue with a thank-you note to express his gratitude for her compassion. He appreciated it very much and he must have asked to be allowed to come some time and thank the sisters in person. Consequently Uncle Tjen came to Salemba Avenue where he was well received and showered with attentions. Of course the *nassi tim* was added to the *obat seriawan* and when he improved she prepared a comprehensive diet for him every day, which Midin brought to Kramat in a *rantang*. "Just leave it to me, Mr. Doblijn. I've always taken care of other people."

He knew what was happening, but offered no resistance. In fact he wanted security. He thought he was all finished with dreams, and if my image of Uncle Tjen is correct, he must have felt that Winny was irreplaceable. The future could only be a compromise and he was prepared to accept it. He did not want to be alone anymore; he needed an atmosphere of caring, kindness, and understanding. He must, therefore, have been defenseless against the zealous attention Aunt Sophie paid him.

My mother said that she saw it coming and that at first she had mixed emotions. Later the notion that it was better this way predominated. Winny's death could not be undone by wearing mourning clothes or by grieving. And on that morning when Uncle Tjen came to our house unexpectedly, my mother was surprised and somewhat taken aback, yet the *will* to accept Aunt Sophie was already there. And Aunt Sophie overcame all difficulties with her warm manner and the considerate way in which she spoke of Uncle Tjen's earlier sorrow. As I noted already, it must have clicked immediately between my mother and Aunt Sophie. And in this way a bond that proved to be unbreakable was forged between the two families.

4

AUNT SOPHIE and Uncle Tjen were married in 1917; she was thirty-five and he thirty, although he looked younger. I remember a photo taken of the wedding couple standing on the marble stairs of the house on Salemba Avenue surrounded by flowers. That photo hung for years in a dark frame in my parents' bedroom. The glass became slightly discolored and the photo itself faded, but the image is still clear to me. Aunt Sophie stood one step below Uncle Tjen. Her dark hair was parted in the middle as it was in the other photo taken of her standing by herself, and she already had a worried look. Uncle Tjen, with the hesitant beginnings of a mustache, was as tall and thin as a schoolboy, and he also looked far from happy. It is as if this seriousness stayed with them, because there were always worries, setbacks, illnesses, death, but very little happiness.

My mother knew the cause: Aunt Sophie attracted misfortune; she said she could "feel" it. Furthermore, her personal maid, Bèot, said to her immediately after she saw Aunt Sophie with Uncle Tjen for the first time: "Nonna Sophie has such dry hands Ma'am. They're 'panas.' They'll scorch happiness." I can still hear my mother telling this to my father, whispering as if she were revealing a great secret. Bèot's words were prophetic. Of course my mother believed in omens, dreams, and fate. She felt that oncoming disaster already hung like a shadow over the happy festivities of the wedding day.

But as a boy of about nine I remember nothing but gaiety. The wedding day was too exciting ever to forget. I especially remember the flowers and the people walking on the verandas: from the light, open front veranda to the one inside, and from there to the rear one where the buffet was. Most of the guests gathered there because the morning was already warm and getting warmer. One could get crushed ice and rose syrup, even *ès puter*, vanilla ice cream in small lilac and pink glasses that had small porcelain figures of shepherds and shepherdesses on them. The small spoons were made of silver.

There were flowers everywhere in silver-plated or white-painted rattan and bamboo stands: white and colored carnations, fragrant roses, big chrysanthemums, and scalloped orchids. The scent of flowers filled the air and there were many gay ribbons. In this otherwise too quiet house, where order was almost measured, there was now a mood of joyous disorder. The furniture was scattered; not a single wardrobe or table was in its usual place. The rooms were unrecognizably festive. Aunt Sophie and Uncle Tjen received their guests on the inner veranda. They stood together as bride and groom while family, friends, and acquaintances came by to wish them well. They were cheerful. Even Uncle Tjen.

Perhaps this was due to the champagne that the *djongosses* brought around on large, silver trays. Or perhaps he really was happy. Time and again he shifted his weight from one long leg to the other, laughing a little foolishly when he bent down to his bride. "Well, Sophie," he'd say, "how are we doing so far?" Aunt Sophie was also cheerful. She was even flushed from a combination of heat, champagne, and the continuous embracing. She kept on saying, "no really, I don't want anymore," but then there would be still another toast. There was a lot of kissing—hard and on both cheeks. Uncle Tjen couldn't escape it either. "All right this time, Sophie?" and then Aunt Sophie gave the stock reply: "Sure, as long as you don't keep on doing it." And each time there was more laughter.

"Grandma" was sitting in a chair beside Aunt Sophie. Uncle Tjen resembled his mother a great deal, both had the same slightly dark skin and the same oval-shaped face. But they were especially alike in their shyness, which they expressed in each gesture and look.

She wore a dark brown satin dress, and as usual her gray hair was combed back in a *kondé*. "I won't get up, all right?" she said. There was something very sweet about her sitting there. She smiled. Everyone bent down to kiss her. She took my mother's hand after the embrace. "Lientje," she said softly but emphatically, as if she wanted to say, "your Aunt's really content."

I also stood beside Aunt Sophie for a while because I was an usher at the wedding. Rienkie was on the other side next to Uncle Tjen. She was a bridesmaid, one of Aunt Sophie's many "nieces." We were about the same age, but she was then much smaller and, especially, thinner. She wore a shimmering white dress, with a crown of small pink flowers in her black hair. What struck me even then was her skin: light-brown but, somehow, fair. I must have thought her very beautiful. She also held a basket in her hand. To my great annoyance and shame, my mother had dressed me in a white satin suit with a lace collar and lace ruffles. We reaped cries of admiration from the aunts, but I heard—and I'll never forget it—one of the men laugh and say: "*kassian* that poor kid." With that I lost control, urgently needing to assert my independence. As my mother expressed it, I became "in-tol-er-a-ble," even insolent. My success was assured, but it was highly necessary so I could reestablish myself as a boy. I didn't stand next to Aunt Sophie so much anymore; for one thing, she often sent me on errands. I mixed with the crowd without wanting to concern myself with Rienkie, although I kept seeing her all day.

There was a very pleasant mood. Everyone from both families was cheerful and happy. They introduced themselves and immediately called each other by their first names. "I'm Christien" or "Just call me Mary." A free and easy atmosphere prevailed without a trace of solemnity or exaggerated formality. A touching sense of belonging together, of being one big family. Typical of the Indies.

There was a lot of noisy activity, but Aunt Christien must have been the most active and excited. On this, her sister's wedding day, she was uncontrollably energetic. She tripped, pattered, and clattered through the house and was unbelievably busy. She dashed over to each imperfection and reproached the servants, all the while turning her head from side to side. My father sometimes said that she resembled a threatened chicken. That is how I imagine her on that day. She was small and nervous with a sharp face and an enormous hairdo that made her head look far too heavy. I can see her gather her skirts up a little, go down the stairs which lead to the outbuildings . . . and fall. This caused great consternation, especially from the bride. Also a lot of sympathy, eau de cologne, and icewater. Only "Grandma" said: "Now, what did I tell you? You shouldn't be so *rèpot!*"

This reminiscence recalls other people from what was first a hazy recollection. In fact so many that I have to make a choice: Uncle Willy. He must already have been bald and fat and always intent on making remarks which my mother used to call "dirty." I can see him standing against the light in a corner of the veranda. There was something both complacent and kindly about him, especially when he laughed. All of a sudden I remember that he wore loose cuffs under his coat sleeves and that they were always slipping down. I learned later—I have no memory of it myself—that while he presented his jokes on that day, his wife (Aunt Lies to me) met the young District Officer Martens, who for many years kept intruding on their marriage.

But I really didn't notice all these incipient dramas, nor the tension among the adults. Not until later did I reconstruct them from vague memories, conversations, and some known facts. But for me there was only a house with festively decorated rooms and verandas. At least this is my most immediate memory of that wedding day, though followed closely by the religious ceremony in the Bethel Church in Meester-Cornelis.

I had never been in church before. I remember sitting in the carriage next to Rienkie and opposite Aunt Sophie and Uncle Tjen. I can remember pulling up in front of the church and seeing the sharp light rebounding off its whitewashed walls. It was a harsh light that disfigured everything. We entered the church. The organ played. The windows transformed the white light into yellow with purple stripes and spots. That was because they were stained-glass windows. I was so awed by the high ceilings and by the stentorian sounds from the organ pipes that I forgot to lift the bridal train. At that moment Rienkie spoke the never-to-be-forgotten words: "Come on, little fellow. Stop day-dreaming." I was dumbfounded and humiliated, but said nothing and picked up the train. I must already have been hopelessly in love with her.

After the church service and the reception, there was a luncheon for family and close friends. There were at least thirty guests. We sat on the veranda in the back, arranged in a horseshoe at a table richly set with the family silver and crystal. We ate from old French porcelain plates that had been brought out of the display cabinets for the occasion.

Then came the incident that caused the only dissonance in what was otherwise a harmonious day. Amidst the noise and the buzzing of voices, just as a flaming pudding was being brought in under the watchful eye of the European cook, someone tapped against a glass and "Uncle De Pauly," one of the older De Paulys, rose from his seat. He was a stately gentleman with a white goatee. He tilted his head back a little, hooked his left thumb behind his lapel, and held his pince-nez in his right hand. He spoke with a refined voice, without a trace of an Indies accent. This man had enjoyed a career of more than forty years in the tropics, yet he always remained every inch a *totok*. He proposed a toast to the bride and groom and addressed himself particularly to Sophie, his niece. He pointed out the De Pauly's strongly developed sense of family, mentioned how much the children were attached to each other, and mentioned the fact that Sophie had not married within the family which was, for him, real proof of her passionate love for Etienne, whom he herewith welcomed wholeheartedly into the family. A storm of applause followed, which soon died down, however, because Aunt Sophie had burst out in uncontrollable sobs. Somebody shouted, "My God," chairs were pushed away, and Christien tried to embrace her sister. Uncle Tjen stood there, looking pitiful and awkward, and made no attempt to console his bride.

The incident disturbed the festive mood of course. No one really understood why Aunt Sophie had started to cry. There must have been something we didn't know about, and it was precisely that which made the event so embarrassing. A gray cloud hung over us, and it was one that did not quickly dissipate. It took a while for the gaiety to return. Some of those present said unequivocally that Aunt Sophie had carried on needlessly, and that she should never have done it, because of the guests and especially not in front of Uncle Tjen. This public display of attachment to others, this concern for family affairs, mortified him. My mother said that Uncle Tjen had looked as only he could: both frightened and shy at the same time.

Nor could he have understood any of it either. It is possible that he didn't give it a second thought, but then again he may have seen the first difficulties looming up ahead. The elder De Pauly admitted his mistake later. Sophie had always been "an overly sensitive child," and he shouldn't have referred to such a sensitive issue. Yet he loved his niece all the more for it, since he very much appreciated her family attachment. As far as Etienne was concerned, he was sorry that he had been the immediate cause of this embarrassing outburst. It didn't seem to occur to him that he also owed an apology to the guests and other family members. After the pudding everyone tried to bring things to a close. The fruit, apples and pears from the cooler, was still eaten at the table, but the coffee and dessert would be served on the inner veranda. This was the easiest way to get away from the table and remove oneself from the incident. Champagne was served once again, but just when a general mood of gaiety had returned, it was time for the bride and groom to change clothes and get ready for the honeymoon trip.

Aunt Sophie returned in a shantung outfit and a veil, holding her gloves in her left hand. A little later Uncle Tjen also appeared. He carried a duster over his arm and smiled shyly. He dreaded the departure a little because he knew what everyone was thinking.

The car pulled up in front with a suitcase on the roofrack. It was the same car that had brought Aunt Sophie and Uncle Tjen the first time they visited us. When the Mercedes drove away, each guest threw a handful of rice. They laughed teasingly because they knew what it meant, but their words were lost in the noise of the engine. "On your way!" "Good luck!" As the car drove off, the young couple looked back through the oval-shaped rear window and waved for a long time.

The road south from Batavia runs like a taut rope past burning plains, orchards, estates, and rubber plantations. It leads to the high Sunda region in the interior of west Java. One must always pass Buitenzorg, that outpost on the border of the lush Priangan district.

One begins to climb, sometimes several hundred feet within a few miles, as soon as Buitenzorg, right at the foot of the mountains. The roads divide here also. The southern route leads to Sukabumi by way of Tjitjurug and Tjibadak, the eastern one ends on the high plains of Tjiandjur by way of Tjipajung and the Puntjak, and the third heads west to the sparsely populated Bantam region. Buitenzorg was known in Indies fashion as a "sweet little town." It always gave a clean and refreshing impression, and especially after it had rained, when it looked as if it had been washed; it rained there all the time.

When it was hot in Batavia, before the monsoon came, and the gray and black clouds came and floated southward again, we would say: "It must be raining in Buitenzorg." Sometimes when it got too bad, when even the nights brought no relief to Batavia, when all nature was simmering and anything that resembled a leaf hung down listlessly, when the grass was withered and the soil cracked, then my father would say after he came home from the office: "We're going to get some fresh air," and then we knew that we were going to Buitenzorg. A long-distance call was placed to the Hotel Bellevue and after the "rijsttafel," around three in the afternoon, the car came to the front of the house and we drove away in a holiday mood. My father could put his worries away and we could hear him sing unintelligibly all the way up. He really knew the tune of only one song: "My Old Kentucky Home." This song, the parched land, the hazy mountains, arriving in Buitenzorg, the Hotel Bellevue, and the view from our room—they all belong to my happiest childhood memories, which in fact, include the entire town.

We always considered Buitenzorg to begin right after we passed the aquaduct, just beyond *paal* 36 [a *paal* is about 1,500 meters, or slightly under a mile]. The coolness had begun long before that. Sometimes we already had rain while we were on the way, and often the trees were still dripping when we entered Buitenzorg. Then everything smelled of earth, moisture, and grass, and it was as if you could breathe deeply again for the first time. But you still had to drive quite a ways before you got to see something of the town. Not until you were past the obelisk at the end of the wide avenue lined with *kenari* trees, could you get a view of the white palace of the governor general. Deer walked on the vast, light green lawn. The famous botanical garden began further on. On the other side, behind palms, lianas, and ferns, were the squat mansions, big and wide. They were old houses from the eighties and nineties, the time of rocking chairs and drooping mustaches. When we passed these houses we knew we were almost there. We took a right before the road itself turned left toward the *pasar*, and then suddenly the hotel would lie before us: a lawn with hundreds of little yellow flowers, the white main building, and, towering over it, the notched peak of Mt. Salak.

Our arrival is connected for me with an image of something very light and clear, mixed with a feeling of anticipation and relief. It was only natural that I assumed that Aunt Sophie and Uncle Tjen also experienced this feeling, because they stopped at the same Hotel Bellevue. The same *mandur* must have met them at the entrance, and brought them upstairs where they had reserved a room with a view of the Tjiliwung and Mt. Salak. They were served tea on the front veranda even though dusk had fallen. A short time later it was dark, but hundreds of lights lay spread out before them. Voices of bathing women and children, and a man's high voice singing a song could be heard until late at night. They would have heard water rushing throughout the night, which must have made them think of cold mountain streams and given them the feeling that they were in the country. Early in the morning they were awakened by a train's whistle, and a little later they heard screeching and grinding as it rounded a curve, followed by the sound of the wheels disappearing in a clickety-clack that could be heard for a long time after. A peaceful sound dying away steadily, disappearing, yet time and again returning for a moment, finally to dissolve in the rushing of the river. When they got up, there was fog over the lower woods and over the swollen river. Mount Salak was whitely veiled, but before long the yellow sunlight broke through and tore the haze into long shreds. It would be a glorious morning like most mornings in Buitenzorg, radiant, bright, and clear.

Early in the morning Aunt Sophie and Uncle Tjen went for a walk in the botanical garden. They walked side by side through the stately, dark green lanes. They descended along winding paths to the splashing fountain and visited the pond with its pink and white water lilies. It was shady and cool there, though nature was full of life. From under the bushes and the grass came the sound of crickets punctuated by the shriek of several *tonggèrets*.

The flower garden with its lilacs and pink asters lay behind the rubber trees. Aunt Sophie and Uncle Tjen probably walked there too.

The sun would have already been higher and it must have been warm, yet it was never so scorching as in the lowlands. You could tell that from the flowers. There were many more there and the colors were more vivid. But the sense of being higher, more in the mountains, came mostly from the many fast-flowing brooks and the brawling river sown with huge mountain boulders. The water wasn't brown and sluggish, as it was on the plain, but clear and fast.

The town itself resembled a large park run wild, a mixture of design and nature, with wide, straight roads and narrow, winding lanes. The sense of being in a garden was never lost; the houses always seemed to be hidden by greenery. They were old and dank under the high *kenari* trees and their walls were splotched with green mold. Some of the street lanterns dated from the last century. It was always dark there at night, and at times some drops of cold water would fall, even hours after the rain had stopped.

Aunt Sophie and Uncle Tjen didn't travel on until the next day. In the afternoon they swam among the holy fish in the natural bath at Tjibatu, with its sparkling water that was clear all the way to the bottom. Aunt Sophie wore a sarong that sometimes bubbled up like a balloon, but they only had to worry about each other, because they were alone. Afterwards they sat in the gazebo and the *mandur* served them black coffee which he poured from a kettle into cracked cups. He brought roasted ears of corn and baked *peujeum* on a white plate. It was a touching gesture that only added to the impression of rustic simplicity.

Right after breakfast the next morning, the car was again brought to the front and Aunt Sophie and Uncle Tjen left for Tjidané, the largest of the De Pauly estates. Although still considered to be in Buitenzorg, it was really in Bantam, about twenty-five miles to the southwest. It was a good hour's drive along a winding road. Tjidané was not the only country estate of the family. There were also some smaller estates and several houses in Batavia—Salemba was one—but for Aunt Sophie, Tjidané was the only place she was always drawn to because she had seen it through a child's eyes: the white house, the dark gardens, and the yellow *sawas*. It was a place imbued with emotions, with melancholy predominating, and she had always wanted to experience it once more. This was the reason she chose Tjidané for her honeymoon. She wanted to spend the first days in those familiar surroundings where she had known her happiest childhood memories. It was as if she wanted to recover some of that former happiness and transfer it to her relationship with Uncle Tjen. As for Uncle Tjen, he had no reason *not* to comply with his bride's wishes. On the contrary, he even agreed with a smile, and was touched by Aunt Sophie's intentions. To be together in her childhood domain meant to be admitted to her most intimate world and this flattered him unintentionally.

Tjidané was a vast property situated for the most part on the plain. It had rice paddies and rubber trees, and a country house that was a peculiar structure with classical columns that seemed to have been brought from another world. Behind the house the land crept up slowly into the mountains. It was sloping and rolling land with deep hollows, huge mountain boulders that had been brought down by old eruptions, and small fast-flowing rivers. During the rainy season these were swollen and roaring. They had been dammed up and their flow controlled to provide water and energy. Still further away, up behind the cloud line where a gray veil of rain hung every afternoon, tea shrubs and quinine trees were cultivated. It was an immense land, broad and majestic, especially when you looked down on it from the high rear veranda of the country house. And to think that everything as far as the eye could see belonged to the De Pauly family. By then they had owned it for three or four generations. Aunt Sophie always said that the original sale to one of her ancestors dated from the time of the British interregnum, when Raffles needed money for his reform plans and sold parcels of land to private individuals.

The house itself was literally a "besaran," a symbol of former power and wealth, of a grand life in the seventies and eighties of the last century. There were feasts at harvest time, for instance, which cost tens of thousands of guilders and lasted two days and two nights. Today one can hardly imagine such a feast. There were hundreds of guests—from Bogor, Sukabumi, and Batavia, as well as from the surrounding estates. Some stayed in the house, others were lodged in the outbuildings and improvised guest cottages, while the rest made do with couches and lounge chairs. There wasn't much real sleeping anyway because the various kettle bands played throughout the day and far past midnight. And the *gamelan* could always be heard because there was of course another feast in progress, the real one as celebrated by the native population, men, women, and children. They were happy in a way different from the Europeans, more quietly attending a *wajang kulit* performance, or watching for hours on end the way the *orang blanda* amused themselves.

By the eighties the dance craze had already reached the Indies, so they must have danced the waltzes, quadrilles, galops, and polkas. The women with their slim waists and long, wide skirts, each with a flower in her hair; the men, complimentary and gallant, with pointed, patent-leather shoes and narrow pants. One can imagine their turning, swaying, and bowing on the platform against a background of Japanese lanterns and a decoration of bamboo and banana leaves in the Sundanese style. They would also have sung their own Dutch songs right in the middle of the Indies. But there haven't been any such feasts for a long time now. It already had changed when Aunt Sophie's father was alive. The golden years of bumper crops and high prices had gone by then. The big house had grown quiet as if turned inward, without yet admitting it publicly. Aunt Sophie said at times that the land yielded more sorrow than profit. That meant that she—with a 3/54 share—received only some two hundred guilders a month. Yet Tjidané was dear to her.

On that day, after rounding a wide curve, the sudden sight of the house must have given her a feeling of delightful recognition and expectation. A little further on they turned right and at the end of the driveway—a tunnel of light through high dark trees—the white building basked in the sun.

Uncle Otto, a great-uncle, lived here. He was in charge, and administered a land so vast that he employed an assistant just for the mountain crops. This man was a kind of family clerk, a taciturn and solitary man who lived in a big, isolated *pondok* against the mountain slope. His name was Niemantsverdriet. An unforgettable name.

Uncle Otto received them hospitably. He had the cordiality of a countryman who was glad to have somebody to talk to again. He met them with open arms and nearly crushed the unknown Uncle Tjen against his enormous chest. "So, you are Tjen," he shouted; and then looked laughingly at them: "You make her happy, hear?" He himself had married within the family, albeit in the wrong way. His wife was an illegitimate daughter of his oldest brother, although she was only ten years younger than her husband. Aunt was friendly, though she did perhaps exhibit some reserve. She must have remembered the family's opposition all too well, and known that they would never regard her highly. But she was a natural hostess and showed little emotion, having been taught from childhood to be attentive and obliging to her guests. The large guest cottage had been prepared. They were always very welcome in the *besaran*, Uncle Otto said, and they should feel completely free to do as they liked. The servants were at their disposal.

I know Tjidané, I have been there as a child with Aunt Sophie and Uncle Tjen, and also with my parents. That must have been two or three years after this, when I was eleven or twelve. The later date accounts for why I can still remember so much: the open space all around me, the plains, and the unforgettable mountains. But it is strange that my impressions are mixed with Aunt Sophie's stories. Especially after Uncle

Tjen's death she spoke often about Tjidané, about those particular days when she was with him ("Only then did I feel completely happy. This all changed later on"). Because of these stories I have an impression of Tjidané that is far more complete and even livelier than my memory alone could have provided. I can give, thanks to Aunt Sophie, an exact description not only of the house, but also of Aunt Sophie and Uncle Tjen as they walked and sat there; otherwise I would have had to be satisfied with such indications as "something light," or "something big," and know that there'd be missing pieces. This is not reality of course, only imagination. So be it, but real nonetheless.

It was a tremendous house and unforgettable. And this is not only due to its size, but also because it was both cool and light at the same time, with countless rooms and verandas. What do I see first? The deep veranda in the back, of course, with its many open doors; something white and bright, with the sunlight streaming in from every side. It must have been early in the morning to have those rays of sun fall obliquely, making bright spots and casting elongated shadows of doors, pedestals, chairs, and even of the plants on the middle table. Later in the day, when it became blazing hot outside, when the mountains were already hazy and the color of the sky had faded to something that was white rather than blue or gray, at such a time it was especially delightful inside. All the slatted doors were closed and the blinds lowered, giving a pleasant, muted atmosphere. Consequently you stayed at the table for a while after the *rijsttafel*. The men opened their collars and the women cooled themselves with native fans of *akar wanggi* (made from scented roots). Aunt Sophie and Uncle Tjen must have sat there this way with Uncle Otto and his wife. But after some time the men will have stood up to go and "write a letter in English." That was a common expression for taking a nap. My father always said it too.

"Well son," I hear him say to Uncle Tjen, "well son, shall we?", and he only needed to make a motion like writing in order to be understood. Uncle Tjen always laughed at this, because he liked that kind of secret language.

The women stayed at the table, of course, but they lowered their voices or even continued in a whisper. After all, the men were sleeping. What could those women have talked about? Well, what else is there than the absent family or how to prepare all kinds of Indies dishes. "Delicious you know, but you have to add a little *ketumbar djienten* to it." I heard such conversations so often that it couldn't have been otherwise.

If Uncle Otto and Uncle Tjen took a nap—as I expect—it wouldn't have been for very long. Around half past three they would already have gone for a bath in their *kabaja tjina* and batik pants, each with a clean towel over an arm. In any case, they would have been present an hour later for tea, again on the rear veranda. But drinking tea was merely one part of what was practically a meal of Indies sweets displayed on plates and dishes: *kwee lupis*, *kwee tjelurut*, *pisang goreng*, *pisang rebus*, roasted *djagung*, and heaven knows what else. By that time the blinds had been pulled up and the doors opened again; the worst of the heat would be over then. And if it rained, that wonderful feeling of relief came earlier, sometimes as early as three-thirty. Even if it was sometimes dry in Tjidané itself, the cool mountain wind with its smell of rain would blow across the plains and then it was wonderful to stand on one of the verandas and be met by the coolness and the smell of wood and soil. While recalling this, I suddenly sense the wide open spaces around the house, and see again the mountains covered with a veil of rain. It must have rained often when we were in Tjidané, because it seems that I can only imagine Aunt Sophie and Uncle Tjen sitting in the house, keeping out of the rain.

Aunt Sophie tells a story about the older natives coming to pay her their respects because they wanted to see the little *nonnie* of the former *Tuan kandjeng*. Some even walked several miles for this. Aunt Sophie gave each of them a coin until Uncle Otto stopped it, knowing full well that the stream of elderly people would be endless. A little later it began to rain and it rained all afternoon, bucketfuls. The sun broke through for a moment between the trunks of the rubber trees, and then evening fell like a thickening veil over the drenched earth. Between the tree trunks in the west it stayed light a little longer, but this too faded to gray and then black. It became chilly, and irrevocably dark. In the country, night steals up on nature, overcomes it, and swallows it so completely and grandiosely that as a child I was always overcome by fear. When the blue, hissing kerosene lamps came on with slight plops and I could stare at the burning mantles, I felt somewhat relieved. Because I was a city child, such an evening in the country always filled me with fears I had not known at home. For as soon as the cheerful light came on, the first insects came at it from out of the pitch darkness, from the fields and bushes. Terrible green monsters with long sticks for limbs and rolling little eyes like those in gruesome fairy tales. They could fly at you very suddenly and scare you by attaching themselves to your clothes. I did recognize them from the city, but at Tjidané they looked more like flying leaves and branches—green as leaves and brown as bark—and were much bigger and certainly far more numerous. But they disappeared as soon as the light was turned off. That is why I believe—at least that's the way I imagine it—that after they had made themselves "more comfortable," and Aunt Sophie and Uncle Tjen sat on the front veranda of their cottage, they sat in the dark. I see Uncle lying on the rattan chair in pajama pants and *kabaja* and Aunt Sophie beside him in her silk Japanese kimono. She had loosened her hair and rocked slowly in her rocking chair. They sat that way until dinner. There was no need to dress. It was wonderful to remain in night clothes, it increased the sense of intimacy and the feeling of being in the country. The four of them sat on the rear veranda, illuminated by the crystal kerosene lamp, the doors open, the impenetrable darkness around them and, in the background, the quiet, peaceful sound of the rain. Afterwards they went to the front veranda, where no lamps were on. There they could sit in the dark, stretched full length in big comfortable chairs. There were ten columns, placed in pairs across the enormous width of the veranda, dividing the darkness into four unequal sections. The heavy furniture was dwarfed by the high spaces that were filled by palm trees.

They said little to each other. Only Uncle Otto might say something occasionally, usually about the family. He wasn't any part of them anymore and really knew very little about the others. "Here in the *udik* you lose track," he said, smiling apologetically. When Aunt Sophie and Uncle Tjen returned to their cottage, it was still raining, a rustling rain that tapped softly on the leaves of the elephant plant in front of the house. By the light of a tall carbide lantern they could see the dripping, brown tree trunks like the backs of crocodiles standing up straight. They had an oiled *pajong* with them and later one of the servants brought a *lampu tèmplèk* as a night light. I well remember the atmosphere during such rainy nights and I can especially recall the ineffable feeling of an empty bedroom with the rain outside, rain that suddenly changed to a rapid and irregular tapping and then again rose toward a steady sound that is really a continuous rustling. I see the room again where Aunt Sophie and Uncle Tjen also stayed, with its high ceiling of heavy, massive beams. Again I see the mobile shadows of the wall lamp moving up along the glass shade, and again I feel the coolness on my skin. Sounds from outside penetrated the tightly shut blinds: a light rustling in the grass, rain pelting on the stone rim around the house, and water swirling in the overburdened gutters. Yet all these sounds are compatible and would have blended together in one reassuring concert if the croaking of the frogs had not been there. The whole damn night. That terrible grunting, that horrible booming noise and insistent reck-ceck-ceck that persisted throughout the night and seemed to rend the air. It penetrated through the blinds, rebounded off the walls and filled the room. And even when the rain stopped in the middle of the night, they kept on croaking enthusiastically for quite some time. After the frogs it was the crickets. You could also find these in the city—the tropical night is never without that well-known, incessant, and needling noise—but in the country their sound seems to be massively intensified until it resembles rhythmic breathing, a powerful block of sound that presses down against the solid earth before bouncing back up again. But all these sounds died down shortly before sunrise, when that great silence falls that announces the break of dawn in the tropics. A silence as grandiose and perfect as the still sleeping land itself.

I have heard Aunt Sophie talk about walks in the area, about trips on horseback, picnicking near a *pasangrahan* higher up, and about bathing in the river. That is how I know that the mornings were dry and that they must have been delightful. She said that she and Uncle Tjen got up very early in Tjidané, that they took a bath in the dark, gray bathroom by the light of a tiny lamp and that they then settled down behind the guest room with a strong cup of coffee and watched the sky getting lighter behind the mountains. After that they went for a walk. They would have gone down the main road that bordered the estate, a wet road with cart tracks and often a view of the light green *sawas*. There were also small Chinese *tokos* along it that sold everything from rice to hair pins. Those shops always smelled of *trassi* and the natives' strong tobacco. The cupboards were made of milk crates piled on top of one another, and had become brown and smooth from years of use, and always contained packs of match boxes with colorful trademarks on them. There was a counter with a Chinese abacus. Long, red strips of paper with Chinese characters were pasted on the wall. They were supposed to be slogans of wisdom or sometimes a few lines of poetry. The food stands must have already been set up along the road with their steaming rice, *sambal*, pieces of *empal* (dry roasted meat) or *rempèjè* on earthen plates, and there was always *ketan* with *kintja* and grated coconut. I have never forgotten that country atmosphere. The house of the assistant *wedana*, with its hedge of red wolf's claw, was also on that road. There was a *tjempaka* tree in the yard. A short cut led from the house into the rice fields. The small *desa* school was there and you could always hear children's voices answering in unison. Or they might have singing lessons and sing Dutch songs: the one about a small cart riding along the sandy road or "Heave Ho, Mates, Hoist the Sails." And this far inland and amidst *sawas* and mountains. How cool it must have been there early in the morning, especially after a rainy night, and it must have smelled everywhere of herbs, resin, and fruit.

A ravine ran along beside the *besaran*, some twenty or twenty-five yards away. It was still within the boundaries of the yard and a small path had been hacked out of the bank that went down to it. The steps were bricked and there were artificial terraces and arbors with hanging stephanotis. This path led to the "bathing place," in reality nothing more than an overgrown part of the fast-flowing mountain stream, with clear, translucent water. Large mountain boulders had dammed up a small natural pool. There was no deep water anywhere, except at the bend where the river was the most sheltered, and where it came to an adult's waist. At any rate, I can see Uncle Tjen standing there, shivering with cold. And that water was very cold, because it came from the mountains, more than three thousand feet up.

To be sure, it was the mornings that made Tjidané so wonderful. Whenever I think about it the first thing I see is a diaphanous morning haze over the rubber trees, and then the rear veranda with that early sunlight streaming in from all sides. And then the mountains. In the morning they stood clear, with all the valleys and furrows clearly etched, while in the afternoon they were faint and hazy, faded to a color that was closer to white than to blue or gray. And they might be purple in the evening, and—when it had rained—even red, as red as wine. The skies in Tjidané were also magnificent. At nightfall there were streaked, frayed clouds with a light in between that sometimes was a pink reminiscent of silk, and also lilac and blue. Black appeared in the east first and darkness fell not long afterward. While the lamps were lit inside, darkness grew outside, too deep to penetrate and buzzing with insects, and lasted until morning came once again and a new cycle began.

In this setting of sun and mountains, of shadows and shining plains, of childhood memories and splashing rain, Aunt Sophie and Uncle Tjen experienced their first, and perhaps only idyllic happiness. She showed her husband the *bungur* tree with lilac blossoms that she had planted beside the house. It had matured by itself, yet it was she who had brought it to life. Together with her husband, she visited the sinister bat caves that haunted her dreams so often, and together they rode on horseback along the small paths up the mountain to the *pasangrahan*. They spent the night there, sleeping under thin blankets. In the *besaran* she showed him the room with the red flagstones where she was born. She walked barefoot on the cool, shiny marble of the veranda and sought the places where she had played as a child: the coach house, the rice sheds, where the harvested rice was left to dry. It was as if she were trying to recover a lost dream. But during that search she was surprised by a telegram from Batavia: "Your presence required." These three words cruelly interrupted the idyl and Aunt Sophie and Uncle Tjen left that very afternoon. When they got out of the car that evening, tired and upset, Aunt Christien was already waiting for them on the veranda. There was some surprise, of course, and Aunt Christien did laugh somewhat embarrassedly, but she said that she really had been "quite sick," and that she had thought she was going to die. Though still sick to her stomach she felt much better, though now that she was expecting a child, the doctor had explained that she might feel this way for quite some time. This despite falling down the stairs. Overcome, the sisters embraced each other. Tears of joy. What a blessing, what happiness. Such a joyous expectation—in more ways than one.

5

THE UNEXPECTED RETURN surprised everyone. However, to continue the honeymoon under these circumstances was out of the question. I don't know how Uncle Tjen had imagined his honeymoon, but instead of four weeks it had lasted only four days.

Because they had to move in a hurry now, there was quite a lot of commotion and therefore enough distraction. Aunt Christien and her husband were to move out of the main building and live in the cottage on the right, while Aunt Sophie and Uncle Tjen remained in the big house. That had already been agreed upon before the wedding. I clearly remember that there had been talk about a house of their own. I even remember my mother and Aunt Sophie going out mornings looking for one. There were many deliberations, but Uncle Tjen finally gave in and agreed to move into the De Pauly house. It was clear that this was the most agreeable solution for Aunt Sophie. It is true, that they were two couples now, but the family bond could remain intact this way. It really could not have worked out better. But the households were to be kept *separate*. Aunt Sophie insisted on this: the two families would lead their "own lives," but at the same time she would be able to see and talk to her sister whenever she wanted to. After all, the walkway connecting the cottage to the house was quite short. Yes, this was the solution. Despite the changes, the familiar ways could be retained.

Aunt Christien refurnished her house completely, she got rid of the rocking chairs and étagères and bought modern, heavy armchairs and a big painting with a smoking, purple volcano against a pink background. It may have been a Dezentjé. She gave her sister the old family pieces, such as the sideboards, the silver water carafes, the crystal chandeliers, and the Chinese wall-plates. She even gave her the family bed, which was enormous, and had lots of brass and scroll work. Uncle Tjen later lay ill in this bed, and Aunt Sophie died in it. Not until after her death was it taken apart, hauled away, and stored in the *gudang*, because it had proven to bring misfortune. But no one knew that yet when it was used as Aunt Sophie and Uncle Tjen's bridal bed. During the time the young couple spent in Tjidané, two *djaits* put the finishing touches on the mosquito net. It was made of the finest mesh, trimmed with lace frills in the Old Indies style and decorated with tufts of orange blossom. The whole room also smelled of *melatti*. Uncle Tjen smiled a little because he knew that the flowers represented the wish for a happy marriage. In the bedroom he watched his bride, her face turned away, let down her heavy hair in front of a beautiful three-sided mirror in a polished brass frame. The furnishings were opulent, old, and costly.

At first, life in that old house still brought new sensations, but soon, all too soon, the everyday events became routine, and life seemed as smooth as the sheets on the beds. Little had really changed for Aunt Sophie. After the wedding, the furniture was back where it was supposed to be, and the verandas smelled once again of carbolic acid, naphthalene, soap, and polish. Little had changed for the servants either. They continued to say "nonna" to Aunt Sophie, and soon she was again walking through the house chattering a mile a minute. "Ajo, Midin, where are you? You were smoking again, weren't you. You're getting dense again, don't you know. That stuff is going to your head. I bet you smoke opium." And then: "Mana kuntji saja?" ("Where are my keys?") Usually she'd put them in her key basket herself or else they were lying close at hand. She was just a little *rèwèl*. The younger servants couldn't stand it; only Midin remained unperturbed, at least outwardly. That's just the way she was ("industrious" she always said of herself). And then I hear again those slippers clicking over the floors. She straightened all the tablecloths, and inspected the tiles for footprints or the walls for ants. Perhaps she did it even more zealously than before. After all, she had assigned herself the role of being an extremely neat housewife, and she had to impress that fact on Uncle Tjen and his family. Her cleanliness knew no limits. Once, when she was rattling on to my mother, she said: "You know Lien, I clean the toilet bowl myself. I wouldn't leave such a thing to the servants." All the romance of the honeymoon in Tjidané had disappeared unnoticed, driven away by the smell of polish and the jingle of keys.

What must have gone through Uncle Tjen's mind at that time? At first he may still have felt protected by Aunt Sophie's overwhelming care, and enjoyed the prosperity that was so obvious in her style of living. They ate sumptuously: a *rijsttafel* at noon and a European-style dinner at night, often with wine. There was always enough for several more people, and a lot of food was given to the servants: "Boleh turun," Aunt Sophie said, looking at the serving platters. It became her habit to say this, because that was understood anyway. No one cared where the leftovers went. It suddenly occurs to me now that the separation of the two families was not quite as absolute as may have been supposed, because I can remember them all sitting at the table—on the large veranda in back of the main building—and Aunt Christien and Dubekart were there too. I'm sure now that they always had their meals together.

There were often guests, though most of them were part of the family in one way or another. Even though Uncle Tjen was included immediately—they discussed all family matters with him—he must have felt more or less like a guest in his own house. After a while it began to bother him that he was never alone with his wife. There were always people around. At any moment he could meet his sister-in-law on the veranda in the back or even in his bedroom. She babbled incessantly about acquaintances, servants, the *tukang kebon*, or about clothes. She questioned the servants and passed the stories along to her sister, whispering as if it were something Uncle Tjen was not part of. Her presence annoyed him, but he understood the relationship between the sisters well enough to hold back what he was about to say sometimes. He trained himself from the very beginning to get used to all kinds of delicate situations, and learned to spare sensibilities, to be tolerant, and not to say anything. He avoided all bickering, just as his mother had done. He also felt that there was little that was worth a fight, and he soon let himself be caught in a network of irrefutable rules which Aunt Sophie pushed through quite tactfully.

She was a gentle tyrant. She never demanded, she only asked, but she did so persistently and never let up. This was what constituted the strength of her regime. What at first seemed impossible to Uncle Tjen became a matter of course. For Sophie's sake he even began to wear a flannel girdle, and risked getting the same kind of rashes that had bothered him as a child. But what always made him finally give in was the obvious care and concern that was behind all her tyranny. And that is how she dealt with many other things. Was Uncle Tjen unhappy with all of this? Probably not, at least the feeling was not intense. It was part of his nature to smooth things over and to continually bend over backwards. He could tolerate a great deal without getting tense. Perhaps his being so easygoing was also part of it. Who can tell? As for Aunt Sophie, she was both married as well as surrounded by her own family. It gave her a feeling of quiet satisfaction, and for the time being she asked for nothing more than that.

Life had become more meaningful for her because of the care she could lavish on Uncle Tjen. Part of her love for him—and she used the word *love* frequently and emphatically—was a kind of instinct, a need to nurture, to attach herself to a person, and now she could focus that desire on Uncle Tjen. She reacted to him with all the care and concern she was capable of, although it seemed sometimes as if Aunt Sophie lived in too much of a rush, lived too superficially to really pay any attention to someone else's existence. She brushed by it, always intent on her own objective. Her care and devotion to Uncle Tjen were undoubtedly sincere, but they did not come from a true understanding of his needs, nor did they lead to his soul. It never occurred to her that relationships were different for him than they were for her, that the memory of Winny might be causing him insecurity and confusion, raising doubts about what he had done. She knew little of this, but experienced instead a new certainty, a determination to have him at her disposal, to decide his freedom, his facial expressions, his gentleness, even his stomach problems. She put him on a diet and she made strong bouillon for him and the *nassi tim* that she cooked with a chicken foot in it. She gave the impression of being busy all day long and asked him all the time: "How do you feel?" "O.K.," he answered and smiled. It seemed as if he always gave in, thereby automatically relieving the tension.

But the memory of Winny must have come back again during this time. Even during those first months, her lovely image must have appeared to him over and over again—loved and mourned more than ever. After his marriage, Uncle Tjen never spoke to my mother about Winny again. He never said a word about her. He carefully guarded her memory, kept it from other people and locked it away like one stores a cherished photograph in a closet because it seems better that way. He came unexpectedly one Sunday morning, and without Aunt Sophie. "What's the matter Tjen, is Sophie sick," my mother asked, because he looked different and serious. He shook his head and asked slowly and haltingly if she would come with him—he wanted to go to the cemetery. My mother was visibly moved. She didn't answer, but summoned one of the servants and said: "Sopir suru madju" ("Have the chauffeur bring the car"). My mother came back quite upset, and told about the short but dramatic scene she had witnessed less than an hour before. I still don't know what exactly happened, but I can still see my father listen to her and then slowly shake his head.

"Goddamn it," he said softly. I had never heard him curse. Even though a child, I knew that there was more to it, that there was something he couldn't immediately accept, something shocking, but I do remember the soft and slowly pronounced words of my mother: "Tjen isn't happy."

My mother was not one to hide anything, she always had trouble keeping secrets, but Aunt Sophie never knew anything about this, not even later on when things had been smoothed over once again. And knowing Uncle Tjen, I'm sure that he never betrayed himself, neither with a glance nor with a single gesture. He kept Aunt Sophie's reality separate from the cherished image of Winny: an untarnished image of infinite loveliness and tranquility. This was a private romance that he kept to himself.

Once in a while Aunt Sophie said: "You know, Tjen is so quiet. I sometimes believe that he's still thinking about his girl." But she said it in a manner that indicated she really sought for an explanation some-where else. As a matter of fact, she was hardly disturbed. As far as she was concerned, Winny was dead and therefore an inconceivable rival because she could not imagine a rivalry other than a realistic one. Aunt Sophie never had the slightest notion what the memory of a dead lover could mean to somebody, and especially not what Winny had meant to Uncle Tjen, with her sad life, her "secret" and her tenderness. Winny was only a name to her, a name Uncle Tjen carefully avoided men-tioning. Aunt Sophie did not share his emotional life, and he left it that way.

As the months went by, Aunt Sophie became less interested in Uncle Tjen and directed her attention more and more at her sister who, as she expressed it, expected a "little bundle from Heaven." The great family event that was approaching began to make increasing demands on her.

Both sisters, especially Aunt Sophie, were preoccupied with all kinds of possibilities. Would it be a boy or a girl? Would it be fair or dark? The odds were incalculable. In the middle of the day, or even at night sometimes, Aunt Sophie would suddenly feel afraid. The image of her grandmother emerged from the distant past, a dark woman she had seen several times in the outbuildings when she was a girl of six or seven. Although Aunt Christien was not completely indifferent, she was cer-tainly less interested in the various possibilities of skin color and, conse-quently, did not indulge as much in somber speculations. The most important thing was that she, like other women, now carried a child, although she had to put up with the usual problems of pregnancy. She became very big, with the result that she had difficulty walking. Several weeks before the delivery she got swollen ankles, looked very pale and tired, and constantly felt *pegel*, or unable to stretch her limbs. She was also troubled by dizziness and an irregular heartbeat, in short, a complete list of the usual complaints. At least several times a day Aunt Christien issued a bulletin: she was stiff and tired in the morning, had swollen legs in the afternoon, a flustered feeling before going to bed, and, in between, light to moderate nausea.

Aunt Sophie worried constantly. She got upset about every symptom and consulted various *dukuns*. They massaged, touched, and scrutinized Aunt Christien attentively, and declared unanimously that it would be a girl because Aunt Christien was not only big but also wide, especially when seen from behind.

Three seamstresses in the meantime worked on the layette, which would be provided by Aunt Sophie, of course. As the time grew nearer the sewing machines, set up on the veranda in the back, whirred faster and Aunt Sophie's slippers clicked on the marble in a manner more harried than ever before. There was no peace for the servants. She drove them mercilessly, and after awhile the atmosphere was like that of "a madhouse," as Dubekart said.

She got entangled in her own fuss and worked herself up to unbelievable heights. Uncle Tjen must have looked at her in bewilderment because it was the first time he saw her like this. He could not have expected this behavior.

A few days before the delivery Aunt Christien fainted, causing great consternation. From that moment on Aunt Sophie hardly left her sister's side. She cared for her completely, washed her twice a day, combed her hair, and oversaw the housekeeping. Aunt Sophie now also slept in the cottage to be with her sister. What Uncle Tjen thought of all this meant little to her. He didn't say anything, but he must have realized by then that her family would always come between them, and that in the future he could only depend on himself. But he was the kind of man who had great difficulty accepting this. His sensitivity as well as his need for understanding and closeness had destined him for a different life.

Kitty's birth will always be known in family lore as Aunt Christien's "mouse delivery." Dear God, we weren't spared any detail. We had to share everything—quite literally.

Kitty was born on a Sunday, this could never be forgotten, because it is associated with the story about the doctor who couldn't make it in time because, as we found out later, he had gone to Priok for a swim in the sea at "Petit Trouville." They called him up three times before he came, arriving just in time to cut the umbilical cord. Aunt Sophie wanted to show him out and "dismiss" him as the family doctor, but

Dubekart acted calmly and with dignity and prevented worse for the sake of the child. And as far as the doctor was concerned, he had laughed and congratulated Aunt Christien on the surprisingly fast delivery and the quick expulsion of the placenta, which Aunt Sophie—in typical Indies fashion—always called "the little sister." But what had really made everything all right and cooled off tempers so quickly was the fact that Kitty proved to be a sweet *white* and *blond* baby. This time her grandfather's European blood had not been denied, thank God, because it really seemed as if a dark complexion and dark hair had established itself forever in the family. In any case, Kitty was not affected and this brought unparalleled joy, which even the servants had to take part in. A *selamatan* would be organized to celebrate this happy event and to thank *Tuan Allah* for the heavenly gift.

But I know that the feast was preceded by lengthy negotiations. A *hadji* from a near-by *kampong* was sent for. He was to lead a prayer of thanks of course and was also responsible for the necessary food, flowers, and coffee. Although he remained standing on the steps in front of the house, he could still be distinguished from the others by his plaid *kain plekat*, a shantung jacket and a white *kopiah*, that signified his exceptional position. Not until Aunt Sophie gave him permission did he begin to speak, but even then in a roundabout way. Everything Aunt Sophie asked for was possible of course. He was more than obliging and accommodating, and during his explanation he managed to display the appropriate attitude of both purveyor and man of distinction. Costs were not mentioned and only when Aunt Sophie, again according to tradition, asked about them at the very last moment, did he answer courteously in terms of mutual benefit. Yet I'm sure that the price caused Aunt Sophie to feign surprise and that they still *tawarded* for quite some time. The negotiations proceeded according to a well known, and set pattern.

Be that as it may, by four in the afternoon the guests were sitting on the "walkway" on *tikars*, listening to the recitation of Arabic prayers, which the lay leader seemed to read from the palms of his hands. From time to time they joined in with a resounding "Amien." An assortment of food lay before them on serving dishes and wrapped in banana leaves. Fragrant incense burned in the center.

Very curious and, of course, very much a topic of conversation, was the extraordinary fact that Kitty, according to Aunt Sophie, had come into the world "totally clean," she hadn't even been "wet." And we could believe it or not, but "do you know why?" Well, Aunt Christien had drunk coconut milk every day before Kitty was born. "And that cleanses," Aunt Sophie added. Though she had let the midwife go ahead ("I didn't want to say anything"), she thought that there was no point in washing the child or putting drops in its eyes. "Oh well, they just want to show that they can do it too."

Kitty proved to be a butterball. Her weight was quite alright in the beginning even though the figures varied from time to time, fluctuating between eight and twelve pounds depending on who was telling the story. She was a good-sized baby, even if you took only the minimum weight into consideration. And that from such a small mother who was also "rather narrow" according to the doctor's statement and Aunt Sophie's information. The short, though very painful, delivery seemed to have taken more out of Aunt Christien than one would have thought at first. The baby cried a lot, right from the beginning. She sometimes howled for hours on end, which made everyone in the house very tense. The servants were driven from pillar to post and were reprimanded even more than usual. After several days the reason became clear: Aunt Christien didn't have enough milk. Only two things were possible now: bottle feeding, with all its problems, or, better yet, to get a good wet nurse, if that was possible.

Recommended by the *dukun*, the latter came with an imperturbable baby in a *slendang*. She was a girl, as Aunt Sophie said, who "looked you straight in the eye," and talked in a loud voice. She was called Waginem, and though her name seemed to indicate it, she could not be Javanese, which proved to be the case. Her father was one of those proud Buginese sailors who "always look you straight in the eye." She was still young, still a girl really, and yet this was her second child. After the doctor had examined her, Waginem and her baby came to live in the outbuildings. "You can never be careful enough with those native girls." A *balé-balé* was put in Aunt Christien's bedroom for Waginem to lie down on when she was nursing. Again her resolution became evident, even to Europeans. She let them know that she was only going to nurse the child while it was in the *slendang*, and despite Aunt Sophie's sputtering to the contrary, that is what happened. It was awful for Aunt Christien to see Waginem sit down on a chair and put the fair Kitty to her big brown breast. Aunt Sophie was there every time to clean the nipples herself with some cotton and boric acid. Waginem sneered at it, but fortunately she let it go this time.

Kitty's crying stopped. Each time the child came back to Aunt Christien's bed she hiccupped from overfeeding. She soon skipped a night feeding, and gained very nicely.

Everything went fine until the incident with Dubekart. One day he came in during a feeding. Perhaps he behaved normally, but then again he might have observed Waginem too long. In any case, she laughed briefly but meaningfully, and both sisters felt cold shivers go up and down their spines. When added to her other recalcitrant ways this was cause enough to give Waginem a good tongue lashing. The result was that she asked for "lepas" and left the very next day with her head up high. None of us knew what explanation she gave to the servants. Aunt Sophie must have asked about it, but they would never have given her the right answer.

There were no other wet nurses after Waginem left. Better to use Bear Brand milk from a can than ever to run such a risk again. Aunt Sophie prepared all the feedings and that is why you could find her busily thinning or warming the milk and boiling bottles and nipples at all hours of the day. And wonder of wonders, this method of feeding also went well, much to the relief of the whole family. Now they could get along without "such a snooty native slut." The only disadvantage was that Kitty grew so accustomed to a bottle that, even when she was three, she still had to take one with her when she went to bed, albeit one filled with vanilla syrup instead of milk. But this could not have been known then.

For a long time after the delivery Aunt Christien continued to feel tired—she proved to be anemic and had to rest a lot. And though she never would have shown it, Aunt Sophie was really thankful that she did, because now she could take the baby to her room on the pretext that her sister needed rest. There she gave her a bottle, changed, and washed her, and after a while, she took over completely. It stayed that way for several weeks until Aunt Christien slowly recovered and reclaimed Kitty. Aunt Sophie found it difficult to give her up. Now that she had taken care of the child for such a long time, had felt her in her arms, carried her for hours in a *slendang*, and had hummed the lullabies to her that she remembered from her own childhood, it was only natural that she felt a strong desire for motherhood herself.

Her disappointment increased with each passing month. When the doctor could not help, my mother went with Aunt Sophie to "the Chinese woman." She lived in the "Chinese Quarter" in the "lower town," and at the time enjoyed a certain reputation. She was a clairvoyant and sold all kinds of *djamus* which, as my mother once said, "had already helped many women." After the other Europeans had withdrawn behind closed blinds against the late afternoon heat, and while my father slept and Uncle Tjen was at the office, they had the carriage hitched up, a mylord, which was rarely used since we had a car. In the burning sun, behind lowered blinds, we rode down the long Molenvliet road. I remember the scorching heat, the whirling clouds of dust, and the strange, empty streets. Aunt Sophie and my mother talked in whispers.

After a while we turned left, because "the Chinese woman" lived far down Gang Kenanga beyond the gasworks. It was a small brick house which from the outside looked uninhabited. Only weeds and damp moss grew in the yard. The front veranda was empty, except for one dusty bulb which may have served as a night light. No human hand had ever brought order here; everything was left to itself, the dust, the weather, and the cobwebs. Behind this veranda lived the woman who, according to the stories, was incredibly rich. She never asked money for a consultation, because she said it would only weaken her power. But she would very much appreciate it if one sacrificed some money to the spirit who enabled her to help people. A small room had been cleared for this spirit. It contained a little bed with a miniature dirty yellow mosquito net, a tiny pillow, and a *guling*. More than once I saw Aunt Sophie put some bank notes on this little bed (it even had little red *klambu* hooks), and they were always gone the next time we came.

Inside this little room it always smelled damp and of native flowers, strong and sweet. To a child, this atmosphere was inexplicably oppressive and frightening. Everything contributed to this feeling: the secrecy that was always maintained during these trips, the ritual upon entering the small room—we had to remove our shoes and Aunt Sophie always asked permission to enter—and especially the Chinese woman herself. She was unbelievably skinny with a horrible mustache that was long and thin. For this reason she was everywhere known as "Njonja kumis." These memories will always remain part of a moldy world, a twilight that hid occult powers and forces.

She sometimes took us to the kitchen which looked like the room of an alchemist with its bottles of magical water, things for abortion, and love potions. I know now that this borders on the criminal, that it was evil and poisonous, but then I felt only the danger of it—a threat that took on extraordinary shapes at night.

Aunt Sophie and my mother sat on low wooden benches during the séance. The Chinese woman sat on a little mat. Incense floated through the room and she had a steamed-up mirror in front of her wherein she saw the images of the future.

"I see three shapes," she kept on saying, "clearly three." This made Aunt Sophie persist again for awhile. She continued to drink the *djamus* which, though born in the Indies, she swallowed with disgust, continued to bring flower offerings to the cemetery, and she had *menjan* burned every *malam djumahat* (the evening between Thursday and Friday) in order to appease the spirits. According to unverified reports in the family (even my mother knew nothing about this), she also paid a visit to the holy cannon in the lower part of town. If that is true, she would have sat on the cannon like the other thousands of barren women before her, leaving an offering of flowers and money.

When all the *dukuns* and offerings continued to fail, and when also the doctor gave her "little hope" in the end, she did not start to breed dogs, or cats, or parrots, but immersed herself in the administration of "the new Office."

Uncle Tjen worked for the postal service in Batavia. He was a head clerk there and, as I was always told, even had a department under him. This was not a bad position, certainly not when we take his age and prior training into account. But for Aunt Sophie, coming from a family of landowners who had earned hundreds of thousands and could lose similar amounts, and who could bend even the mighty Department of the Interior to their will, for her, such a subordinate job was not worthwhile. When he was still living in Painan, Uncle Tjen had begun studying to become a notary. Well, he had to pick it up again, and she would take on the daily management of an office for the administration of houses and estates to be organized by Uncle Tjen. This would be financed with family money and could perhaps later on be turned into a notary's office. This was decided during a family meeting.

The other cottage, the one on the left, was cleared out and an office was established there that quickly flourished, and was later incorporated. It is no wonder, because Aunt Sophie put all her energy into the new business, especially in the beginning. She turned out to be an excellent business woman and under her supervision no clerk dared to waste time. Her high and piercing voice exhorted them to ever greater conscientiousness, while all the activity completely occupied her time, thereby channeling her desire for motherhood into different directions. This work also informed her of her husband's worries and problems and soon led to a more intimate partnership. It gave her a sense of being closer to him, and Uncle Tjen, in turn, praised her to everyone for her support.

Whenever time permitted, she concerned herself with the little girl Kitty, who, fair and with lustrous blond hair, was beginning to look very cute. Aunt Sophie captivated her and bound her to her in many different ways. In the afternoon Kitty was allowed to sleep between Aunt Sophie and Uncle Tjen in the big bed and soon she was more with Aunt Sophie than with her own mother. She no longer distinguished between them anymore and called them both "aunt." It was hard on Aunt Christien but she let it pass, both for her sister's sake and because she was expecting for the second time. It turned out to be a boy with a dark complexion and dark hair, and his birth was in no way a "mouse delivery." There was no *selamatan* either. Not only that, but Aunt Christien was so worn out that a blood transfusion was necessary. She was brought to the hospital in the middle of the night. For days she "hovered between life and death" as they say, and did not come home with her baby until three weeks later, although she was even then extremely weak.

In the meantime Kitty was allowed to sleep with Aunt Sophie in the main house. At first only the crib was moved, but gradually the other furniture was also brought to the new nursery. When Aunt Christien was on her feet again at last and began cautiously to resume her daily tasks—especially taking care of the baby—it seemed reasonable for Kitty to stay in the main house. This went on for several months and after that it didn't seem to make much sense to change again.

A time of relative happiness followed. Aunt Sophie found satisfaction in carrying out the double task she had set for herself, and was calmer than ever before. This of course influenced Uncle Tjen. He smiled with relief and even agreed to another plan: the construction of a tennis court in the back yard. Shrubs were cleared away, bird cages moved, fences taken down, and a lawn cultivated. I remember coolies working with a roller at the time. I recall a lawn sprinkler and can still see the seeding of the lawn with grass seed from Singapore. Uncle Tjen taught me to play tennis on this delicious smelling court. He was the best player. I can still picture him waiting for the ball: a tall thin figure in a pair of narrow white pants and white tennis shoes, though strangely enough always with black socks. During that time I know that not only family came to play, but also acquaintances such as the young people from Dubekart's office, although he himself did not play.

Sometimes they talked for a long time afterwards in the big rattan chairs on the grass, waiting for nightfall. And sometimes a lamp was also brought outside, and it happened that people stayed for dinner. I also remember simply sitting outside on a moonlit evening. The moon itself was a mysterious, yellow globe, always with the same markings of its craters, mountain peaks, and deep seas: a phosphorescent eye that cast a sulphurous light over the tree tops. Beneath them the shadows were as black as ink. Against the side of the house ivy and the pure white bridal wreath grew against a background of stirring leaves dotted with black spots. To the side, orchids hung in the pergolas, again the purest white, almost like flesh, half animal and half plant, but in the evening sweetly fragrant, as glorious as one could wish for. On such a moonlit night the peacefulness also came over the people, and their voices were subdued. Everyone enjoyed such lazing around.

Peace had descended from heaven . . . until the event that has always been described within the family as "*the* transfer." We would say to each other: "Oh, yes, that happened before the transfer" or "that came after it." A milestone.

Dubekart was appointed agent for the Blauwhoeden Warehouse Company in Bandjermasin, in Borneo. It was an important promotion that must have meant a lot to him, but it also meant moving. He knew about the appointment months in advance, but he had kept it quiet in order to keep peace at home. "I believe I acted properly in doing so," he is said to have stated later. But when the news reached the sisters, it hit like a bolt of lightning. There was an uproar in the Salemba house that several hours later spread to our house and inflamed my mother too. Aunt Sophie heaped reproaches on Dubekart and carried on like a lunatic. She insisted that a separation from Kitty would mean her death, but she was no match for his calm stubbornness. "Then I regret," he concluded in his usual manner of speaking that sounded as if it had been written, "that I cannot make you see the irrationality of your attitude."

A month later he left for his new post. Aunt Christien would follow several weeks later. The weeks became months, but she did leave finally, and Kitty went with her.

The day of the departure must have been a difficult day for the whole family, especially for Uncle Tjen. Little imagination is needed to realize how intractable Aunt Sophie must have been. She did not die though. Instead she threw herself more than ever into her work at the office. All day long her voice crackled through the house. The clerks made mistakes, the messengers delivered the wrong letters, and, when her husband came home, she overwhelmed him with complaints and grievances. She reproached him for his halfheartedness, his lack of initiative, and for being in league with the servants. No matter how unreasonable the reproaches may have seemed to him, he was once again the sensible one who avoided arguments because he knew that they would only end in big fights.

Except for that short hysterical interval, I really don't remember Aunt Sophie as being anything more than "nervous." I know that she took bromides and God knows what other drugs. She suffered from headaches—"bad tension headaches"—and from dozens of other ailments. She always spoke vehemently about "terrible pain," "been so sick," and so forth. And yet, according to my mother, these recurring laments came later, after "*the* transfer." I only remember the tension and the sometimes boundless self-glorification.

As long as I can remember, there was always a feeling of turmoil, a tension that was ready to discharge at any moment. The whole house was permeated with it; it clung to the walls and was spread over the furniture. I can still hear my mother say: "It's like there's electricity in the air." And once lightning struck, the clamor was everywhere: servants running, dogs crawling away, chickens cackling, and cockatoos screaming. But Uncle Tjen remained silent. You only needed to experience such an outburst once in order to pity Uncle Tjen, the servants, the animals, and Aunt Sophie as well. And just as thunder is followed by a huge downpour, so was the explosion always followed by the inevitable crying fit, an uncontrollable sobbing that I needed to watch only once. And just as the sky clears up afterwards and is wiped clean, so too peace returned to the house for a while. The storm had blown over again and Aunt Sophie was as amiable, friendly, and as solicitous as ever; she'd laugh her short laugh again and Uncle Tjen was overwhelmed with expressions of affection. But she never wanted to be reminded of scenes like these. She eliminated them from her life each time and expected others to forget them too. These outbursts simply did not fit the person she wanted to be.

Although she may have always been that way, the forced manner and the continuous need to build a separate person around her real self could only have come later. Which is what my mother said too. It dehumanized her, made her unapproachable, and made her lose any ability to see anything but herself: *her* life, *her* fate, *her* problems. But there was despair and torment in the grim manner she played her role, in the way she aired her complaints, and in the way her endless talking always brought her eventually, by way of other people and things, back to herself.

In that state we left Aunt Sophie behind in 1922.

6

AUNT SOPHIE AND Uncle Tjen were standing beside each other on the quay in Priok. It would be the last time that we saw them together. Uncle Tjen was as thin as ever, and Aunt Sophie, slightly heavier since her marriage, was sniffling a little. We were on the promenade deck of the *Rembrandt*, the steamer that would bring us to Holland. Although I had never seen it, this was the country I was accustomed to call "my fatherland." Perhaps that's why I expected so much.

It was blazing hot and the light was unbearable. We waved with our handkerchiefs to all the family and friends we were leaving behind in the Indies. From behind the backs of the people hanging over the railing I looked for Aunt Sophie and Uncle Tjen who were standing on the bright quay among the white and colorfully dressed figures who were getting smaller and smaller. They were still there, but when I tried again a minute later, I could no longer find them. We steamed out of the harbor at half speed, slipping by the breakwaters. Suddenly I saw my father hurry after my mother, who was sobbing quietly. He took her to their cabin. Only now do I realize that at that moment she must have felt completely abandoned. Until then she had lived within a large Indies family of brothers, sisters, first cousins, and cousins by marriage. This is where she belonged and she could only "function," think, feel, and act, when she was a part of it. This was the first time she had been uprooted, and she must have felt helpless and lost. My father was the only one left from that familiar context, yet he did not really belong to the family. He could not make up for the lost environment. She would now have to do without her usual way of life: not only her morning visits and her eternal fussing, but also her family *perkaras*, her conversations with *babu* Bèot, her predictions, and her garden with its *melatti* shrubs and *tjempaka* trees. All of this sank away behind a foggy horizon of masts, ships, smoke, and tin roofs, while in front of her was the even fainter horizon of a faded blue sky and a pale sea.

The quay would be empty now. The people were in their cars again, and Aunt Sophie and Uncle Tjen would be driving home on the Priok road like all the others who had seen people off. They would reach Salemba Avenue, turn into the yard, and perhaps sit on the rear veranda to talk a little about us. But we wouldn't be there anymore. We were now on the deck of the ship. This was the only reality: the ship, the sound of the waves, and the wind.

The beginning of the voyage was not very encouraging, especially for my mother. The rolling had already begun in the Straits of Malacca. The Indian Ocean was choppy, and we were going against the current. The ship lurched, pitched, groaned, and squealed so much that, as a joke, the passengers began to talk about the "drunken" *Rembrandt*. It even reached my mother. She was lying pale and sick in her bunk in a broiling cabin that smelled of varnish, eau de cologne, and peppermint. She did not come up on deck until we reached the Red Sea.

She quickly made friends with a group of people that included the unforgettable Roos Blondeau whose way of laughing figured in my mother's stories for years afterward. According to her that laugh was like "Ke-ke-ke-ke-ke-ke-ke . . ."—just like squeaking woodwork in stormy weather. "You're too much, Roos!" Roos clearly had Chinese blood. She was small, fat, cheerful, and very jealous of her much younger husband, a "charmer" as my mother said, not without satisfaction. The other ladies said he was "naughty," but I only remember an old Indies hand, tall and stiff with a small mustache, who always tried to behave correctly. He was courteous in an old-fashioned way, especially toward the younger ladies, and in particular to one of them called Jeanne Dom, who came from Djokja. Then there was an older officer who had served in Atjeh, with a *klewang* scar across his forehead that looked really rather innocent. In the company of ladies he always said that he had another scar, but that it was one he couldn't show. He could be very funny.

The last one I remember was a broker from Surabaja, called Bloot. He always introduced himself as: "I am Bloot." The funny officer made a face that was priceless. He could always count on Roos to cheer him on. In short, it was an interesting and lively group of old Indies hands who were looking forward to their leave in Europe, though with the strangest expectations. The high point came when we steamed through the Suez Canal. In the evening we danced on deck and the next morning we were in Port Said. The group went ashore together and spent their money on jugglers, snake-charmers, souvenirs, and Egyptian cigarettes. We were going to leave that evening, but the funny officer could not be found. We were already under way when he was brought alongside in the launch of the harbor police. He had been robbed. He was upset and somewhat depressed, but he still had enough presence of mind not to mention where the theft had taken place.

The *Rembrandt* was brought into the harbor at Genoa a week later, early in the morning, against a strong wind. The officer from Atjeh left for Paris, "La Ville Lumière" as he said in French. We met him there later. He had his hair dyed and was manicured and pedicured. Paris was "terrific," he said, but the women disappointed him, and he praised his young Sundanese mistress whom he had so casually left behind in the Indies. He whispered something in my father's ear and almost died laughing. My mother didn't like "such things," she said later, but my father smiled shyly and only said: "What do you expect from such a man?"

We traveled directly from Paris to The Hague where we arrived in the evening, and registered at the Vieux Doelen. It was raw and windy and the branches of the trees along the Voorhout thrashed wildly. My mother shivered and was cold.

The next morning there was a knock on the door and the bellboy delivered a telegram. It came from Batavia, and was from Aunt Sophie and Uncle Tjen to welcome us home. My mother was very moved and said, "It is so nice to know that they are thinking of us in the Indies." My father didn't answer, and was more quiet than ever.

We were already living in our own house when the first letter arrived. It had come on the next boat and consequently contained little worth mentioning. "Life is going on as usual" Aunt Sophie wrote. She had driven past our house and noticed that the new residents had already moved in, and that the *melatti* shrubs in the front yard had been removed, probably because they blocked the view. And my mother had always taken care of them with such love. Very early every morning she'd walk along the fragrant hedge and pick the flowers, and always stick a couple of them in her hair. The new people had to be *totoks* according to her, and they had no feeling for a tropical garden. They were always so *kasar*. She bore a grudge against the *totoks* from the day she arrived in Holland, and did not consider the fact that my father was one too. "Those *totoks* are dirty," she always began, not only didn't they *tjèbok* themselves, but they also didn't believe in personal hygiene in other ways. She also said that it would be better if I never married a "real Dutch girl." "Bau banké," she snorted.

My mother wasn't happy in Holland. She wanted to go back even before the leave was over, because she was homesick for the Indies. But circumstances forced my parents to stay much longer, even years longer. When, after much deliberation and doubt, the decision was made to stay, we moved to the section of The Hague called the Statenkwartier. We moved into a large house on a quiet square. In addition to my own bedroom I also had a separate "study" which looked out on a few trees which I can only picture in rainy weather. There I continued to live the life of a spoiled and only son, which carried the disadvantage of my mother's doting surveillance.

And so we lived for several years among Dutch houses, Dutch people, and through the usual succession of seasons, but on the horizon always loomed my parents', as well as my own, "country of origin." There were evenings when right through everything—through the beams, the walls, and the doors—I suddenly saw the windblown coconut trees alongside our old house against the background of a light evening sky. The moon was part of this scene, of course—a bright yellow moon in a wide circle of light. This always portended disruptions, difficulties, disasters, and misfortune, and once again I sensed its ominous power. But sometimes the memory of that same moon evoked that irreplaceable feeling of tranquility and happiness, of consolation and reconciliation, and of deep satisfaction.

But if this was true for me, how difficult it must have been for my mother. The ties to the Indies were never absent. They could be found in recollections, in meeting other Indies people, and in letters. We were kept up to date by Aunt Sophie's long and confusing stories, while our memory took care of "integrating" nature and our former surroundings. For instance, Aunt Sophie wrote that there had been a heavy thunderstorm, and that lightning had struck one of the coconut trees in the back yard. "You know, the middle one," she wrote, and of course we did. And I would automatically correct the image out of some sort of need to "keep up." Along the road, Aunt Sophie continued, several *kenari* trees were being cut down, the large Chinese pot had fallen over, the *rambutan* tree was again covered with clusters of red fruits, "Lizzy" (one of the dogs) was in heat again, and the toilet was plugged up ("our cesspools are filled to overflowing!"). And on it went: one uninterrupted stream of trivial facts, events, and interests, interspersed with commentary.

One day Midin had run away. He had not given notice, but he simply wasn't there one morning. His room was empty, and he had taken everything he owned. I suddenly saw his small, mouselike face before me. He was always being reprimanded, and he endured it in silence, with a kind of resignation that had almost become routine for him. Any

rebelliousness would have been useless anyway, because he was firmly
tied to the family. He had run away a few times before because Aunt
Sophie's treatment of him had made him *malu* in front of the other
servants, but he always came back "with his tail between his legs" as
Aunt Sophie put it. He always fled to the *udik*, also, I am convinced,
because he yearned for the rural life he had left. But it inevitably became
clear in the long run that he no longer belonged there. He'd lose weight
and become sick because life in the *desa* and the plain food no longer
agreed with him. Then he would admit defeat and soon he would be back
in the old routine. After each defeat in a long series of defeats that Midin
came to accept as a natural process of ebb and flow, he became more
firmly tied to the family and more than ever at the mercy of Aunt
Sophie's and Aunt Christien's whims. He hadn't been away for years but
now, Aunt Sophie wrote, he had suddenly left again. She had already
noticed that something was wrong and one day he had run *amok* and had
left "in an angry mood." At first Aunt Sophie waited calmly for his
return, but when he stayed away for weeks, she lost her assurance. Each
letter spoke of her concern because the household functioned poorly
without Midin. When he suddenly appeared again, Aunt Sophie informed us immediately. She reveled in it, though she was at the same
time relieved and grateful. He was thinner and more destitute than ever
before, unwashed, and forsaken—forsaken by his young girl friend! He
had met her at a circumcision ceremony in the *kampong* behind Salemba
Avenue and she was attracted by his wise, reassuring words and his
prestige as a prosperous man. And he probably saw a sudden chance to
add some color to his monotonous life of servitude. He must have forced
a confrontation with Aunt Sophie just to be free. Within two months the
process had taken its natural course. He had stayed all that time in the
kampong, living off his savings until the inevitable end followed by
the humiliating return to Salemba Avenue. Aunt Sophie read him the
riot act this time, because she now possessed a powerful weapon. She
wrote us all of this and also what she had told him: "Who'd want to
marry such an old *kakèh?* Aren't you ashamed of yourself?" I remember
that when I read this I felt pity and sympathy for poor Midin. Faithful
old Midin had been led astray by his romantic feelings, and now had to
pay for it by spending the rest of his life indentured to the family. He was
no longer allowed to spend his own savings. It was deducted from his
salary by Aunt Sophie and put in a savings account in the bank. Her
passion to put things in order, to have a finger in every pie, to take care of
things, and to dominate, drove her to usurp his freedom. She simply
made herself Midin's guardian.

At another time Aunt Sophie wrote that on New Year's Eve Uncle Alex had come from Sukabumi to celebrate the New Year with the family. Aunt Sophie had enjoyed it very much, although being together on such days had lost much of its charm since Aunt Christien had left for Bandjermasin and since we were also gone. "We drank to all of you, Lien, to your health, and to seeing you here again very soon."

On the New Year's Eve in question Alex had carefully prepared his sister for the news that he was going to be a father. In Aunt Sophie's words: "with that native woman he lives with." It turned out later that the girl had already been born. This shocked Aunt Sophie and reminded her of something she preferred not to think about. "I'm ashamed of my own brother, Lien," she added. It seemed so strange, she said, that she and Aunt Christien "had turned out so well," while Uncle Alex had never paid much attention to the good name of the family and to its traditions. She had to admit that "that woman" was rather good for him and took excellent care of him, but Aunt Sophie still had to say that she'd never thought it was "nice." She always lowered her voice when she talked about *the* question, and usually began to whisper, at times even moving only her lips emphatically when she said: "A pity, huh, with— a—*native*—woman," while her face expressed ineffable sorrow. "Terrible," she said and invariably closed her eyes. And one time she said, as if expressing something profound: "Our family could better practice racial improvement, Lien, not that. . . ." And now it had happened: a child. A "native branch" had again sprouted and a dark skin was now even more prominent in the family. Just terrible!

It was always very noticeable that it was difficult for Aunt Sophie to talk about this sore point. She held something back, an embarrassment so characteristic of the sensibilities that dominated people like Aunt Sophie. But it was precisely her secrecy and distortion that gave her away. Her notion of marriage and of mistresses, of race and skin color, was no different from that of others of her class, and it was this very same prejudice that made Aunt Sophie and Aunt Christien urge Uncle Alex to "recognize" the child legally, so that it would become "European." He did resist a little, because he knew, of course, that it also meant a European upbringing and, sooner or later, taking the child from the mother, not to mention the expense and other obligations. Uncle Alex had already lived for years with Titi—that was the name of "that" woman— but this was their first child. Only it didn't end there. After Fonnie came Joyce and after Joyce, Deetje. They followed each other at intervals of one and a half to two years. After the last one, however, Aunt Sophie told her brother in no uncertain terms that it had to stop. Perhaps Aunt

Sophie managed to wrest a promise from him, but I do not know if he kept it. In any case, he only recognized those three. Aunt Sophie raced by car to Sukabumi each time one of the children was born, but it was always a disappointment. "Black, Lien," she reported to Holland, "and not just a little either, but really dark!"

Aunt Sophie's letters indicated her emotional barometer. There were lots of fluctuations, and a depression was often followed by a cloudless sky, rain was followed by sunshine, and sadness by joy. The joy came with the return of Aunt Christien and her children from Bandjermasin. For Aunt Sophie that meant first and foremost, Kitty. She never said a word about her brother-in-law, Dubekart. It was such a happy letter. Although she'd never given a thought to any religious obligations or allowed a minister into the house, and although she held decidedly unchristian ideas about the hereafter, Aunt Sophie wrote that she had folded her hands for joy and had thanked God. Now she would get "her child" back. What spoiled her pleasure somewhat was when Aunt Christien forewarned her sister that they were not returning to Salemba Avenue, but were instead moving into their own house. But Aunt Sophie was not easily defeated by this setback. This time she was quite prepared to take on Dubekart, because she had no doubt that he was behind this. And this time she had some powerful weapons, because circumstances were in her favor. Just wait until they were in Batavia and were staying temporarily on Salemba Avenue. Using the same gentle tyranny that conquered Uncle Tjen, she now overcame Dubekart: she was friendly, sweet, and exerted a gentle pressure, and she never let up, not even for a minute. In any case, I can only remember Aunt Christien and Dubekart living in the large cottage, even later on, and remember that Kitty lived in the main house as the child of two mothers.

The return and the meeting at the boat were described to us in minute detail. Aunt Christien did not look well but was tired and pale, and had grown noticeably older in those few years. She had not been happy there and was overjoyed to be back. One doesn't need much imagination to reconstruct the reunion. The emotion and the tears of joy were probably mutual. Dubekart must have been watching it with Uncle Tjen. And then there were the children. They were ten and eight now. Kitty had become lovely with her beautiful "golden blond" hair and her soft, pale complexion. "And Lien," she wrote, "you wouldn't say so of a ten-year old, but she's already something of a woman, you know." Tjalie also appeared to be "a nice boy," but it seemed to her that he had become darker and began to resemble Uncle Alex's girls. But not even this could dampen the joy of those first few days. Uncle Tjen was also happy.

"Maybe you'll calm down a bit now," he had said. "I think so too," Aunt Sophie added. But the nicest detail was the description of Midin, who, with tears in his eyes, had embraced both children. He had gone down on his knees, calling out, "Allah, njò . . . nòn. . . ." And time and again he gripped their hands and caressed their arms. "It was really moving, Lien." Midin had suddenly been canonized. How faithful and devoted native servants could be—at least the older ones like Midin, who had not yet been stirred up by the "Communists." This was followed by a somewhat alarming story about impudent fruit vendors, and a devastating critique of the ethical policy of the government. Yes, the natives were getting more and more impertinent. Why just the other day when she was in the post office, a native had said to her (in Dutch mind you!): "Ma'am you should wait your turn." Can you imagine that! She had immediately put him in his place, in Malay of course. They were really getting insolent.

"Really, Lien," Aunt Sophie wrote, "they don't know their place anymore." And the government didn't do anything about it. On the contrary, they did many things that the natives could interpret as weakness. Especially the governor general gave the example. He was so much on the side of the natives that he had given the palace personnel one afternoon off per week. And *she* was also so wishy-washy. Imagine, when the chauffeur was sick, Madam Governor had visited him with a bouquet of flowers. And do you know what he is supposed to have said: "Njonja perliep sama saja" ("Madam is in love with me"). Which only goes to show how little these ethical *totoks* understand the natives.

After these political opinions, and I suppose that they were influenced by Dubekart, Aunt Sophie's letter would suddenly switch over to the birds or the servants. The cockatoo with the pink crest was dead and —just imagine—Alimah ("you remember Lien, that young maid you knew") had come to her again for "leave." She was pregnant once more. That was the fourth time already, even though something had gone wrong the other three times. The children were simply not meant to live. They had died either at birth or shortly thereafter. All three of them. "*Kassian*, those people, don't you think so, Lien?" It was indeed a sad case, and Aunt Sophie thought it necessary to act this time. She simply told Alimah: "I don't want that to happen anymore, do you hear!"

In one of the letters Aunt Sophie wrote that Uncle Tjen had caught "a bad cold." He had driven around in an open car, and in the rain mind you. She had kept him in bed, she wrote, the way you write about a child. Several weeks later the cold had developed into bronchitis. He felt quite well, though, and went to the office in the morning, but by evening he always had a temperature. It "bothered" her a little, she wrote, but the doctor had said that bronchitis could sometimes last a long time. In addition Uncle Tjen proved to have a real *kepala batu*. He obstinately stuck to his habit of not taking a bath until dark. And the night air could not be good for him, of course. After an interval of two weeks, the letter arrived that caused such a commotion: Uncle Tjen had "something wrong with his lungs." It was a letter of despair, and I still remember one sentence from it: "Oh, Lien, if you only knew what I feel now. As if I'm suffocating." That letter already contained plans to go to Holland, but for weeks nothing further was said about it. But Uncle Tjen did not improve. Even staying for a month in a cooler place had not done him any good.

We had anticipated a letter from Aunt Sophie saying that Uncle Tjen's condition had deteriorated so much that he had to leave immediately for Europe. Hence there was no surprise when it really did arrive. The difficulty was to find a replacement. Without one they could not make plans. You cannot give up a business just like that! The delay made Uncle Tjen nervous as well as Aunt Sophie, but at last they found one— Versteeg was his name—a man not quite thirty yet. He had excellent references and made a favorable impression. Even so, they had taken a chance, but they had to. He was taken immediately into the business and was to get a share of the profits. He had made that a condition.

Aunt Sophie's letters were somber, but how could they have been otherwise? She wrote about fearful premonitions and terrible omens and dreams. Her letters sometimes complained bitterly. Being a woman from the Indies it was only natural that she dreaded going to Europe without all her family. And then there was being alone in a foreign country. And above all, the departure meant that she would be too far away from her sister and from Kitty. And yet it went without saying that she would follow Uncle Tjen, there wasn't even an undertone of doubt or hesitation in her letters on this score. All she did was complain. Once the difficult decision had been made, she must have been the one who pushed it through and made the decision to go directly to Switzerland. There was determination behind these actions, a toughness that made her a business woman, and represented the other side of her tyranny. She often mentioned money and expenses, but we knew that this was not of paramount importance. Nor did it really matter to her, although she'd always talk about financial matters and always mentioned how much things cost. That's the way she was.

They left on the *J.P. Coen* and traveled first class. We received a telegram from Genoa that they had arrived safely, and a week later one from Davos. It came from a hotel fortunately, not a sanatorium. Uncle Tjen needed treatment for only one winter, and they would come to Holland in the summer. They had taken X-rays, and Aunt Sophie would write as soon as possible about the results. There was no word for ten days. Then the other lung appeared "not in order" either.

The disease progressed in its usual way. Sometimes it seemed that Uncle Tjen was beginning to feel better, and then he was worse again; or his sedimentation rate went down but his temperature went up to 101; another time the temperature was down, but Uncle Tjen had not gained any weight despite all the rest. And so it went, week after week, up and down, down and up.

In the spring it seemed advisable that Uncle Tjen stay for another winter. There was some progress, but recovery was a slow process. I knew about those careful wordings that avoided the seriousness of the case.

Aunt Sophie's letters were long, but she never wrote anything about her surroundings. Uncle Tjen's illness and the news relayed to us from the Indies took up everything. She left all to our imagination, and we never got to see or feel anything directly. Only once in a while did we get something more. For instance: "Do you know what's so terrible? The silence, especially at night. You never hear a cricket here, Lien, and it is so still you can hear the silence ring. Is it like that in Holland too? And then the *udjan kapok*, all that white, and the doors always closed. I could scream sometimes, Lien."

After those few sentences I could imagine it for the first time: a window, and beyond the glass the mountains shining in the moonlight. I really imagined tropical mountains, and merely retouched the picture a little. For the first time I felt Aunt Sophie's loneliness. But a passage like that was an exception and stood out immediately. I read *Magic Mountain* during this time and the novel supplied what was missing from Aunt Sophie's letters, especially the atmosphere of a sanatorium and the slow deterioration of the nervous system. This book formed the background for Aunt Sophie and Uncle Tjen's life during those months. And now I also know that the feelings I attributed to Uncle Tjen were those of Thomas Mann's characters. I was constantly thinking "So this is the way he is being consumed and is wasting away."

I don't know if it was really true in Uncle Tjen's case. He hardly ever wrote except for a few sentences once in a while. I supplied him with reading material from Holland and this sometimes elicited a note in his own handwriting. I remember that he wrote about insomnia and about how you could overcome it by doing math in your head, though this should not require too great an effort. And then I really felt the emptiness and the torture of being awake all night long.

I no longer remember how the first symptoms of the final stage manifested themselves. I believe that he began to complain about headaches. In any case, shortly thereafter his kidneys were affected. An operation that was finally decided upon brought the end.

We could have foreseen Uncle Tjen's death, and yet I can still remember how the news hit like a bomb. I see myself accept and sign for the telegram. My mother stood by the door, my father behind her. They had been alerted by the bell.

"Poor devil," was all my father could say, but he said it in a tone I hadn't heard from him before. Then I looked at my mother's distorted face. She cried very strangely, without a sound. Everything in the house had suddenly changed. Even the living room seemed to be different from the moment before.

The next day we sent a long telegram to Davos. It was a given of course that Aunt Sophie was going to stay with us.

7

AUNT SOPHIE REALLY knew all along that she was pursued by fate, though, of course, she never dared to say so. And yet, on that fall afternoon when she was sitting with us in the front room—was it days or weeks after Uncle Tjen's death? Suddenly I see everything before me again.

It was dusk but the drapes were not drawn yet. The streetlight in front of our house was already on and lit up the raindrops which raced down the globe. They struck the glass, disintegrated, and were blown away. In this autumnal atmosphere of rain and rustling darkness, Aunt Sophie began to talk. She was apparently looking back over her life, weighing the pros and cons. There had not been much happiness.

"Oh, Lien," she said, and each word seemed to dissolve in the darkness, "oh, Lien, what did I really get out of life? Everything I loved and everything I've looked after has died: my plants, my orchids, my animals, and now even Tjen. My hands are *sĕbĕl* Lien, really."

"Come now, you shouldn't talk like that," my mother said, but her tone and her entire attitude indicated the opposite.

She sat there pale and rigid. Hearing Aunt Sophie talk about her own fate like that brought her suddenly closer to those dark, invisible powers she always talked about but which up until now she had always been able to keep at a distance. Aunt Sophie attracted adversity. Suddenly fear and panic dominated all other feelings. Would it extend its influence to our house and family as well? I am sure that my mother considered this. She believed that a person could "attract" good fortune or misfortune, believed in conjuring, putting a hex on people, and believed in lucky and unlucky days. It was not only because her hands were *panas* that all this adversity had happened to Aunt Sophie; she had also married on a "wrong day." My mother had warned about it.

"Fie, shouldn't you go to Mrs. Huffenreuter first?" (The woman was renowned for "calculating" and determining lucky days.) But this time Aunt Sophie, smiling and overly confident in her temporary happiness, said: "Oh, you shouldn't be so superstitious Lien." My mother was somewhat surprised, if not a little offended. That of all people Aunt Sophie would say this. And my mother was right. When you came right down to it, she, Aunt Sophie, and a dozen other women with the same Indies upbringing were all alike. All of them had a strange faith in preternatural things. They all believed that the soul lived on in living and dead objects, that spirits can "materialize" themselves, in short, they believed in the efficacy of mysterious powers, but also that it was possible to defend yourself against them. In any case, when I came home one afternoon I smelled *menjan* on the landing (in a Dutch house, mind you) and knew immediately that it was Thursday. It seemed that it had become necessary to revert to an almost forgotten rite: to commune with the spirits and ancestors whom one could beseech for aid and support. The feeling, the mood that was always present on Thursday afternoons was suddenly back again, when Bèot went through all the rooms of the house, swinging the censer. And even I was susceptible to it.

But when my father came up to me, smiling as if in mutual understanding, I nodded to him meaningfully. I realized that in a way I was dishonest to myself. He shook his head. "There is that stench again," he said, but he knew that my mother would not be deterred by anything. I heard her and Aunt Sophie talking softly in the kitchen, as I had heard so often before, as if they were planning a conspiracy.

". . . Last night he came again, Lien. He stood next to me." And then with increasing emotion, "It was just as if he was with me again. Then he suddenly said in his sweet voice: 'Don't be sad, Fietje, I'm very happy here. . . .'"

My mother was startled and didn't really know what to say except: "That's nice for you Fie."

"Not *nice*, Lien . . . because I miss him so, my boy."

"I mean . . . it's nice that he came back to you again."

"Yes, that's true. . . ."

Then there was silence, probably because she was crying or sobbing. After a while they began to talk again, but now too softly to be understood.

When we were alone that afternoon, my mother, still moved by the conversation in the kitchen, told us that Aunt Sophie had expressed the wish to go to a séance. Their mutual friend, Toetie R., had managed to convince them "that there's something more than what we can see or hear." She had also lost her husband, but was in contact with him again thanks to the psychic gifts of a certain Mr. H. C. Treves. Within a few days Mr. Treves was going to hold a public séance at De Ruijter Street. My mother said that you didn't have to believe in it in order to want to experience it. I had to reserve seats. Did we want to go too? Because my father remained skeptical I went with my mother and Aunt Sophie on that unforgettable Thursday night (it happened to be a Thursday again) to De Ruijter Street. I remember that there were only a few dozen chairs. The small number bothered me. I could now easily be asked to join, and that would betray my ignorance and disbelief. There were religious pictures on the wall, among them what looked to be a picture of Christ with very feminine features, but it could have been some Yogi. At the other end of the hall was a mysterious, transcendental symbol, something with an elongated cross sticking through a ring. There was already an ethereal mood of detachment and transcendence present, partly due to the poor lighting and the uncomfortable chairs. When the hall was full, mostly with older women, a man and a woman stepped forward. The man— still young—proved to be Mr. Treves; the older woman, most likely one of his disciples, would introduce him. She spoke slowly, and sprinkled her Dutch with many strange words that were probably very common in her circle. I must say that I was eagerly waiting for it to begin. But Mr. Treves also gave a long introduction, speaking as softly and sympathetically as possible. In conclusion he said that we could begin by bringing him an object. Aunt Sophie and my mother had apparently prepared for this and each took an envelope out of her handbag. A letter or a portrait? I don't know. I had to bring them to Mr. Treves. I saw that his hair had not been cut for a long time. At the back of his neck he had two *buntut djangkrik*, and I saw white flakes on his collar. He probably had dandruff.

It was completely quiet in the hall when he took the first object and felt it carefully. It seemed to belong to a middle-aged lady who looked very worried. It was wrapped in paper and could not be seen. It belonged to a child, Mr. Treves said. About three or four years old, with blond curls. Now he was saying something. He mentioned a name: "Sonny" or "Johnny." The woman nodded in silence. The child had "crossed over" long ago, years and years already. And now he had a message for his mother. She'd better see Treves afterwards. The mother was understandably very moved. It was a good start for Mr. Treves, but he acted quite normally, as if it was nothing special. Aunt Sophie and my mother looked at each other meaningfully. This was followed by even more convincing examples. Mr. Treves even indicated where a disease was precisely located. He would add that it should be brought to a doctor's attention. Then suddenly it was our turn, although in a somewhat different way than before. Mr. Treves started into the audience and pointed slowly in our direction. "There," he said, "behind those ladies a figure manifests itself." It was an older woman (not Uncle Tjen as I had feared) with white hair combed back, a rather long face. . . . Wait, now she moved. She stopped directly behind my mother. I shivered at the thought that she had moved past me, and I have to admit that the tension mounted. Yet at first my mother could not place this "older woman."

"Has she crossed over already?" she asked, immediately adopting the jargon.

"Yes," said Mr. Treves, and then: "Does the name Betty mean anything?" My mother shook her head slowly. "Or Betsy?" he asked. At that moment my mother and I knew it almost simultaneously. It was Betsy Huffenreuter, the one who was so adept at predicting lucky days. But she was not dead. My mother said so.

"I'm sorry Madam," he replied, "she *has* crossed over."

"Yes, but I received a letter from her only a couple of days ago, from the Indies," my mother said. He shrugged his shoulders slowly and took another object from the table.

Nevertheless, we were all very impressed. We didn't say a word in the streetcar so we could think things over again. But when we came home, everybody began to talk at once. My mother and Aunt Sophie together against my father, with me butting in every so often, already much less skeptical. But the unresolved point remained: had she crossed over or not?

"Let's wait," my mother said. And she was justified in waiting, because a week or so later the letter she had written to Betsy Huffenreuter in Bandung was returned by the post office. On the back was written in pencil: "sudah mati" ("deceased").

There couldn't have been more convincing proof that the soul continued to exist after death, and that it was possible to get in contact with it. And even though Uncle Tjen had not been contacted, Aunt Sophie's conversion and air of arrogant secrecy date from this time. She was a true believer. Aunt Sophie consulted Mr. Treves privately. He even came to our house.

"He's still so modest," my mother remarked. Which was true, considering that he was someone who had such close and continuous communication with the transcendental. After some time Aunt Sophie also managed to get into contact with Uncle Tjen through Mr. Treves. It gave her great satisfaction. Treves showed her letters that were written by an invisible hand. The handwriting really did resemble Uncle Tjen's a little, except that it was much bigger. Several messages were passed on in these letters, though I never managed to learn what they were. My mother and Aunt Sophie were communicative enough, but on this point they maintained silence and kept me out of it.

After some more time had passed, Aunt Sophie proved to be psychic herself. Now the messages could be communicated directly to her. In her room were numerous sheets of paper with all kinds of large scrawls on them. It did resemble handwriting somewhat, but not really, and I've never been able to deciper a single word. Aunt Sophie, however, read several messages right off the page. It seemed almost supernatural.

During that time our house buzzed with words like "materialization," "materialized spirit," "spiritualism," "transport," and the like. My mother and Aunt Sophie spoke in a shockingly normal tone of voice about "communication" and "messages" coming from family members who had "crossed over" long ago. It did not stop with Uncle Tjen of course, and the contacts became more numerous, especially at first.

But the excitement gradually faded. It's true that a number of new words enriched our vocabulary forever, but otherwise the old words and notions returned, and the conversation once again concerned itself with such familiar topics as family matters, inheritances, graves, the "lousy Dutch climate," and how to prepare *rijsttafel*. Also the letters from the Indies—from Aunt Christien, Kitty and even Tjalie—demanded once again more and more of our attention. My mother also explained that it wasn't good to associate with that other world too much. It demanded too much of you, and in the end it made you nervous and physically exhausted. Aunt Sophie was advised, by Treves himself no less, that she should restrict her contacts and, as the weeks and months passed, the need for them faded. It had been proven that one could communicate with the supernatural, and that in itself was enough of a consolation for Aunt Sophie. Gradually normal life reasserted itself. You can't keep on worrying all the time.

"You have to live with the living and not with the dead," according to my mother.

Months passed and Aunt Sophie was still staying with us. She did speak about "renting an apartment" and, especially later on, about "going back to the Indies." But my mother told her: "Oh come, Fie, why so soon? The business is going well, and after all the things you've been through you should stay here until you're completely on your feet again." Aunt Sophie raised some vague objections—she longed so much for her sister and the children, she said—but she stayed. It was really because of Aunt Sophie's staying with us that I was allowed to get my own room in Leyden. My mother always tried to make me realize how pointless it was to move, but now that I had given up my room for Aunt Sophie, she dropped her opposition and I was permitted to move to Leyden, although a small room was always kept for me—and that was nice, I have to admit. I studied the so-called Indies Law without much interest or enthusiasm. Though I was living now in Leyden, I was often in The Hague, partly because my mother expected me to be, although nothing was ever said, but also because I had trouble getting used to life in a student's room. The atmosphere of such a room, with its hodge-podge of secondhand furniture that was so typically bourgeois, drove me often out of the house. Coming from the Indies, although by then we had lived in Holland for years, I had a peculiar notion of what student life was like. At least in the beginning, I saw it as an obligatory string of parties and celebrations, exactly as my mother had warned me it would be. It seemed, particularly the first year, that I felt obliged to live that myth, but I was never really suited for this kind of life. Having come from the Indies I was not used to drinking, and I could never get used to a bois-terous and rowdy atmosphere. I always felt a little ill at ease and each time was a struggle. I never felt more strongly that I was leading a double life than during this first year, perhaps even more so because I lived in such a mythical world. I wasn't cut loose from home or my parents yet, and sometimes I felt a great urge to go home for dinner. No sooner was I back there than I felt stifled by my mother's sweet but coercive regime, and I would go back to Leyden again.

Among my friends during that first year was another loner, a Jav-anese classmate from the elementary school in Batavia. He was a quiet fellow by the name of Sudarpo, the son of a *doctor djawa*. Later, during the revolution, he played an important role in the Madiun uprising of 1948. I never knew the whole story, but I was told that after the revolt was put down, they hanged him, in the *alun-alun* of Magelang. He apparently remained faithful to his own myth during all those years, the myth of Communism.

I visited him rather often when I first lived in Leyden. He never came to see me. He added yet one more "life" to my "other life" as a student, and looking back this dimension was perhaps the best part of it. I spent hours in his shabby, messy room where a faded *sarong* hanging on the wall was the only decoration. He never talked about his studies, or anything else for that matter except politics, although for him this in-cluded everything anyway. What he said shocked me. I had lived for so long in the protective society of Europeans, where I had been brought up with the idea of the obvious justice of Dutch rule that it was completely new to me to hear this same rule, quite as obviously, called *un*just. Our conversations must have annoyed him, although at the same time they must have given him a quiet satisfaction. In defeating me he could defeat the colonialism that he saw embodied in me, and at the same time verify what he believed in. He attacked my conventional opinions with pent-up rage, and he did it so straightforwardly, in the form of personal attacks, that he instilled a sense of personal responsibility in me. There were times when I was surprised to find myself going back to him over and over again. Then I thought I did this because, of all the students I knew, he was the most reserved and the most refined; only later did I understand that there must have been another reason. I know now that I needed to make amends. That I didn't get up and walk out was due, I think, to the fact that I wanted to justify myself to him as a Dutchman. And it was probably also from a feeling of guilt (from which I suffered a lot in those days), that I wanted him to accept me as a person and even as a friend, no matter what the cost.

How did he feel about me? I don't know. I remember only one remark in this regard: "I ought to hate you," he said.

One day he disappeared from his room. According to rumor he was still in Leyden, but I never saw him again. I did not abandon him, but he left me. I felt that my affection for him had been betrayed. Not until later did I understand that the "betrayal" lay elsewhere and that, if he ever considered such a thing, it must have been Sudarpo who felt that a sympathy for me was a "betrayal" of himself. I even wonder sometimes if he fled because of me. In any case, he had already learned enough Marxism to know that one must be able to sacrifice personal feelings. After all, he was not allowed to tolerate weakness in the impersonal and difficult battle against "colonial exploitation," "domination" and "oppression." If what I've been told is true, he must even have died in the armor of this terminology.

I don't think we would have understood each other any better as adults, and I never made an attempt to meet him again even though the opportunity twice presented itself. But sometimes I do regret—now that it is too late of course—that I was not able to let him know that he had a decisive influence on me during a particular period of my life and, when you came right down to it, how much I was spared. Because of him I was saved from the bitterness and regret others experienced about "the loss of the Indies." Doesn't that alone give me enough reason to be grateful to him?

I cannot say that the first months in Leyden were pleasant for me; even the conversations with Sudarpo caused me to return to my room crushed and defeated, continuing the discussion with myself until I fell asleep from exhaustion. His disappearance relieved me momentarily of a burden because it seemed as if he had become my conscience, reminding me continuously of "necessities," "consequences," "obligations," and "responsibility," and I really could not handle all that at the time. I went back to The Hague with a heavy heart and almost against my will, but I soon allowed myself to be caught again in the web my mother always managed to spin with experienced finesse. She did her utmost to make me see that it was nicer to be home than to be anywhere else. And Aunt Sophie did her part to bring me to the same conclusion. The care, generosity, prosperity, and, perhaps above all, the familiarity—including the free and easy Indies way of life—all had me in its grip again.

With these feelings and in this mood I saw Rienkie again for the first time since we had posed together for the photographer as bridal escorts: she in tule and lace and I in satin with lace ruffles. I had heard her name mentioned occasionally, and I also knew that her parents were divorced now and that she and her mother lived in The Hague. Yet I had never met her, although I expected to run into her on a street corner, or on Frederik Hendrik Avenue. But it never happened. I hadn't even seen her during the two or three months that Aunt Sophie had been staying with us, although more than once during the long evenings the conversation had turned to Rienkie and her mother. Aunt Sophie: "Beautiful girl, Lien. She's become practically white here in Holland." But Rienkie was only one among many who were discussed; the whole family was dragged up during such evenings.

One day I came home and headed upstairs immediately because I saw that there were visitors in the front room. The door opened and I turned around. Aunt Sophie beckoned me. "Guess who's here," she called out with a laugh. I said that I didn't know, but I knew at once: Rienkie. Slowly I went down the stairs again and put my hand on the door knob. I could already hear the lively, though muffled, talking inside. The sound was suddenly louder; I caught words and even sentences which appeared to concern me. I saw Rienkie immediately. She was bent over a little, her back toward me. I think she was helping with the tea. But before she turned around and I could see her face, I was in the circle of women standing opposite her mother, a typical Indies woman in Holland, dressed with care. The first thing that entered my mind was what my mother would say *later*, after the visit. "Rienkie's mother is still handsome, and so neat and proper!" She was more than "neat and proper"; she had the air of a woman who, though growing older, isn't quite finished with life yet. I introduced myself and she extended her hand, though while doing so she looked at Aunt Sophie and not at me. She made a gesture that was meant to indicate that I had become big and tall. When I went over to greet the other women, I noticed that she was looking me over. She was gauging me of course, and again she made a gesture to indicate tall and broad as if she wanted to say: "He's a man already."

For Rienkie? I don't think so. I was then a second-year student and she must have had someone in mind for her daughter, someone who had, at least, a "position" already.

There was nothing left of the little girl I had once known, but even at first sight Rienkie still embodied all that was familiar from the Indies of my childhood. So strong was the recognition that I readily found the right tone. We really should have been strangers to each other, but it seemed as if we had known each other for years already. At least I had that feeling, and I think that the way I acted made Rienkie feel the same way. There was no question of surprise anymore.

This meeting, which I so often had imagined in a different way, went almost too smoothly, and the tension I had noticed when I came in gradually dissipated. In any case, it began differently than I had either assumed, or even hoped it would: a relaxed mood with some nice conversation that all the aunts participated in, laughing, cooing, and teasing.

"What do you think of Rienkie?" Aunt Sophie asked.

"Lovely" I said immediately, without hesitation and without being flustered. I knew I was playing the game as these people expected me to. And I did think her "lovely" as she sat there with a smile saying "Ah . . . ah . . ." to me. Rienkie laughed and played with her lace handkerchief, and once, when she wanted attention, she did it with such a typical gesture—a movement of her limp wrist—that I had to smile in spite of myself. It was so specific and inimitable, in a way that revealed her origin, her upbringing, and her social circle. And all of this suddenly seemed dear to me again. I had no trouble in continuing this renewed acquaintance. It happened naturally.

"Just drop by after your classes," her mother said. "You can stay for dinner. I'll make you *rijsttafel*.

When I went for the first time to where they lived, on Columbus Street, it was the mother who talked. This time Rienkie seemed somewhat shy and withdrawn. We were sitting in a room with Japanese vases, Rozenburg plates, and a large painting in a dark, varnished frame. It was a memento of "our Indies," of course, with the inevitable purple volcano and yellow *sawas* and among them several smears or spots of color that were meant to represent people. It was a painting of the kind I knew so well from the Christmas issues of the Indies illustrated magazines. Whether the magazine was called *De Zweep*, *De Reflector*, or *D'Orient*, all the pictures resembled each other. Always the same *sawas*, the same mountains (with or without smoke), blue skies, pink skies, purple skies, ravines, *kampong* huts, and so on.

"What do you think of that?" asked Rienkie's mother, pointing at the painting. "A real Indies sky, don't you think?" And only a few people could reproduce an Indies sky, she went on to say. To do that you must have lived in the Indies for a long time. In fact, you really had to be born in the Indies. And Nol Dézentjé, the painter, certainly had been. From a Djokja family, you know. As if I didn't know that immediately from his name.

Rienkie did not say much. She sat on the floor curled up among the pillows like a cat. There was also a piano in the room, and after the rice with *sajur lodeh*, *babi ketjap*, *sambelans* and the *serundeng* I loved so much, Rienkie got up as if by prearrangement, and sat down on the stool. She struck the first notes, then took a run, and, accompanying herself, started to sing (just like the RCA record):

Blue skies
Smilin' at me,
Nothin' but blue skies
Do I see.

She had heard her idol, Jack Smith, at the Kurhaus and was delighted by the "whispering baritone." The poor man had cancer, she added, that's why he sang in a whisper. Rienkie also sang with a low voice, half talking, half whispering, as if she was extremely tired. And I must confess that she made a great impression on me. She kept on playing and singing like that while I sat beside her and asked her to play one song after another. We even sang our mutual favorite, "Dinah," together:

Di-nah, is there anyone fi-na'
In the State of Carolina . . . ?

And in the places where I could not remember the words anymore, I filled in with "pa-papa-papa . . ." imitating a saxophone a little. Rienkie had lots of fun because I couldn't keep the tune, but Jack Smith, the Ramblers, and "Dinah" broke the ice again. From then on Rienkie's mother could do little more than shout her approval (it was clear that she felt she had to be part of her daughter's life and be young with the young). It seemed as if a change had come over Rienkie. She not only sang, but she also talked now in a lively manner, rapidly and enthusiastically. Then she suddenly got up, walked out of the room, and indicated that I should follow. We went upstairs to her room, where she had a record player. We rolled up the rug a little and pushed several chairs to the side. Rienkie clearly wanted to dance, and laughing, she pulled me by the sleeve saying only "ajo." We danced fox trots, waltzes, tangos, and even the Charleston, which was already out of date by then. It was remarkable how she changed while she was dancing. Her slow and languid way of moving had suddenly disappeared, along with her hesitation and reserve. She had become another person under the straight-cut dress that was fashionable in those years. I saw then a different Rienkie, one who was no longer the symbol from a child's dream, but a desirable young woman.

It became late, but we went on talking and smoking, even long after we heard Rienkie's mother rummaging around in the next room. Rienkie talked about movies and movie stars and crooners and band leaders, about the office where she worked, her treatment by "the boss" (as she still said in Indies fashion), and briefly about her father. He had a different wife now, one who always walked around with a little monkey on her arm. She and her mother had met them on the Scheveningen Pier and her father had greeted them by tipping his hat, like a stranger. But from Scheveningen we got talking about the jazz concert at the Kurhaus, and then of course about the Saturday tea dances, the Ramblers, and the Argentinian tango band with the singer who could sing "La Plegaria" so beautifully ("terrific," Rienkie said). All this led to another date of course.

For that occasion I wore a kind of outfit that I created especially for tea dances, consisting of a short, chocolate-brown jacket and a striped pair of pants that was very wide at the bottom, even for the fashion of that time.

We sat down near the window in the room where the tango band played and looked out over the terrace to the sea. It was bright and sunny outside. There were tables all around us and people who, just like us, wanted to dance. That's all I remember. I don't even remember anything of our conversation. After all, we came to dance. As far as I was concerned, it was only important to be an ideal partner for Rienkie. I danced with as much control as possible, listening attentively to the music, and constantly keeping an eye on Rienkie. I introduced each new step cautiously in order to prevent misunderstandings, while at the same time trying to adjust myself to her way of moving. I had heard a dancing teacher say that a couple who dance well form a unit. Well, sometimes we succeeded in realizing a little of that. It was as if the music moved us

in unison. We really did form a couple. Rienkie enjoyed it, and this gave
me great satisfaction. More afternoons like this one followed. We saw
each other on Saturday or Sunday, and later even during the week. I
seldom went to Leyden anymore. At five o'clock, after the offices closed,
I could see Rienkie coming in the distance through the window of my
room. This was usually on Tuesday, but sometimes on Friday too. After a
while I waited every afternoon at the same time, and I was able to recognize her immediately because she walked differently from other girls.
She always wore high heels, never sport shoes. I sometimes teased her
and said that her mincing little steps were affected. "That's all right,"
she said, "I don't want to be like those Dutch girls."

She stole my mother's heart with such remarks, thereby giving her
the opportunity for yet another harangue. "Oh yes Rienk, they are so
clumsy and heavy. They always walk like this . . . ," which was followed by a successful imitation. And they found themselves in complete
agreement.

Some people might have regretted the development of our relationship, such as her mother perhaps, but mine didn't and neither did Aunt
Sophie. It was Aunt Sophie, and not my mother, who was the first to take
me aside and ask me straightforwardly if there was anything between
Rienkie and me. Without waiting for an answer she said that it was
something she would very much like to see.

I was never much interested in the family relationships, and when
Aunt Sophie began talking about the De Pauly family tree, I usually
found an excuse to escape her endless discussions of the "rich branch" and
the "poor branch," or the "golden De Pauly" and the "silver De Pauly,"
or the family patriarch, the notorious Geraerdt Knol (the man in the
portrait with the sly little eyes and the low forehead), or the many other
family members, both dead and alive. It never became clear to me where
Rienkie fit in, but she definitely belonged to the "Indies branch" and the
"poor branch." Aunt Sophie declared quite frankly that, with my white
skin and blond hair, I would be the ideal candidate for Rienkie. That's
the way Aunt Sophie was in those things.

When Rienkie visited us in the middle of the week, she sat among
the family, poured tea, did the honors (as my mother would say), and took
part in the general conversation about family matters. It was remarkable
how easily she adapted herself to the usual conversation, and how, with
little trouble, she managed to adopt the prevalent views, opinions, and
prejudices of these older ladies from the Indies. Most of the time there
was a general consensus because she, like the others, held the same opinion about things such as skin color, money, marriage, nationalism, the

totoks, and the Dutch climate. When Aunt Sophie spoke about Uncle Alex's children, "the girls," whom she later, as she said, would take into her home (they were De Paulys so they had to have a European upbringing) then Rienkie could put on a face just as grave as any of the other aunts and say in a resigned tone: "Yes, Aunt Sophie, it really is too bad that they're so dark."

It annoyed me more than I could, wanted, or was allowed to show at such a moment. But these were the things that bothered me. Everything in Rienkie attracted me, her loveliness, elegance, love of ease, and her spoiled nature. And, of course, I secretly wanted her like any boy that age wants a girl—with all that was romantic about it. Yet there was always an undercurrent of disappointment, especially when Rienkie talked that way. But I said nothing. I had no right to reproach her for anything because I had no claims on her, and because I myself was guilty of avoiding anything that might be a matter of disagreement. Our relationship had developed on a different basis, yet had developed into a feeling of belonging together, of affection, and, on my part, of desire. But there was still a large area we had never explored together, and one where we might perhaps never meet. I had always been careful to avoid this, although I knew that the moment was approaching when avoidance would no longer be possible. There was nothing for me to do but to make emphatically clear what were *my* interests, *my* discoveries, *my* disapproval, and *my* obstinacy. I was aware of hurting her sometimes, but it was the only way that I could revenge my disappointment. It also gave me a sense of power over Rienkie, who would look at me quietly, almost fearfully. She remained silent then and had that brooding wait-and-see attitude that I was also familiar with. I could be sure that she would stay away until I called her again for another date. She never referred to what happened, although I don't think that she easily forgot such things. I knew that after each of these times, it would be necessary for us to go dancing again, because it was then easier for her to regain self-control and drop her reticence. These were our silly quarrels, without either of us ever saying a word.

That was also the way things went in the Palais de Danse that memorable Friday night. I had called her the day before and asked if she wanted to go with me, but she made excuses. She had been so tired lately she said, because the office was so busy, and she didn't have a suitable evening dress. No matter how much I persisted over the phone, this time she emphatically declined.

"Another time then, all right?" she said, cutting the conversation short. We had not agreed on anything definite.

That evening I overcame my aversion for her mother (why did she always try to belittle me?) and went to Columbus Street after dinner. Rienkie herself opened the door. "Oh, it's you" she said tonelessly. Her mother was out. She brought me into the living room which was badly lighted, cheerless, and messy. I had never seen her without make-up before, and it made her more human and yet more vulnerable too. And that night I was apparently in a mood to be moved by this. Rienkie— and I can remember it precisely, even the lighting—sat down on the edge of a chair, her hands in her lap.

"I came to ask you again to go to the Palais de Danse." And then the sentence I had formulated while walking in the street, complete with its appropriate delivery: "I want to dance with you again, and I want to be alone with you, without other people around us, without my mother and without those damned aunts."

My vehemence frightened her, because it seemed almost like a proposal. She didn't say a word at first, but then answered slowly and in a husky voice: "Well, all right then. See you tomorrow night." A moment later she was completely recovered. Her voice sounded almost cheerful when she asked: "Be a sweetheart tomorrow and pick me up in a car, will you? Then my dress won't wrinkle so much." When she walked ahead of me to the door I saw her small, bare neck under her short, cropped hair.

The next morning I called a florist and had him deliver a corsage, a purple orchid. I had also included a note, saying: "To be worn with your pink dress."

For weeks our relationship had been up in the air. I had noticed by her attitude—especially that previous evening—that I could not leave it that way without the risk of losing her, and, truthfully, I was already much too used to her to take this loss with indifference. In spite of my uncertainty and my uneasiness about that unexplored area, I was determined to use the evening to make our relationship official. I dressed with extra care because I knew how much Rienkie appreciated it. I took the time to do it right. Each action, even tying my black tie, seemed directed toward my intended goal of that evening. In any case, I concentrated as much as possible on what was supposed to happen. And I must say that while sitting in the car after undergoing the inspection of my mother and Aunt Sophie ("Aduh, you look so nice"), I managed to foster a feeling of certainty with, what was for me, a very unusual sense of determination.

The light in the hall of her house came on by itself when I got out of the taxi. She had heard me arrive, of course, and had not waited for the door bell. I peered through the glass in the door and saw her shadow behind the frosted glass of the storm door. She was standing still as if suddenly hesitant (though perhaps she was only looking quickly into the mirror), and then walked straight to the front door. Yes, she had the pink dress on as I had ordered. And my purple orchid as the required corsage.

Rienkie made an exaggerated bow in front of me and asked, "Is this to your liking?"

I nodded slowly, "Yes." It was indeed. Completely. It was rather cold outside, it might even snow. Rienkie shivered as she walked to the car in her dress coat.

We arrived at the Palais de Danse a little too early. The doorman was walking slowly back and forth in the lobby, and a portly lady stood watch in the cloak room. Everything was still in a state of expectancy. The lighting in the lobby pretended to be intimate and there was a thick carpet that muffled every sound. By now two other women had also entered, and stood in front of a mirror inspecting their eyeshadow. Their skirts were as short as Rienkie's (the fashion was even above the knee then), and their hair was also cut short, but both were redheads with a very white skin. The waxen complexion and rust color repelled me. In the meantime I waited for Rienkie, who was spending a long time in the powder room. Her skin was light brown. There she was, with her white Spanish shawl around her shoulders. "Kassian," I heard her say while still at a distance. "Of course you were waiting for me, weren't you?" Then teasingly, "You're a sweetheart," and confidentially, "I had some trouble, but the attendant helped me." She put her arm through mine, "Ajo then . . ." The dance floor was lighted. We crossed it and chose a place on the other side, somewhat away from the center.

The band members trickled in slowly. One by one they put their instruments behind their stands. There was an elegant silver R on each stand. Rienkie knew the first-trumpet player. He laughed and nodded in recognition. The second nod was for me. Rienkie waved back, though it resembled the way Dutch people beckon someone. "That's Harry C.," Rienkie said, "did you know that he's even related to us, and to Aunt Sophie too?" He had started to study for a position in the colonial service, but the government stopped his allowance because he neglected to take exams. Now he played in the band. That was really "terrific" for an Indies boy, but he had always been musically inclined. He had taught himself to play, and so well that he was now playing in a professional band.

She kept on talking in a soft voice, nearly a whisper. But the high pitch betrayed her increasing excitement. It was as if she did not want me to get a word in; she gave me no chance to take over the conversation. Was she following a plan? Did she want to avoid something she felt was sure to come? Or was it only agitation? I don't know. But the words she spoke and the words I wanted to say had nothing in common. For the time being there was nothing for me to do but listen attentively and observe her movements and gestures. Only in this way could I guess her feelings, I thought.

We saw the band members getting ready to begin. We heard three taps, then a soft rustle that a moment later became a loud splashing of sounds. Suddenly the hall changed, transformed from a space of boredom and expectation to a cheerful garden with violets:

Sweet violets,
sweeter than all the roses . . .

"Ed!" Rienkie called out. "Ajo Ed . . . like that other time." That other time was the first evening in her room when I'd improvised all kinds of variations to this same tune, and which always threatened to get me in trouble, though we managed to extricate ourselves each time. It had amused Rienkie very much then, and did so this time too. It was as if she didn't want to think about anything anymore, not about "silent quarrels" or about what she could expect from me that night, especially after my short outburst of the day before. She only wanted to dance and lose herself in that. It was the only semblance of belonging together.

It was a different evening than I had imagined, an evening when we were together with the familiarity that always grew so easily between us, but without even a moment's illusion of real understanding. I wanted her, as they say, but my hands seemed paralyzed and my mouth remained closed. Even now I don't know exactly what I felt, but I must have slowly driven Rienkie to desperation. As the evening progressed, I felt her excitement wane while we danced. Our dancing became pointless, although we went on without saying a word. Right up to the end, we both kept waiting for the liberating intimacy. It did not come. I was dejected, and ashamed to look at Rienkie. For a finale, the band played in a slow, almost comical tempo:

Sho-o-w me - the way - to go - home,
I'm tired - I want - to go - to bed . . .

While we were leaving, I put my arm loosely around Rienkie, just as I had done when we left the house, still full of expectation. Some wet snow had fallen, and under the big arched streetlights we could still see some flakes swirling. It had become wet, cold, and raw. A taxi drove up we hadn't asked for. The doorman of the Palais de Danse opened the door and we automatically got in. As we drove away, I gave the driver Rienkie's address. At the same time I was thinking: the evening cannot end like this, I have to save something of the illusion. Anxiously—because what would the result be?—yet purposely, I stretched out my arm and tried to put it as naturally as possible around her shoulders. She scrutinized me for a moment. I saw her do so with the same amazing clarity that I would see everything else that followed. Then, with her back half turned toward me, she edged slowly to my side and leaned back. A little later I felt her cheek and smelled the sweet perfume she had worn all evening, only stronger now. At first it went as is usual on such occasions: rapprochement but at the same time restraint, and not only from her side. Our faces were close now, side by side, and I watched hers because I did not want to miss anything. I saw the light from the street glide over it, time and again sliding away along her cheek and over her lips, narrowly missing her eyes. There were rapidly moving squares or bands and ever-changing shapes running along her coat, my jacket, or the upholstery of the car. The mood was perfect now. Something had to happen before this also would be gone. I moved my hands. At first I sensed that she would allow it, then, at the very last moment, she withdrew from my hands and kissed me in the way one places a period at the end of a sentence. She shook her head slowly. Nothing else. It was gone. I was forced to let everything that had just flashed through my mind, along with all the tension, ebb into a feeling of resentment. What was this all about? What made her stop what she herself must have been expecting? How had I offended her? They were just *tinkas*, and I didn't want anything to do with them. They would have defeated me in the long run anyway. Instead of this typical Indies way of messing around with feelings and hidden motives, I wanted an honest game without the complications which, I thought at the time, came from a heightened sensuality. Above all I felt humiliated, the victim of a calculated game she had wanted to win. But the game had been too obvious to allow her the prize.

These were my thoughts then, but I did not express them. I did not reproach Rienkie at all and I cowardly opened the front door for her and let her in. I demanded no explanation. I let her go, and even let her thank me. She pressed my hand, looked at me for a moment, bent forward, and kissed me on the cheek. I must have stood there frozen rigid. Then I watched her go up the stairs, slowly, but without hesitation. It was the last I ever saw of Rienkie.

Looking back years later, I am less certain that my thoughts and assumptions during that time were correct. Now I sometimes wonder if Rienkie's intuition or calculation (or should I say intuitive calculation) at a well-chosen moment did not save us both from the maze of feelings, misunderstanding, and mistakes that we were in danger of getting lost in. But by then I was already too far removed from her and, consequently, too far removed from anything that had to do with the Indies. Perhaps.

At breakfast the next morning, sitting across from my parents and Aunt Sophie after a sleepless night, I ate silently, absent-mindedly, and was totally self-absorbed. I feared only one thing: my mother's curiosity.

"What's the matter, Ed?"

There it was. "Nothing," I answered brusquely.

"Did you two have a fight?"

"A fight? No."

An hour later, when my mother was in the kitchen and my father stood beside her (they were talking about me of course), I went in and announced that I was taking a trip. My mother stared at me, horrified. My father didn't say a word and looked straight ahead.

"Where are you going?"

"Brussels."

"Are you going with Rienkie?" Even now she had to ask, God help us!

"No," I said impatiently. "Alone."

I turned around and opened the door.

"Ed," she began again. "Why are you suddenly . . . ?"

But my father restrained her.

"Leave him alone . . . ," I heard him say.

8

KITTY'S BIRTH and the hectic activity it unleashed, the endless stories about the delivery, the late arrival of the doctor, the feeding, and who knows what else, are properly speaking, not memory, but fiction, legend. But what intrigues me is that at times I don't really know anymore where memory ends and legend begins. Be that as it may, both combine to form the earliest images of my childhood and can only be separated again by reason. Thus I know that I could never have seen the baby although I remember her, nor the cradle (though I could describe it), or Kitty's wet nurse, a Javanese women with some Buginese in her, whom I can visualize. Perhaps I could have known the small child of three who threw herself in a tantrum on the floor, kicking and crying for rage; but on the other hand I cannot be completely sure, because this scene is too much like the classic image of the spoiled Indies child that I'd always heard about. Also the old *babu*, who looked on silently and picked up Kitty's toys, fits right into this scene. But who was she? She was never mentioned in the exhaustive conversations about the family, so that what is called the element of "legend" can't be excluded from this memory either.

But then there is the image I can be absolutely certain about: a two- or three-year-old girl in a white undershirt and pants trimmed with lace, a round little face turned up, with something like recognition and hesitant expectation in her eyes. It is too clear and too sharp not to be my own memory, and perhaps also because there is a feeling of desperate embarrassment attached to it. Aunt Sophie's famous statement came at the moment Kitty looked up at me. It was announced loudly and with a laugh and repeated a thousand times within the family: "Do you know what Kit said yesterday? 'I don't want to marry anyone but Eddy when I grow up. He's such a sweet little boy.'" To the adolescent I was then in the process of becoming, it was as if someone had pulled a rug from under me. I felt that Aunt Sophie had cowardly betrayed me. She had made my feelings public, and displayed what I felt was worse than physical nakedness. Kitty will always be connected to this public disgrace, yet the image of the little girl may be lovelier because of it. All of this happened before *"the* transfer" to Bandjermasin. Thereafter Kitty disappeared from my life for a number of years, and wouldn't be part of it again until she was a young woman of sixteen or seventeen. I saw her again for the first time on the quay in Priok when I returned from Holland twelve years after we had left the same quay on the "drunken *Rembrandt.*" I had satisfied the family's requirement for a "European education," and it was a matter of course that I'd return to the Indies after I was finished. Besides, my parents had left for the Indies two years earlier and it would have been unthinkable as well as unbearable for them if I hadn't followed.

On that gray morning as the boat swung around one more time before being slowly pulled to the quay, I looked for them first, of course, and found them with a girl beside them. It had to be Kitty. Aunt Sophie was a little further away. A quarter of an hour later I was hanging over the railing like all the other passengers, looking down. Now I could clearly see them and even yell to them at the top of my lungs. My parents had changed little in those two years, and Aunt Sophie seemed even younger, although her hair was clearly getting gray. She had become fat during the months that she spent with us in Holland, but now she seemed thinner again, and dressed with an obvious care that I didn't remember her taking before. Yet I immediately spotted her, even from a distance. Only Kitty was unfamiliar to me. She didn't at all resemble the little girl I remembered. Her physical maturity was actually a disappointment. She even seemed somewhat big for her age. Only her blond hair reminded me of the past.

I noticed that Aunt Sophie was trying to get my attention behind Kitty's back. She pointed to her niece with the same gesture as she used to point at a precious heirloom in the display cabinet. It was as if she wanted to say: "And . . . don't you think she has become nice looking?"

We all met on the crowded deck, and I could see them more closely. My father was in his white suit. I noticed how much he perspired. My mother was laughing continuously and gave me her arm which meant: "Now you're with us again." They were both very cheerful. After all, they had waited two years for me.

I also saw Kitty more closely now. She was blond and fair, yet undeniably from the Indies, for instance, in the way she walked, that typical gait we call "lèngang," or her somewhat faded complexion (despite her red lipstick) that so many of her type have. And last, but not least, it sounded in her voice and the way she talked.

"She's getting to be a flirt you know," Aunt Sophie teased. What did I think of her? I had an undeniable feeling of disappointment, and the feeling remained.

We went to the smoking-room. It was very warm and buzzed with excited voices. Because of the way she sat and walked and in the way she was continuously aware of the impression she was making, Kitty had become a typical precocious teenager of the Indies, something unthinkable without the abundant movies imported from Hollywood. Later, I could always recognize this type easily. It was as if at a certain stage all these fifteen-, sixteen-, and seventeen-year-old girls had chosen a role model, with varying degrees of success. And, to Kitty's credit, it must be said that she also succeeded only partially. Fortunately, she was too lazy. It was clear that Mae West was her model because of her blondness, height, and size. She placed her hand on her hip, leaned against the doorpost and, her head lowered as much as possible, gazed up to us like a tiger or some indolent female animal. Later I noticed that Kitty often forgot her role and became the sweet, warmhearted girl again that she was by nature. But that day on board the ship, she played her role to the hilt. Probably to prove to me how mature she was.

"John's comin' to pick us up, you know," she said suddenly. Then she got up and wiggled out of the room. I had never heard the name, but I could guess that John was Versteeg, the partner who had taken Uncle Tjen's place.

We had to wait quite a while for him, and Aunt Sophie took the opportunity to brief me on Kitty. It turned into a story that was interrupted by short exclamations and questions. What did I think of her? "Did you notice what delicate ankles she had." And then the incontestable evidence of Kitty's childlike innocence. "Ah, well," she said, "Kit just has something, you know, that makes all the boys swarm around her. And not only boys, but even . . . men." Hadn't she recently been approached by an older man ("a man with five children!"), whom she had never seen before, but who had confessed to her that he watched her ride her bicycle to school every day. From that moment on she never dared to take that same road again. And imagine . . . he wanted to go to the movies with that child! But fortunately Kitty is made from the right stuff. She had simply burst out laughing and said: "You must be crazy, old man!" And at home she added: "Aunt Sophie, imagine if he kissed you . . . he'd have such an old man's smell!"

Oh, that innocent Kitty, what a child she still was!

And all that in the smoking-room amidst the buzz, the heat, and my concern for my luggage.

"There he is at last," Aunt Sophie suddenly shouted.

John came into the room. It was so crowded that he had to squeeze between people and say "sorry" several times. He acted very energetically and businesslike. Apologizing for being late, he greeted my parents first: "Hello Aunt, Uncle." I was surprised. So he was part of the family. Then to me: "You must be Eduard. Well I'm John." He smelled of brilliantine and English cigarettes. He had a can of Capstan in his left hand and I saw that he had long, tapered nails. Soon I noticed that he interspersed his Dutch with all kinds of British words. During the conversation he said that he would "get in touch" with one of his connections for me. He didn't drink beer either, but whiskey and soda. And when he brought the glass to his lips he said "cheers" to me. At the time I still saw him as an individual, but later I learned how to classify him. He was the Indies *klontong* type, the office-*budjang*; a friendly guy but one who overdid everything. He was too animated, too friendly, too polite, and overdressed. He had his suits made by a first-class European tailor of course, but his lapels were a little too wide and his pants just a little too flared. He wore expensive American sport shoes of a strange design. He had learned to keep quiet about the price, but he couldn't resist saying something about the soft leather. Later I would meet many more young men of his kind. Almost all of them came from the lower middle class and, once in the Indies, they were freed from the dependent position of those who are only partially mature, and released into a society where they held a privileged status by virtue of their white skin alone. Within a short time they learned to discard their submissive attitude. They became "sir," "tuan besar" even, and they soon adopted from their elders the Indies way of snapping at their chauffeur, caretaker, or *djongos*. John had also gone astray like so many of these bourgeois boys, hence the exaggeration and that "little too much" that characterized everything he did. He was generous, helpful and, in a pinch, kindhearted and easily moved, but he had something of the parvenu and pursued everything by which people in his circle measured prestige: money, comfort, and the attitude of a man who knows the world.

There wasn't a seat for him in the smoking-room, so he sat on the arm rest of Aunt Sophie's chair. He put his right hand around the back of the chair. Aunt Sophie looked up at him, smiling, with an expression of happiness on her face.

"The doctor doesn't want you to drink whiskey," she said, and then to us: "He has dysentery."

"Oh, come on," he said to Aunt Sophie, patting her amicably on the back, "you look after your dogs or Kitty, but not after me."

Aunt Sophie laughed: "Stubborn, you know, really stubborn, but who'll have to take care of his diet later? Me, of course." And she laughed again. Apparently she took pleasure in showing how informal their relationship was and how she had to take care of him. I don't know why, but without thinking I looked at Kitty. She was looking intently at John. Being still so very young, she wasn't yet able to hide her envy, and a few words and a single glance that morning revealed a small drama in the making. Aunt Sophie, Kitty, and John. My God! The result of that might lead to a family tragedy and it wouldn't be hard to guess who the loser would be.

That first evening back in the Indies, I sat outside with my parents until late at night. The first time in so many years. In Holland I had often longed for the Indies, for the mountains in the distance behind a white veil of rain, but I had yearned even more just to be able to sit outside again with the enormous starry night all around me. And now I was sitting there just as I had wanted. Nothing was missing. Something rustled in the grass as of old, and I listened to the crickets. I sat in a low rattan chair between my mother and father. The street was quiet and there was only the high, thin buzzing of the mosquitos in the garden.

There was almost the same atmosphere as on the night after Winny's death when I had also sat alone with my parents outside, and my father had showed me the stars. Suddenly I had a strong feeling of belonging to them again, of "being at home"—in a double sense. We sat quietly after all the talking and questions of that day, and could breathe more freely. I could have let this mood continue for quite a while, but a force stronger than I was impelled me to bring up what we had not yet spoken of.

"I think Aunt Sophie's changed quite a bit," I said.

"Yes," my mother replied, smiling briefly, "nowadays she pays a lot of attention to her appearance. I think she's afraid of getting older."

"Who's she doing it for?" I asked, getting straight to the point.

She waited a minute, searching for words. "Well . . . the family says that it's because of John, but the family says so many things."

I in turn was quiet for awhile. "What do you think about it?" I asked my father who'd have preferred to keep out of it.

"I really don't know," he answered, using almost exactly the words

I'd expected, and he puffed on his cigar, suddenly lighting up the darkness like a firefly.

"That's a partial confirmation," I said.

"Personally, I've *never* noticed anything," my mother said, this time unasked, as if she wanted to take her initial words back again.

"Hasn't Aunt Sophie ever talked to you about it?"

"No, of course not. . . ."

"But you know her well enough, don't you?"

"She'd never do such a thing. You know how she is," she began slowly, "you never get very close to Aunt Sophie. There's always something she won't tell you. And this, for example, she'll never tell, not to anyone."

"So you think that there is something after all?"

"Well, yes . . . no. . . . I don't think so."

Then she looked straight ahead again. My father was the first to speak again, almost mumbling, and mostly to himself. "It's really *kassian*."

And with that our conversation was ended for the day. I was tired and sleepy and no longer able to probe someone else's feelings.

That night I undressed slowly, strangely conscious of my own presence. The awareness of standing in a typical Indies bedroom with its whitewashed walls never left me for a moment. An electric light without a shade spread a harsh light from the middle of the room. When I turned it off and opened the mosquito netting, it was pitch-dark. It took some time before I could distinguish outlines. I lay on my back, arms crossed on my chest, and I felt myself lying on the lumpy mattress of an old Indies bed. Yes, even now I can almost physically remember this, as well as the awareness that I was behind the double protection of the mosquito netting and the wall, and that the nocturnal world only began beyond this. My body rested while I was lying there, but my mind began to work, slowly at first, then more and more rapidly: images, images, and even more images (I believe that I'm even doomed to *think* in images).

Kitty. The way she had looked at John early that morning. Kitty, swaying her hips when she left the room, and then suddenly backwards in time: Kitty as a four-year-old girl. It seemed as if I were changing portraits over and over again, sliding one in front of another. Kitty was gone. Now I put Rienkie's portrait over hers, also as a little girl, the little bridesmaid I had been so madly in love with. Then I pushed this image away too. I saw Rienkie look up at me while we were dancing and then slowly go up the stairs with her back turned to me. Kitty, Rienkie, even Winny (the loveliest of all), then Uncle Tjen, and after him, Aunt Sophie. A series revolving without interruption. I wanted to go to sleep, but all sleep had left me. Perhaps it was only the heat. It was as if I had to wait for something. I listened to the sounds outside. There were bats. They chased through the leaves, squeaking, and almost simultaneously I heard ripe fruit thudding on the ground. Then suddenly all the crickets were silent, and it was quiet for a moment. Afterward the short, prickling sound began again, like steel needles that vibrate. But worst of all that night was the persistent calling of an owl. For hours.

Sometimes dreams seem to be a continuation of quotidian life into another world, translated into another language, into other images. But sometimes a dream can invade our daily existence. It can hover for a while at the edge of our consciousness and determine our mood for that entire day. Eventually it fades away, sometimes lasting for hours, sometimes less.

That's what happened to me that night and the next morning. I probably fell asleep in the "mood" that determined the dream I would have that night. I had seen a darker side of Aunt Sophie that she herself had betrayed to us. It seemed to me that I had glanced through an open door and, against my will, had seen Aunt Sophie's intimacy as well as her shame. She appeared to me in my sleep that night: younger, darker, lying down in the light of a boudoir, laughing and acting seductively as I had never seen her do in reality. A little later she shriveled up into a naked, brown, wrinkled dwarf. There were sheets, bows, and pink colors, followed suddenly by quiet, godforsaken streets with shining rails beneath deep purple light, a reddish purple streaked with green and yellow. There must have been a fire in the distance. I sensed a deep mystery and a noiseless motion as landscapes and events changed slowly. Floating over a brown sea, I chanced upon a nocturnal harbor. Somewhere I pushed off and felt myself sinking into a boundless depth.

When I woke up it was almost morning. The sounds of night had disappeared, and it was perfectly still at the threshold between night and day. Darkness faded slowly. Suddenly, the twittering of a bird, shortly thereafter another, and then another. Within ten minutes day had arrived. I heard a door squeak somewhere in the house and then the bright sound of teaspoons against cups. My mother was making coffee for me of course. She suddenly seemed to be dear to me again. When I heard my father talking in hushed tones too—"Let him sleep late"—I got out of bed. He had put three rattan chairs in the garden. We talked a little about the laundry man who would come to pick up my dirty clothes, about financial matters, about my future, and what I wanted to eat

("babi kètjap"), but not a word was said about what we had discussed the
night before. It was of no use, and what business was it of mine anyway?
That's what I thought. But all day long, something of that dream kept
running through my mind, more as a feeling than anything else. It was a
feeling of embarrassment (the same as that morning on board ship) that
in the dream I had apparently translated into other symbols that involved me more than was true in reality. Even though I had come back to
the Indies as an adult, I continued to be a child to my parents and, to a
lesser extent, to Aunt Sophie. Because they were my elders I still held
them above reproach, and it gave me a shock when I caught Aunt Sophie
displaying her most intimate feelings that morning. That irreproach-
ability disappeared and she suddenly lost that impassive, almost impersonal, quality. She had descended from a pedestal and had become my
equal. With that, my whole relationship to her had changed. It was a
change that might have been dormant in me for a long time, but it
happened quite suddenly. But now, so many years later, when I think
back in wonderment to the confusion of feelings at that time (all out of
proportion of course) I realize that I could not have written about Aunt
Sophie until after that change had taken place, one accompanied by the
aforementioned confusion.

The following days and weeks brought me to "Salemba House" many
times. The big house seemed much smaller to me, less stately and not as
high, even somewhat dilapidated. Yet it was the same house. It still
smelled of brass polish and carbolic acid, it was still cool there, and the
floors shone as of old.

But inside something had changed. Some of the servants were new
and the old ones seemed to be different. Midin was still alive, but he was
old now, skinny and shriveled up. As he was standing there to pay his
respects I noticed a blue film over his eyes. He seemed more humble than
ever. Experience had apparently made him meek and tired, especially
tired I think.

Alimah was still there too. "Tabééh Tuan muda. . . ." You
couldn't tell that this stooped and toothless little woman had been pregnant in the past with the natural regularity of a cat. The other servants
were new, and still young and strong. They did the real work in the
house and yard. Midin only served at the table, sharpened the knives,
and polished the spoons and forks, and otherwise puttered around a
little. "That little old man, he dozes off so much, you know," said Aunt
Sophie, half apologetically. "I just don't say anything anymore." But she

did not keep her word because a little later I witnessed a good old-fashioned tongue lashing: ". . . did you forget it again? . . . The toilet's not clean, again. . . . You should do it yourself. . . . Don't leave it to the *kebon*. . . . You should do it this way . . . with your hands . . . like I've showed you so many times already. . . ."

New to me were "the girls," Uncle Alex's daughters, who were given a European upbringing by Aunt Sophie.

"Girls! Where are you? *Ajo*, come here, say hello. Aunt Sophie taught you that much, didn't she. You aren't in the *kampong*." And then one by one they appeared. They were dark indeed, with big, black eyes. They looked timidly at me and extended their hands shyly. They mumbled something and then retreated again. "Very different from Kitty, these girls, don't you think?" She meant: Kitty is so white and the girls are so dark, with *hidung pèsèk*. They had been in the house for over a year already, but they were still shy in front of other Europeans. They only seemed to be at ease with the servants. Aunt Sophie, however, had strictly forbidden them to go the outbuildings. They learned the wrong things there, like laziness and indolence. They had already been in the *udik* so long anyway. "And well, you know how Lex is, he's good, you know, but he can't bring up the girls. After all he's the father."

The children had lacked the care of a European mother for too long. Their own didn't know a word of Dutch. She did love the children, but well . . . she let them grow up like real natives of course. They had been allowed to go barefoot all day, and they were used to eating sweets continually, especially *rudjak*. No wonder the oldest one always had stomach trouble. Neglected amoebic dysentery, the doctor had said. Ah, "that woman" hadn't paid attention to anything! Now *she* prepared the child's diet. And *she* prepared the *obat*. It was the classic diet of *nassi tim* cooked with a chicken foot in it, and the inevitable *obat seriawan*. No *pedis*—but imagine! One afternoon when she had unexpectedly gone to the bathroom, she found the child eating *sambal* with rice as if it were normal. Those stupid servants had given it to her. What did she sacrifice herself for then? She couldn't be everywhere at the same time, could she? And invariably her final argument was: "You don't live in the *kampong*, you know."

"Girls, Aunt Sophie does all she can to give you a European upbringing. But you have to cooperate. What else do you want? . . . To marry a native?" Once she started in on them that way, she soon got out of hand. She had made up her mind to cut the native shoot off the family tree and graft it onto a Dutch branch, preferably one from a different family tree. But for that to happen they first had to be brought up as Europeans.

According to her, Uncle Alex had resisted at first and tried to keep the children for Titi. She had expressly asked for it, he said, but Aunt Sophie had again pointed out to him the necessity of a European upbringing (the words were always on her tongue). What would happen to the girls later on? He ought to bear in mind that he had legitimatized them and that meant that they carried the De Pauly name. They were too much like natives already, anyway.

"You decide then," Uncle Alex said. It was clear that he was afraid of scenes, and didn't want to take the responsibility.

"Let her come by some time, then I'll talk to her," Aunt Sophie answered. And one day he came by car from Sukabumi with Titi. She sat in front with the chauffeur, he in the back. When they arrived on Salemba Avenue, she walked around to the back of the house, and went to the outbuildings. Uncle Alex came in through the front.

The conference took place in Aunt Sophie's room. A *tikar* was spread out for Titi to sit on; her exceptional position entitled her to that. She behaved as all women from the *udik* do in the presence of their superiors or authority: she sat down, crossed her legs, put her hands in her lap and lowered her eyes. Aunt Sophie sat on the edge of a chair, bent forward, and began to talk. After some formal questions and a few reassuring phrases, the subject of separation was broached. She pointed out to Titi that, above all, it would be in the girls' best interest. What was more, Titi could see her children regularly. During vacations they would be allowed to stay in Sukabumi and she herself could come to Batavia whenever she wished. Titi answered everything with, "Saja njonja" ("Yes Ma'am"). She had already surrendered her opposition when Uncle Alex told her that she had been summoned to Batavia. That night she slept with the servants. When she left the next morning, Aunt Sophie gave her money, twenty-five guilders. "Terima kasih njonja" ("Thank you, Ma'am") she said, showing her benefactress the *hormat* she was due.

Several days later Aunt Sophie herself came to pick up the children. No stories have been handed down about any scenes on Titi's part, but I only have to imagine Aunt Sophie to know how miserable the children must have felt under such bulldozing. She must have begun immediately with detailed instructions, impressing upon them how privileged they were to receive a European upbringing, and she must have implied that the children should feel obligated and thankful, a feeling that they could not possibly have realized at the time. They had been torn from their familiar half-native, half-European surroundings and were frightened and insecure when they were confronted by all the domestic rules of order and cleanliness that Aunt Sophie assailed them with, even on the first day.

"Remember, girls! Aunt Sophie does *not* want you to walk barefoot. And *no* sweets in between meals, girls. You eat at the table. And correctly, with knife and fork, and not with your fingers. Where are your toothbrushes? You don't have any? Aunt Sophie will buy them for you and then, every time after eating, girls, brush thoroughly and gargle well. Like this, 'gaaarrr.' Girls! Keep your kimonos closed. Think of the servants! And lock the bathroom door." And once, when she went into the bathroom: "Girls! Who peed in the *mandi* room? Aunt Sophie does not like such things, understand? You smell strange enough as it is."

The children must have sought refuge with each other from this terrible outside threat that curtailed their lives and stifled them. Whenever I recall these girls, I always see them together sitting quietly in a corner, doing their homework, or whispering. Like "frightened little birds," an image I already used once in the beginning.

For them Aunt Sophie represented a foreign and even hostile world because her method of upbringing was based on a strange mixture of frantic care and Indies prejudice. She probably had no idea that her constant remarks about "the kampong," "natives," or race and skin color, might deeply hurt the children. *They* were not natives after all, but De Paulys! Once she got going, she could speak in the children's presence as if they were impersonal creatures without an emotional life of their own. One day—we were at the table—she was apparently speaking with my mother about the family, heaven knows about which branch of it. I had been following their conversation only half-heartedly, but suddenly I saw her point to the girls for further emphasis and heard her say slowly but clearly: "Yes, dark, Lien, but still not so dark as these girls." If one of us showed concern about such remarks, she waved away our objections with a single gesture and said reassuringly: "Oh, those children feel that differently than we do anyway." And another time: "*Ajo*, girls, you have to try harder in school; Aunt Sophie wants you to be able to take care of yourselves later." Because—and then it came again—they had to understand that their native descent and Indies appearance sharply decreased their chances for marriage. And she would never permit them to marry a "klipsteen"! [I didn't know this word either, but Aunt Sophie used it to describe any Indo with dark skin.—Author's note] The children must learn to think and feel "European," Aunt Sophie said again on another occasion, but she herself consulted *dukuns* and burned incense, practiced conjuring spirits, and believed in lucky and unlucky days. She ate sweets in her bedroom (the *rudjak* forbidden to the girls), drank *djamus*, and was squeezed and *pidjited* for hours by Alimah.

Raising the children brought many disappointments and irritations. She was seldom gratified. Only the oldest one gave her any satisfaction because she turned out to be a robust young woman with a stately way of walking. Completely European! Aunt Sophie spoke about her as "the crown of the family," but of the other two children she could only say with all the more disdain: "just look at those hips and that stomach . . . a real native build, don't you think?" According to Aunt Sophie, the youngest one, Deetje, sometimes had a very strong, penetrating smell, just as if she was always eating *petéh*. Every month she had the child purged—one spoonful of Epsom salts—but that peculiar perspiration smell remained. At her wit's end she took the problem of the "real native smell" to Van Braam, the gynecologist, who lived at the corner of Raden Saleh. He examined the child for three quarters of an hour, externally and internally. And do you know how little he charged? Three and a half guilders! Internal neglect, Van Braam said, but she had protested: "It's not my fault Doctor, but their native mother's. She never paid attention to anything. That always took care of itself. . . ." She, *she* always noted the dates precisely. And she did. On the calendar over the sink, in an easily decipherable code. Three crosses for the oldest, two for the one in the middle, and one for the youngest. The calendar sometimes gave the impression of having been used as a board game. Deetje, who as the doctor explained was "very dry" internally, had to have injections. Twelve! Ten guilders each! But she would do it for the children.

"You know, Lien, nothing is too much for me as far as the children are concerned. I've said: 'Girls, even if you'd cost me hundreds of guilders, I wouldn't begrudge it.'" She didn't mention the reasonable compensation Uncle Alex paid, simply because at the moment it didn't suit her purposes to include it in the long list of reasons for her sacrifices.

She never skimped on their material well-being and, in her own way, she also expressed her affection. "Come, girls, get dressed, we'll go to Pasar Baru. Then you can pick out material for a dress." "And," she said to Deetje, "you also have to have a new pair of shoes, we'll look by Sapi-Ie in a little while."

But she never got anything in return. Never, *never* were those girls nice to her, nor did they ever do anything unasked; it was as if they avoided her. She did not mention affection, or mutual love, because she had not received it yet from the children. She racked her brain about this for nights on end but found no explanation other than their "native origin." We'll never learn to understand them, she said, speaking in general, and they'll never become attached to us. Bitter experience lay behind this declaration and what was worse, it never got any better. The children who were at first so silent and submissive, became rebellious and insolent, and Aunt Sophie was especially hurt by the coolness with which they treated her. Sometimes this unduly provoked her. The confrontations between her and the girls became more frequent, though it was almost always Aunt Sophie who talked while the girls said nothing. But a glimmer in their eyes or a slight shrug of their shoulders were the means they used to express their hatred, their grievances, and contempt. And this was far more effective than if they had contradicted her. Aunt Sophie could not get a hold on it.

Sometimes Titi came from Sukabumi. Because the girls were living there she was allowed to go through the house, even when the others were at the table. While she was there, the girls were allowed to go to the outbuildings in the afternoon and stay with their mother. Titi never stayed more than a day or two. All that mattered to her was seeing her children again, and after that she withdrew as quickly as possible from the place where they forced her into a subordinate position.

We saw Uncle Alex more often because he had to be in Batavia regularly, usually to sell his products or sometimes to withdraw money from the bank, and then he always stopped by for a while to show he was interested, and to eat. If we were there, he ate first. Like Titi, he usually remained invisible. "Lex has to eat early, because he has to go back rightaway, otherwise he'll run into rain." When he came to town he wore an immense brownish *djas tutup*, though the collar was always wide open so that his undershirt showed. He accented his words in a peculiar way:

"Well—how are you?—*Panàs*, right?—Fie, Fie!—D'ya have—a *kipàs*—for me?" He always groaned when he sat down or got up again. He pushed himself up with difficulty and the rattan chair creaked. "*Allàh tobat, panàs!*"

"That Lex!" Aunt Sophie said when he was gone, "he's become so much part of the Indies. What a shame."

His life was superb: primitive and idyllic at the same time, in completely rural surroundings. His house was not on the main road, but a few hundred yards down a country road. And even then it was still somewhat hidden behind a hedge of flowering shrubs. A simple house, rather spacious, but not too big. It was surrounded by trees and greenery. Only the front had been left clear because of the view toward the mountains. By the time he returned from Batavia the worst of the heat was over already. I can imagine his arrival. As the car drives into the yard, the servants come to take the luggage: an old-fashioned, oblong "citybag," a raincoat, and a pith helmet. As was his way, Uncle Alex won't have carried anything himself. As *Tuan kandjeng*, he had to leave that to his subordinates. With a single call from the front veranda, he'd have ordered Titi to come so that she could take off his shoes and socks, and prepare everything for his bath: his pajama pants, a bar of soap, and his towel. He will only have felt human again after *siraming* himself for a long time, and drinking a cup of coffee. He never drank tea in the afternoon, always coffee, the well-known, native *koppie tubruk*. Titi must have stayed near him, probably sitting on the steps while he lay in his lounge chair on the front veranda. In that position, hardly looking at one another, they will have spoken in short Sundanese sentences, the language Uncle Alex was already more familiar with than Dutch. Long conversations were unnecessary anyway. His relationship with Titi was really typical of an *orang udik*; it involved few words.

By that time Uncle Alex had lived for many years a planter's life, getting up early and going to bed early. Every morning he saw the sun come up over the mountains, and saw the same row of bare *kapok* trees along the other side of the road. Every morning the grass was wet with dew and there were the same sounds: chickens cackling, goats bleating, and the sound of running water. Every morning a breakfast of *ketan* rice and the trip through the *kebonan*, always with his favorite dogs, Item and Matjan. Orders to the *mandurs*, discussions with the *desa* chief, all in a few words. Overseeing the harvest, paying the cutters and pickers, arranging transportation to Bogor and Batavia, and all of this over again day after day. Every day the same sunlight, the same shadows, the same trees, the same sounds, and the same voices.

It was a life without obligation or much tension. Those were only forced on him when he was in Batavia. His sisters always started in again about money matters, the children's upbringing, and his "responsibility." Their reproaches meant little to him, they spoke from another world and in a language he no longer understood. They talked about "going native" and "sinking low." It's "fun" he once said to my father as if he could smell where he could find understanding, because my father also liked to evade responsibility. When he was younger, they had tried more than once to persuade Uncle Alex to marry. They had one of his second cousins in mind, a European of course. He never said "no" and never said "yes," he didn't contradict them nor oppose them, he just let it be. And that was his strength. He saw no reason to change his life. He was really afraid of European women. He wouldn't have known how to behave toward them, and he must have had that characteristic, uncomfortable feeling about white skin, about what he called the *kulit bulé*. I don't know how much sisterly tyranny influenced his feelings of aversion. I can only guess. He also felt—with a mixture of intuition and understanding—that in a relationship with a European woman his role would be totally different from what it was with Titi. He would have had to talk with a European, to account for himself, and be obliged to do this and to do that. Now he was only served, and there was no one to demand his attention and urge him to act. It was good this way. By not acting and by letting everything go its own way, he proved to be as firm as a rock. Perhaps his only rebellion against the pressure of his sisters was to father children. I'm not entirely sure, I would first have to place the girls' dates of birth in certain periods and I cannot do that anymore. But I wouldn't at all rule out that he would do so just to frustrate them. He must have taken devilish pleasure in it.

His death was pitiful and lonely. He died one year after Aunt Sophie did, several months before the Japanese invasion. But death would have overtaken him anyway, because imprisonment would certainly have been the end of him. He had been losing weight for a long time, and he said that he didn't feel too well. That's why he didn't come to Batavia anymore. It made him too tired. But Titi appeared one day to get some *obat*, and her news was alarming. His jackets were much too large for him now and he walked slowly and carefully as if he was going to fall at any moment. His large neck (size 18) seemed long and wrinkled. Stooped and shuffling, his old and ruined body made a sad and hopeless impression. Until he couldn't walk anymore. Then he came to town by car. He just couldn't make it anymore. He was practically carried, but when they tried to help him, he began to cry. He no longer feared doctors and lay down obediently on the bed in the guest room, at the mercy of a specialist. That same day they brought him to Tjikini Hospital. A surgeon was consulted. Only a gallbladder operation could save him, but they wouldn't promise anything. He refused slowly but firmly, warding off the doctor with his hands. "I'll just die," he said softly, "no knife." Aunt Christien was struck by the way he said it. He died two days later, on a hot afternoon, behind a white screen in a room that was much too bright. Just like Aunt Sophie, the death struggle was terrible, but he didn't have pain. He didn't say a word. He didn't ask for his wife, he didn't even ask for his children. When he finally gasped his last, because no organ seemed to work anymore, no one from the family was with him. Not Aunt Christien ("Oh, I can't bear to watch"), not the children, nor Titi. She didn't arrive from Sukabumi until evening. They had sent for her by car. She came to Salemba Avenue first where they would prepare her for what she probably knew was inevitable. They took her into the bedroom and Dubekart had to tell her. Titi threw herself on the bed and sobbed violently. Aunt Christien watched, aghast because of the unexpected reaction and because she would have to change the bed-sheets now. She bent over Titi, took her by the shoulders, and led her to the outbuildings.

From a chronological viewpoint however, I am now overtaking my own story. I have to return again to what happened to Kitty and John shortly after my arrival in the Indies. These events are intertwined with the major and minor conflicts with the girls and happened at the same time. In themselves they are not very important, but they must have been excruciating to Aunt Sophie, so much so that she eventually succumbed to them. Her anguish, despair, and inner rage date from this time, though she still skirted along the edge of these emotions which had not yet taken the upperhand.

After my return from Holland it soon became clear to me that I was witness to a new situation, a change in the relationships on Salemba Avenue. Up until that time Kitty had only been a little girl for Versteeg, Aunt Sophie's "child" who was referred to all day in terms of delight. But he slowly discovered the woman in the child, and this meant that Kitty became Aunt Sophie's rival. The dramatic and tragic aspects were lacking as yet, but it was not difficult for us to imagine what Aunt Sophie must have felt. Sometimes she told my mother that she had to swallow a lot, but she could never express her feelings. She transferred all her disappointments to Uncle Alex's children without ever realizing what she was doing to them, and ignorant of the hatred she aroused.

In the meantime, the relationship between Kitty and John developed in a way that caused a lot of talk within the family. In the first weeks after my return I heard many stories from my mother. The child Kitty revealed herself as a flirt, something even Aunt Christien had to admit, though regretfully.

It had started whenever John came to Salemba Avenue. Kitty would appear on the rear veranda in her shiny, black silk pajamas, greeting those present with the languid gestures so characteristic of an Indies girl. There was immediately an atmosphere that my mother called "sultry" (which it wasn't). I've witnessed several of these entrances, but they were rather laughable, especially because the spectacle was judged with seriousness, and followed with such interest by the family. Not only that, but Kitty played her role without much subtlety or refinement; she was really only irresistible to John. Perhaps she thought she was as coolly passionate and love-hungry as Mae West, but in reality she was only coquettish. In any case, she was too young, too silly, and too lazy to be able to experience love as a real compelling force, to say nothing of anything more meaningful.

One day Kitty got a new bathing suit with a pattern of flames on it, a novelty from the Gerzon House of Fashion. Of course John had to admire it before they christened it together in the swimming pool. It consisted of a top and bottom connected only by a small strip of material. As it passed from Kitty's hands to John's and back again, it was nothing more than a modest little suit that certainly did not seem worth the price, but Kitty showed its elasticity by stretching it out against her body and then letting it spring back. The family appeared dumbfounded again, but Kitty and John did not seem to notice, so engrossed were they in their own activity. Then, finally, after a long drawn-out game, came the climax: "Try it on!" Kitty's excitement completely matched the expectation.

There was an even more disquieting event, however. One day John had come again to take Kitty for a ride in his light gray car. She was still getting dressed (Kitty was never on time), and he waited for her on the rear veranda. From where John was sitting one could see where the bedrooms opened onto the inner veranda. At first they yelled at each other for quite a while, as if the whole family had not been there.

"Aren't you ready yet?"

"No-o-oo!"

"How far are you?"

"None of your business!"

"Almost?"

"Ye-e-es!"

The bedroom door opened and Kitty, barefoot, with nothing on but a slip, toddled across to Aunt Sophie's room, apparently to finish dressing in front of the large mirror. And as if planned by the devil—or perhaps a friendly spirit—the door was locked. John, who had immediately jumped up, witnessed the retreat from a very short distance. Kitty cooed a little but, unfortunately, the story ends here.

Whenever my mother returned from a visit, she had always something new to tell, always something to report about Kitty and John. She could convey what happened with enough feigned restraint to equal her real pleasure in telling it. And she always added comments such as: "Filthy, you know, Mommy thinks it's sickening!" One day something was really bothering her. That morning she had been to Aunt Sophie's, and found the house on Salemba Avenue in an uproar. It had really been "too much"! Just imagine . . . and then came the story, told so colorfully that even now I can easily write it down. Kitty had been ill, or "unwell" as they usually called it, and lay on the couch in her unforgettable black pajamas. Aunt Sophie, my mother, and a few other aunts, were sitting around her, this time without taking Kitty's complaints too seriously. These were too familiar by now. Whether or not Kitty knew about the coming visit ("why else had she put on her black silk pajamas again?"), the fact is that John's car suddenly appeared, just when everyone expected him to be in the office. He entered ignorant, or seemingly ignorant, of Kitty's "illness"—we have to leave that up in the air. He had been alarmed when he heard the word "pain," and acted very worried. After being reassured by the aunts that it was not very serious, he sat down at the foot of the couch, now merely interested. He offered to get canned fruit (Kitty really wanted some), and returned with both the fruit and a box of bonbons. What my father called "utter nonsense" and my mother "strange goings-on" didn't start until then. Kitty, who up until then had only been languid, pale, and meek, closed her eyes and gave clear signs of physical suffering including, among other things, soft little groans. The women looked at each other, embarrassed by the whole thing, and also embarrassed by John, who constantly urged her to explain the nature of the pains. He wanted to call the doctor, but even Kitty objected to this. Then came the big moment. He asked her to locate the cramps in her abdomen, and after Kitty had pointed to several areas at once with a vague and tired gesture, he, backed up by his first-aid diploma, took immediate action. He knelt down beside the couch and, to the great horror of those present, began to examine Kitty's stomach. He did it very decently, though probably not very knowledgeably. But this went "too far," even more so because Kitty closed her eyes and let him go ahead. Both sisters were furious, they even pressed their thin lips together to show their indignation as clearly as possible, but unfortunately they kept silent, thereby sacrificing their right to reproach others.

"It's no good, you know," Aunt Christien said later to my mother, "to have those young people always in the house like that. Kitty is already so," and she seemed to have to look for words, "so . . . voluptuous, let's say."

Whether she was looking for a description or not, what it boiled down to was that Kitty was already too much of a woman to be able to play that game without danger. Of course Kitty and John didn't know each other or themselves very well and would have unleashed forces which they wouldn't have been able to control. In other words, a kind of fatal passion that would lead straight to the specter of an early pregnancy. The women had often talked together about it, but they didn't know how innocent and barren Kitty's passion would prove to be. Eventually the relationship led to a normal engagement and a legal wedding complete with veil and the church's blessing (even though they saw the minister for the first time at the ceremony). The marriage, however, remained childless, and was dissolved later on.

In any case, her relationship with John promised Kitty a decent future. She was certainly not blasé or calculating, only inexperienced. So many other things besides coquetry were involved. Certainly an excess of movie romance (with the ideal protector for a husband, of course), but also the relics of an ultra-bourgeois tradition, the eternal longing for the immaculate wedding gown, for the treasured family life, and for a cradle decorated most charmingly with ribbons (pale pink or sky blue): in short, a perpetual idyl.

Kitty's room, really a bedroom and separate boudoir, was a faithful reflection of her dreams. A real girl's room in spite of the expensive, green lacquered furniture with shiny steel knobs that Aunt Sophie had put in it. There were portraits and framed pictures on small tables and cupboards. The light green walls were also dotted with them. Everywhere you looked there were movie stars with their everlasting shiny hairdos, accomplished by excessive back-lighting—stereotypical photos sold in the Pasar Baru. And among all those smiling and seductive mouths and sparkling eyes, were photos from Hedda Walther's book *Mutter und Kind*. Close-ups of babies, too big to be real: bare bottoms and round tummies, with or without mothers who were mostly just as naked, bathing in "Licht, Luft und Sonne," prototypes of Hitler's suntanned and blond "Deutsche Jungen und Maedel." And next to them were family photos of children again, either on an arm, a lap, or in the cradle.

Two almost hostile worlds, each with its own romanticism, contended for mastery in Kitty's room. It would have been amusing, if Kitty had not fallen victim to it. Poor Kitty. For what became of that immortal idyl? A completely shattered marriage.

At the time, Kitty seemed suited for John. She shared his desire for luxury and an extensive wardrobe, and she loved to go out. This new life of going out, dancing, and entertaining seemed so new and attractive to her that she became possessed by fashion, manicure, and make-up. For her eighteenth birthday—that was shortly before her wedding—she asked for a visit to a beauty salon as a present from her parents. She

returned with plucked eyebrows, many jars of cream, and a big bottle of
Soir de Paris. Only John also thought that everything was as beautiful
and modern as she did, and that same afternoon he took her out riding in
his open two-seater past Noordwijk and Rijswijk to the Pasar Baru
where, early in the evening, luxury cars were parked in long rows.

Once a week she did her hair differently: parted on the left, parted
on the right, not parted, parted in the middle; hair down her neck with
bangs, no bangs; a small thin bow in her hair, a big wide ribbon, and so
on, and so forth. On Sunday mornings Kitty might change her clothes
three times, blaming the heat: from pajamas to dressing gown, and from
dressing gown to housecoat. Piles of unfinished patterns were lying on
the veranda in the rear, and fashion and movie magazines were scattered
throughout the house. She had marked several pictures with a red pencil
along with directions for the Chinese seamstress, a certain Mrs. Tik, who
made dresses for almost everyone in the family. It was she who once told
my mother in very poor and rapid Dutch: "Just terrible, Ma'am, such a
young girl and now already with such big tits. She shouldn't use ready-
wear anymore, I'll make bras to fit her." My mother was a little shocked
about the word "tits," but still had to laugh; she knew that dear Mrs. Tik
meant it well.

No matter how much Kitty was absorbed by the role she could play
all too easily for John, and no matter how he tried to make her into the
worldly woman he had always wanted as a bourgeois youth, there was
still a lot of the former sweet and kindhearted child left in Kitty. At
times there were still those unexpected expressions of sincere affection for
Aunt Sophie and her mother, as well as for my parents. Whenever Kitty
visited them, with or without John and his showy car, she always
brought something with her. Sometimes it was flowers, sometimes eau
de cologne, another time—in Indies fashion—a braided basket filled
with all kinds of food, from Nestlé bars to butter. My father smoked a
lot, and countless times Kitty arrived with a box or tin of cigars, or with
a pipe for him. "Here Uncle, that's for you." I can hear her say it in a tone
of genuine tenderness.

At such times there was not a trace of affectation left. If she was not
obliged by a male to display her feathers, she could be herself. And she
was at her loveliest when she was natural that way, when she wasn't
constrained to be someone else. It was the same side of her character that
loved ease, indolence, and mental laziness. Seated in a rattan chair which
she would not leave again for the entire morning, and with little more
than a faded kimono on, she could lose herself in a relaxed conversation
about ailments, doctor's bills, family and friends, shopping for clothes,

or about the seamstress. While she talked she painted her nails red or massaged her fingers. She easily gave in to inertia, a condition that was to annoy John a lot, later on. "Goddamn it," we heard him yell once, "where's my towel? You sit in a chair on your ass all day long and don't know where anything is." Kitty smiled wanly, but stayed in her chair. What else were servants for? From childhood on a *babu* had been trailing after her, picking up her mess. When Kitty's marriage broke up there were many arguments in the family about who was at fault, but Kitty really couldn't have acted differently.

No doubt the failure of her marriage really bothered her. She must have been deeply hurt ("You're too fat, too big, too lazy, and too stupid for marriage," he had yelled). She was humiliated by his unfaithfulness and felt that especially her teen-age illusions had been betrayed, but the same inertia and indolence that had contributed to the breakdown of her marriage now protected her from the unbearable tension that intense hatred can provoke. She was not the kind of person who could remain distraught. That was really rather strange because when I think back over her marriage—which did not last more than a year—I recall any number of outbursts, hers included. I remember one time when Kitty tried to play an all too obvious game with one of John's friends which, though petty, was derived from a quite understandable need for revenge. I can still see John's foot shoot out when she squeezed by his chair, and I'll never forget her look of suddenly intense hatred, nor her voiced reaction: "Adu, John, don't be so rude when there are people here!" That was all, but it disclosed a world of pent-up humiliation, so much so that it almost scared me. Kitty could hate, hate intensely, and was capable of completely losing control. She could carry on in a way that even Aunt Sophie couldn't improve upon, but either God or heaven had granted her a protective layer that absorbed the shocks and lessened the inner turmoil. After her divorce was an accomplished fact and she had returned to her parents' house, she said that, above all, she felt a sense of relief. She had announced this, partly smiling, some time later, on a day when the whole family was sitting together peacefully again on the familiar veranda with the blinds lowered.

"Don't you think that's strange, Aunt Sophie?"

"You're one of a kind, Kit!"

"Rumah sial," my mother always said about Salemba, meaning that there was a curse on the house. In spite of all the *selamatans*, there could never be happiness there. Frustration, moodiness, illness, death, and always the tensions, quarrels, and confrontations: explosive material that slowly increased in the house before thunderously exploding again. I have already mentioned such emotional eruptions, and how they could develop into fits of hysteria. Aunt Sophie did not have a layer of inertia to protect her; everything seemed to be just beneath her skin, threatening to burst open at any moment. Each new outburst brought her closer to insanity. This was the "mental illness" that Aunt Christien referred to on the day of Aunt Sophie's funeral.

During that time my mother was often summoned to Salemba Avenue. According to Aunt Christien she had a calming influence on Aunt Sophie—something that, on the surface, could hardly be the case. For she could hardly influence fate, or change anything in Aunt Sophie's life. "The girls, the girls drive me crazy," she'd scream, but what she meant was: Kitty . . . John . . . and I. "What is to become of me?" Sometimes she mumbled gibberish, consciously or unconsciously. She uttered maledictions or addressed spirits, evoking both fear and pity. Everyone was considerate of her and restored peace for her sake. But she was consumed by her destructive sense of fighting a "silent battle."

For a while it seemed—perhaps only to us outsiders—as if the tensions would dissolve, as if Aunt Sophie had finally managed to control herself and had relinquished John to Kitty forever. The umpteenth sacrifice! Until John suddenly got sick. The fever was high enough to be alarming, and because he was "so alone" without anyone to take care of him, Aunt Sophie took him into the house. The doctor diagnosed malaria tropica. John needed nursing care, and it would be best if he were taken to a hospital. But Aunt Sophie didn't want to hear of it. She would take care of him. She had already done it so many years for her husband that she could also take on this task. And she carried it out with devotion and infinite patience, watched over him part of the night when the fever went above 104. She dabbed his forehead, filled the ice bags, gave him something to drink, and changed him. At night she wandered through the dark verandas and, for the first time in a long time, she felt happy again. Finally someone to take care of again! There was suddenly a new determination in her, a decisiveness, and a willingness for self-sacrifice that was almost frightening. She spoke about John and his illness in the same way she had once talked about Uncle Tjen. That bothered the family. Dubekart expressed it openly, saying that she was "in love" with John, but her feeling for him was really much more complicated. It was totally different from Kitty's feeling, more profound, but also more confusing. Many things were part of it, such as the disappointment of her marriage, her childlessness, and the eternal suppression of her feelings.

Something of both the female and mother instinct in her had been re-awakened and, though coming so late, it was worth defending against any outside threat.

During this time, Kitty appeared and demanded her rights. After the fever broke, and John could once more be refreshed by sleep and enjoy mornings free of fever, she stole into the sickroom in spite of Aunt Sophie's prohibition. She entered the forbidden domain and saw John lying there, pale and greatly emaciated. She felt strange and embarrassed, he almost seemed to be someone else. Tears came to Kitty's eyes. She approached the bed slowly and bent over him. Perhaps she wanted to embrace him, perhaps she only wanted to fluff up his pillows, but at this moment Aunt Sophie came in. Kitty did not yet have the self-possession of an adult, and quickly straightened up. Like a child caught in the act. Then the rivalry broke out into the open. Aunt Sophie literally chased Kitty out of the room, and on the back veranda a scene developed that bordered on idiocy. It took place in full view of the horrified servants, and only several yards from the sickroom. That same afternoon John asked to be brought to Tjikini. Luckily the girls were in Sukabumi for their summer vacation.

Peace had already returned when my mother arrived on Salemba Avenue after she had immediately been summoned by telephone, of course. Whispering, Aunt Christien brought her up to date, but my mother could not do anything because Aunt Sophie had locked herself up in her room and had given orders that she was to be left alone. No one from the household, not even Aunt Christien, was allowed in. Only Alimah brought some food to her, but it was returned untouched. At Aunt Christien's orders, Alimah had to sleep in front of Aunt Sophie's door that first night. The next morning she reported continuous moving about, mumbling and talking, and strange sounds of vomiting and hic-cuping. After two days the door opened and Aunt Sophie reappeared: pale, haggard, and obviously suffering. My mother was alerted the same day, and she had a long conversation with her. Only the symptoms and the measures that had to be taken were discussed, not a word was mentioned about the reasons for what had happened.

"Really, Fie, you're overwrought." My mother had only one solution in mind and she pursued it with determination: get away! Not only from her room, but also away from the house and its surroundings where those evil spirits were at work. First they had to be exorcized, and then a big, new *selamatan* had to be held before Aunt Sophie would be allowed to return. My parents were about to leave for Lembang, for a vacation in "the mountains," and Aunt Sophie was to come with them.

"It's best, Fie. You have to get away for a while, away from this house. It'll do you good. The girls aren't around anyway." It couldn't come at a better time, now could it? Aunt Sophie had never been to "the mountains," she had only been to Sukabumi, to Uncle Alex, and sometimes—before it had been sold—to Tjidané. But to stay in a hotel as my parents suggested, no, that was not for her. That she finally agreed to go certainly proves that she also recognized that her presence on Salemba Avenue would only make the situation more difficult, not for her alone, but for the others as well. She also realized that she needed time to get a hold on her self again, and could do so in a place that would not remind her of the tensions of those last few weeks. And so it happened that my parents traveled by car to Lembang, and that Aunt Sophie went with them.

There was yet another conversation. Not between my mother and Aunt Sophie, but between Dubekart and John. Dubekart must have told John that he wished to have "a serious discussion" which, as it turned out, John only welcomed. In the hospital he told Dubekart that he loved Kitty and wanted her for his wife. If he only had come out with his declaration earlier! The relationship between John and Kitty was sanctioned in Batavia, while Aunt Sophie was staying in Lembang. Dubekart must have directed Kitty's attention to the fact that John was many years older than she was, that she ought to consider this in all of its ramifications, that she had to consult her own heart, and so on, and so forth; but I really don't think that even Dubekart believed that his words would do any good. This manner simply suited his personality. A letter was sent to my parents wherein Dubekart, on behalf of Aunt Christien, informed them of Kitty's intended marriage and in which he asked them to prepare Aunt Sophie as gently as possible. But there was no need for it. The change of surroundings, the cool climate, and the diversions, all had their desired effect. Aunt Sophie had calmed down, was quieter than she had been in months, and was able to evaluate her position. She followed a course which, thanks to the cooperation of all the others, was to lead to a complete reconciliation. Stories about Kitty began to fill her conversations again, soon even John appeared in them but, right from the start, only as Kitty's future husband "who would make her happy." At first my mother was somewhat surprised by this "about-face" as she called it, but she was immediately willing to play the same game. She saw it as a good sign, or at least as a willingness on Aunt Sophie's part to end "that crazy relationship." My mother cannot have readily understood that the solution was only possible because Aunt Sophie had identified with Kitty ("my child"). And she also cannot have understood that there was no question here of an about-face, but only the confirmation of a trans-ference. This was the reason for her great sympathy for Kitty, why she followed Kitty's life so closely, and why she always took Kitty's side when there was a marital conflict. Only in this way did Aunt Sophie manage to save herself, though a certain rigidity remained, a continuous element of unrest and tension, and an increasing need to justify herself. And I can hear her rattling on again:

"Oh no, nothing's too much for me as far as the children are concerned. I don't ask for thanks. I sacrifice myself gladly." According to Aunt Sophie herself, one of her friends told her: "Fie, you're a noble woman." Aunt Sophie said this because we didn't, and because she needed to hear it in order to build an image of herself as the self-sacrificing woman, full of love and devotion, devoting herself with all her strength to the difficult task of raising children. How could she turn three native children into three well brought-up European girls, worthy of the De Pauly family? It was a noble task demanding her utmost energy, care, and attention. It was all worthwhile to her, she exclaimed. *She* would do this and *she* would do that. . . . But this need to fashion a different image of herself only showed that she lacked happiness and satisfaction, and that she was powerless to help herself. She was unhappy. She felt that life had slipped through her fingers without ever having been able to hold on to some happiness, and it made her desperate at times. And indeed, in the end there was something tormented about her.

And I see her again in a frequently recurring scene of the last few months: the front veranda of the house on Salemba Avenue at twilight and, later, at night. We almost always had our regular places: Aunt Sophie sat with her back to the traffic, and I usually sat opposite her. It was also customary to leave the lamps unlit, always making it lighter outside than in. I usually saw Aunt Sophie's silhouette partially illuminated, her face in darkness. I can easily recall, of course, what her face really looked like in the last months before her death, but on such evenings I saw it vaguely. Only when there was a certain kind of light could I sometimes see her eyes and the slow blinking, and once in a while the flash of teeth, but not much more, *not* the deep wrinkles around her mouth or the large, dark circles under her eyes—in short, I could not see that weariness which now, looking back at it, was so obvious.

Behind her moved people in an unbroken stream past the food stalls garlanded with tiny oil-lamps, *sados* and *deelemans* with their twinkling candle lamps, and cars with far-reaching headlights. Yet Aunt Sophie saw and heard nothing of all this, she only talked, hardly to us anymore, but rather to herself about herself, and about illness and death, deliveries and miscarriages, marriage and divorce, the maintenance of family graves, the servants, Aunt Christien, and God knows who and what else. It always, literally *always*, included Kitty, especially the pity and indignation she felt about the treatment Kitty had had to endure from John. That's how strong the identification was. And when she spoke, sometimes whispering and then again raising her voice, she bent forward and supported her head with her right hand. Then the golden bracelet—a snake with diamonds for eyes—would slide down her wrist, and she would push it back again, and she'd talk right through everything, the ringing of bells and the calling of the street vendors and the clanging of the *sados*, and right through the buzzing and droning traffic that went by on Salemba Avenue, one of the main traffic arteries leading inland from the city. Aunt Sophie's silhouette became clearly visible each time a car flashed by. The gray hairs sticking out against the white light added to the impression of something wild and tormented, without ever allowing a good look at the face itself.

It must have been shortly before her death, which brings me automatically to the last image, the image of death with its dark eye sockets and intertwined white fingers, just as I described in detail at the beginning: the sweet smell of flowers, the tempered light, and my mother's tear-stained face. A typical death mask, taut and glassy, without a trace of previous physical suffering, but also without the "serene peace" which had granted Aunt Christien the needed consolation. The first signs of decay and the total immobility of the body, a state more earthy than earth itself, but also without even a single observable sign from higher regions. In any case, an irrevocable farewell to life.

With this last portrait before me, I realize that I did arrive at a place in this story where I'd resolved never to arrive: to that useless emotion. . . .

Epilogue

BETWEEN THE BEGINNING of this chronicle and its completion lie quite a number of years—thirteen to be exact. All the characters have now disappeared from my daily life; the older ones are dead and the younger ones are invisible somewhere beyond the horizon.

I should really begin with a kind of death list: Aunt Sophie died in 1940, Uncle Alex in 1941, my father in 1942, my mother in 1944, Aunt Christien in 1946. Titi also died last year. Only Dubekart is still alive.

Uncle Alex and Aunt Christien are entombed in the family grave at Tanah Abang, of course. It is the most inhospitable cemetery I know of, a vast wasteland of columns, cupolas, pyramids, flower tendrils, figures of angels, and an enormous amount of plaster work which is tarred at the edges and whitewashed above, yet stained, overgrown, gnawed, scorched, wet, and split asunder. It is nature's ultimate triumph over man, over every human attempt to artificially lengthen what is temporal with marble and stone.

On a hot afternoon once I visited the graves with Aunt Sophie. She walked through the cemetery like a twittering bird pointing out graves left and right with her parasol, continually talking, calling, and grumbling. She apparently followed a habitual route with regular stopping places on her tour of inspection, because she not only took care of the big family gravesite, but also of the graves of more distant family.

"Look, over there. Do you see? That's where Aunt Jozien and Uncle Léon are lying. . . . God, is that roof dirty again . . . *Kebòn*!!" (It was the caretaker she called.) "Why didn't you clean that roof? Those stupid birds. Why do they always have to go on the roofs," and rattling on, she continued on her way until she came to the family tomb. From a distance it did have something of a small, inviting garden house; it resembled a pergola with ivy that had attached itself to the zinc roof with very fine tentacles. Closer up, however, it proved to be too heavy and massive. At this spot she came to her senses, at least she was quiet for a while. Then she pointed with her ringed left hand (she had her bag and parasol in the right) to the vault underneath and spoke the prophetic words. "I too will lie there."

Did Uncle Alex have the same thought on that afternoon when Aunt Sophie was buried? And Aunt Christien too? If so, their expectations were realized. They are now lying together with Aunt Sophie and several other family members (family with family!) in the moist vault with the heavy concrete slabs above them, and over that, the peculiar marble, stone, and zinc structure. My parents are buried elsewhere, without marble and zinc, closer to nature. When I think of their graves, I always hear wind rustling through bamboo, and it contents me though I never go there anymore.

But of them all, Titi will lie in the most beautiful cemetery, the one in the *desa* where she died. There is nothing more beautiful than an Islamic cemetery planted with *kembodja* trees.

Dubekart, who had a splendid chance of being laid to rest in the family tomb too, missed his chance by staying alive and going to Holland. He, the *totok* in the Indies, now lives in The Hague as an old Indies hand. I imagine you can see him walking regularly along Frederik Hendrik or Meerdervoort Avenue on his way to the Hotel De Kroon or L'Espérance. There he and several companions from the same generation preserve an old world, a ghost world set against a purely colonial decor.

And the younger ones? All of them also live in Holland, even the girls. They live somewhere near Beuk Square or Thomson Avenue, that typical Indies quarter where they have formed their own community and follow their own way of life with its endless visits and dinners ("*Ajo*, come again soon, Toet; I'll make you some delicious *gado-gado*"). Kitty remarried and now lives in Arnhem, the other city where old Indies hands can meet each other regularly. All these children left the Indies after 1950. They left because that country no longer offered them anything, because it was not *their* country anymore. And they are right, the world of their parents, and thus their world too, has come to an end. It is beyond retrieval. In The Hague alone there are thousands like them: uprooted Indies emigrés. Some of them sit aimlessly in front of a window looking out at the wet streets and leafless branches and thinking of their *kebonan* with its fruit trees and *melatti* bushes, flower beds, and palm trees. They are homesick, and have an aching desire for *their* Indies and say to each other: "Too bad it went the way it did, it used to be so good over there." Others sit all day near a red hot stove in their pajamas and slippers. Rolling papers and a package of shag tobacco lie handy on a small table. They read the "Report of the Committee for Overdue Payments," and are bitter about the government. They feel betrayed and abandoned, and an old rancor grows. Yet they will still partially adjust—at least the younger ones will—and sooner or later they will find their place in Dutch society. From them will come the next generation, with a lighter complexion, until they will all be indistinguishable from the *totoks*, both in appearance and opinion. Aunt Sophie cannot have suspected that her most fervent desire has a good chance of thus some day being realized—albeit in a way different from what she could have imagined.

Even though the people have disappeared, the house on Salemba Avenue is still there, but the rural and stately road has become cluttered, busy, and noisy. Piles of sand and lime, and stacks of beams and red bricks now lie in the yard. The house and grounds have been rented to a business in building materials. The stones in the driveway are sunken, deep wheel ruts lead to the back yard. The lawn that the gardener watered daily now shows bare spots as if it had mange. The house has fallen into decay and lost its purpose. The walls sweat in black and green patches, the woodwork is moldered, and the gutters sag; the marble floors are dull and cracked. A sad demise.

December 1953.

Notes

If a Malay word is not discussed in the notes, refer to the glossary.

For practical reasons the old Dutch spelling of Indonesian words and phrases has been kept. Not only is it appropriate to the age when these texts were written, but it also will aid a student of this literature in finding other sources pertaining to this genre. All such secondary literature will have this spelling, including dictionaries, atlasses, and other references. For those who would wish to follow the modern orthography of Bahasa Indonesia, the following changes should be noted:

The old spelling tj [tjemar] is now c [cemar]; dj [djeroek] is now j [jeruk]; ch [chas] is now kh [khas]; nj [njai] is now ny [nyai]; sj [sjak] is now sy [syak]; and oe [soedah] is now u [sudah]. Only the latter change was adopted in this series because the diphthong [oe] is not familiar to readers who do not know Dutch.

1   That his *mother* had native blood, was always a source of pride for Nieuwenhuys. See his own biographical statement in *Singel 262* (Amsterdam: Querido, 1955), p. 7, and his lecture "De houding van de Nederlanders in Indonesië zoals deze weerspiegeld wordt in de toenmalige letterkunde," in *Bijdragen en Mededelingen betreffende de geschiedenis der Nederlanden* (The Hague: Martinus Nijhoff, 1971), 86: 68. He notes there that his mother and the *babu* Nènèh Tidjah lived together "in a completely Javanese magical world."

2   For evidence that his *love for nature* was nurtured by Nènèh Tidjah, and that he easily recalled the way she smelled see: Lisette Lewin, "Portretschrijver," *Vrij Nederland* 41 (12 July 1980): 7–8.

3   *Kipling's comment on England* from Charles Carrington, *Rudyard Kipling: His Life and Work* (London: Macmillan, 1955), p. 369.
    The quote from Henry Adams is from *The Education of Henry Adams*, ed. Ernest Samuels (Boston: Houghton Mifflin, 1974), p. 9
    T. S. Eliot on Kipling from the introductory essay of *A Choice of Kipling's Verse*, made by T. S. Eliot (New York: Charles Scribner's Sons, 1943), p. 30.

5   *Family as atmosphere* from *The Education of Henry Adams*, p. 36.

5   For *Geraerdt Knol* see note on p. 159.

6   *Kipling's phrase* quoted in Martin Fido, *Rudyard Kipling* (New York: Viking, 1974), p. 106.
    Nieuwenhuys' comments on his own style see: Rob Nieuwenhuys, *Een beetje oorlog*

(Amsterdam: Querido, 1979), pp. 9–10. Cf. E. Breton de Nijs, "Kroniek of Roman?", in *Singel 262* (Amsterdam: Querido, 1957), esp. pp. 16–18.

For quote from Burgess see: Anthony Burgess, *Earthly Powers* (New York: Simon and Schuster, 1980), p. 40.

The quote from Yourcenar is from an article: Deborah Trustman, "France's First Woman 'Immortal,'" *New York Times Magazine*, January 18, 1981, p. 20.

The quote about Kipling from Angus Wilson, *The Strange Ride of Rudyard Kipling: His Life and Works* (New York: Viking Press, 1978), pp. 38, 103, 3.

7   The phrase about *Clothilde's managing* in John P. Marquand, *Wickford Point* (Boston: Little, Brown, 1939), p. 252. One may mention here that families are indeed similar, no matter what the setting is. In a recent novel from modern India—Anita Desai, *Clear Light of Day* (New York: Harper & Row, 1980)—one finds yet another, fine portrait of a decaying family, this time in Delhi. Bim is remarkably similar to Aunt Sophie. She runs the household, keeps everyone going, while denying herself a life of her own. It is a novel constructed around carefully delineated detail, with a convincing picture of the oppressive atmosphere resulting from the merciless heat of India, combined with a passive subjection to the past.

8   *The passage about pictures* from Marquand, *Wickford Point*, p. 51.

9   *Writers not understanding New England:* Ibid., p. 156.

10 *Parlando.* Du Perron collected his poetry under this title: E. Du Perron, *Parlando,* in *Verzameld Werk* (Amsterdam: Van Oorschot, 1955), 1:6–162.

11 *Walraven's comments on Nieuwenhuys' story* may be found in: Willem Walraven, *Brieven aan familie en vrienden 1919–1941* (Amsterdam: Van Oorschot, 1966), pp. 815–22. Walraven's letters to Nieuwenhuys are on pp. 707–870.

For *mention made of English authors* by Walraven, see for instance *Brieven*, p. 258 (on Conrad), p. 816 (on Kipling); he mentions Dickens in his story "The Clan" (see the anthology in this series).

The phrase about *Daum's work* is from his daughter and was quoted by Nieuwenhuys: Rob Nieuwenhuys, *Tussen twee vaderlanden* (Amsterdam: Van Oorschot, 1967), p. 89.

12 The *passage describing Haverschmidt's style* is from Nieuwenhuys' fine book about him with the expressive title (which sounds much better in the original) *The Minister and his Angelic Strangler* (R. Nieuwenhuys, *De Dominee en zijn worgengel* [Amsterdam: Van Oorschot, 1964], p. 112).

13 *Batavia* is the name the Dutch gave to the city they built on the shores of the Tjiliwung River on the northwestern shore of Java. The city began as a warehouse near a Javanese settlement called Jakarta, which was subsequently turned into a fortification. In 1619 it was given the name of Batavia, after the "Batavi," a Germanic tribe in Holland mentioned by Tacitus. The word became synonymous with the Dutch nation. During the seventeenth century, Batavia grew to become the capital of the colonial Indies, acquiring the sobriquet of "Queen of the East," although it also became known as "the graveyard for Europeans." The original city was constructed like a Dutch town with gabled, narrow houses built wall to wall, with canals and drawbridges, and its design was quite unsuitable for the tropics. The unhealthy climate of the coastal plain made physical survival precarious and from about 1733 wealthy Dutchmen began to move away from the city, going

further inland to profit from a higher elevation. By the end of the eighteenth century the old city of Batavia had lost its splendor as well as its European community. It became known as the "lower city" and was primarily populated by Chinese. Governor General Daendels moved the seat of government further inland in the beginning of the nineteenth century, to *Weltevreden* (Dutch for "Sans Souci") which had a more beneficial mountain climate. By 1870 the old city no longer had a European population. Along a canal called *Molenvliet* ("Mill River") new and larger houses were built, forming suburbs which kept expanding further inland. These spacious houses were better suited for a tropical climate. They had stone or marble floors, were never more than one story high, had covered verandas in front and back, and were surrounded by large shade trees. These suburbs were also given typically Dutch names such as Noordwijk or Rijswijk, and branched out from two huge squares called Koningsplein and Waterlooplein. Collectively these new settlements were known as the "upper city." Today Batavia is, of course, the capital of Indonesia and has resumed its original Javanese name of Jakarta. A great deal has been written about Batavia in one form or another. The best work on old Batavia is: F. de Haan, *Oud Batavia*, 2 vols. (Batavia: Bataviaasch Genootschap van Kunsten en Wetenschappen, 1922–1923). A brief description of the city, illustrated with contemporary prints, may be found in *Reizend door Oost-Indië. Prenten en Verhalen uit de 19e Eeuw*, ed. B. Brommer (Utrecht: Spectrum, 1979), pp. 11–50. For photographic material from the nineteenth century and the beginning of this century see E. Breton de Nijs, *Tempo Doeloe* (Amsterdam: Querido, 1973) and R. Nieuwenhuys, *Batavia, Koningin van het Oosten* (The Hague: Thomas Eras, 1976). *Salemba* was the name of both a wide avenue and a suburban district south (further inland) of the old city of Batavia, and north of Meester-Cornelis (now called Jatinegara).

14   *Sukabumi* is both a city and a former administrative district in southwestern Java. In the north it is demarcated by the slopes of the volcanoes Gedé, Salak, and Halimun, and its southwestern border is formed by the Indian Ocean, particularly the two bays: Wijnkoops Bay and Zand Bay. This region was also described in E. du Perron, *Country of Origin*, forthcoming in this series.

15   *Tanah Abang* was the name of a district in the greater Batavia area, and was once a fashionable European quarter. The name means "red" (*abang*) "earth" (*tanah*) in both Malay and Javanese, and refers to the reddish soil frequently found there. The passage alludes specifically to the European cemetery in that district, which dates from the end of the eighteenth century. It was recently removed by Indonesian authorities to make room for more housing units.

        De Pauly and *Dubekart*. Such names were not, of course, the names of Nieuwenhuys' family, but one does find them as historical names of the colonial Indies. "Dubekart" for instance, was taken from a man called A. M. Courier dit Dubekart (1839–1885) who spent most of his life in Java. He had a wide variety of jobs, was constantly in trouble with his superiors, and offended the small Dutch communities in which he lived. He married a native woman from the island of Nias and refused to let his children go to school. In 1872 he published a book in Semarang, which kept his memory alive. It was called *Facts of Brata-Yuda or Conditions in the Netherlands Indies (Feiten van Brata-Yoeda of Nederlandsch-Indische toestanden)* and contained some seven hundred pages of criticism of colonial policy.

Multatuli discussed this book at length in his *Ideeën* (Vierde Bundel), nos. 1024 to 1030 (Multatuli, *Volledige Werken*, 7 vols. [Amsterdam: Van Oorschot, 1973], 6:313–27).

For detailed information on the names of colonial families see P. C. Bloys van Treslong Prins, *Genealogische en heraldische gedenkwaardigheden betreffende Europeanen op Java*, 4 vols. (Batavia, Weltevreden: Drukkerij Albrecht, 1934).

17   *Buitenzorg*. This city, now called Bogor, became the residence of the governor general of the Indies after the unhealthy climate of coastal Batavia urged the removal of the seat of colonial government to this spot in the mountains with an elevation of over 800 feet above sea level. Although it has a rainfall of nearly 170 inches a year, Buitenzorg was famous for its climate and beautiful scenery. Besides being the residence of the highest official in the colonial Indies, Buitenzorg was also known for its botanical garden.

17   *Djati* is the name for what is probably the most famous wood of the Indies, known as "Java teak" in English, or generally referred to as "teak." The *djati* trees are particularly abundant in Java. It was especially sought after as a wood for furniture and, because of its hardness and resilience to climatic changes, it was also favored as a wood for the decks of ships. It is dark brown in color and was considered by the Javanese as "true wood," for *kaju djati* means "sound wood" in Malay and Javanese. The word itself is of Arabic origin meaning "real," "genuine," or "pure."

18   *Kramat* and *Senen* and *Museum Avenue* were names for streets in Batavia. Salemba Avenue becomes Kramat Avenue, then Senen. *Kramat* means "holy" and *senen* means "Monday" (market day was Monday).

19   *Tjemaras* is the *Casuarina equisetifolia* tree. It is noteworthy for its thin branches and its little scalelike leaves. The general appearance is reminiscent of pine trees. *Purple* is a color of mourning in Asia.

21   *Saté* is a native dish resembling miniature shishkabob. Small cubes of goat's meat (*kambing*), or beef (*saté manis*) are skewered on small sticks and roasted over a charcoal fire. *Saté* was a standard dish for *rijsttafel* and was also a common food sold by street vendors.

Menggirip is the brief period of time between the setting of the sun and the onset of darkness. Night falls very quickly in the tropics. This period of time was associated with bathing, for cleansing oneself both physically and emotionally. The word derives from Arabic *maghrib* which is the Mohammedan term for the fourth daily meditation performed at sunset, and also means, as a geographical term, the West.

Sundanese is the language spoken in western Java, the area that includes primarily the southern portions of what were formerly known as the districts of Bantam, Batavia, Cheribon, and the Preanger regions. This is mountain country and some Sundanese refer to their language as *Basa Gunung* or "Mountain Langauge." It was spoken at the time of this novel by about four million people.

26   *Pasar-Baru-East* is the name of a street in greater Batavia, the furthest east of the district called *Pasar Baru*, which ran along the river Tjiliwung (which cut through Batavia) and across from the canal called Gunung Sari (or Sahari). *Pasar Baru*, which means "new market," was a Chinese shopping street.

Djeruk is Malay for a citrus fruit that is related to the grapefruit, and also as a generic term for citrus fruit.

Melatti, also spelled *melati*, is in Malay, Javanese, and Sundanese, the word for a variety of jasmine (*Jasminum sambac*). It is a climbing shrub with white, sweetly fragrant flowers, which Javanese women liked to wear in their hair. The flowers were particulary associated with marriage ceremonies. The *melatti* flower was at one time almost synonymous with the exotic beauty of Javanese or Malay women. The flower was adopted as a pseudonym by a Dutch woman, N. M. C. Sloot (1853–1927), who wrote romantic tales and novels as "Melati of Java."

27   *Gendih*, a jug with a long neck ("goglet") usually to keep water in. It was made of porous unglazed earthenware.

Sarong, the skirt of the Indies, worn by both men and women. *Sarong* (properly: *sarung*) was more commonly used by Europeans, while *kain* was the general word used by the native population with countless combinations, so that *kain sarung* would probably be more correct. *Sarong* means "sheath" or "covering" (e.g., *sarung kaki* means "sock" or "foot covering"). *Sarongs* could be woven or batiked, and were either cotton or silk. A *sarong* was divided into a "head" or *kain kepala* (the beginning of the woven cloth), the "body" or *kain badan*, which represents the rest of the garment, and the *pinggir* or "border." Each had its specific design, usually of an abstract nature.

With the sarong a jacket was commonly worn, by both men and women; known as a *badju* (*baju*), it traditionally was meant to cover the upper body from the neck to the knees. A *badju* that reaches just below the hips is called a *kabaja*. This is fairly loose, open in front, with long and narrow sleeves fastened at the wrists. The front does not have buttons and is closed by three brooches connected by little chains, often silver, called *kerosang*. Because the combination of *sarong* and *kabaja* is both elegant and comfortable, it was adopted by European women as a relief from the unpractical and stifling European dresses. In Java a *kabaja* is never batiked.

When the European men wanted to get comfortable they put on a *slaapbroek*, which literally translates as "sleeping pants," but which were not, properly speaking, pajamas, but loose trousers of batiked cloth. Over that they wore a *kabaja tjina* or loose cotton jacket with an upright collar.

28   *Hoffman drops* were popular medicine, composed of equal parts of alcohol and sulphur-ether. They were a remedy against "nerves" and fainting.

Kantjil is a small deerlike ruminant called "mouse deer" or "chevrotain" in English. It is indigenous to the Malay archipelago, and is also called *pelanduk* in Malay. It belongs to the family *Tragulus*, is small, usually no longer than twenty inches, does not have horns, but the male has two canine teeth protruding past the lips. It lives in hilly or mountainous terrain and is found usually alone or in pairs, never in herds. The *kantjil* or *pelanduk* is the Brer Rabbit or Reynard the Fox of Indonesian fables, and *pelanduk* can also mean the "wily one."

30   *Indo* is the abbreviation of "Indo-European," which meant in the Indies a person with one native and one European parent, a Eurasian.

Sauers and *Bayards* are rifles.

31   *Tjempaka, kenanga, melatti,* and *ramping* are tropical flowers. *Tjempaka* is a kind of magnolia (*Michelia champaca*), with fragrant yellow flowers; *kenanga* is a tree with fragrant flowers (*Canangium odoratum*); *melatti* is a kind of jasmine (*Jasminum sambac*). *Kembang ramping* is a fragrant mixture of leaves from the *Pandanus dubius* tree. This tree grows on beaches as well as in the mountains. The leaves are dried, crumbled, and mixed with the petals of the other odoriferous flowers.

32   *Blekok* is a kind of heron (*Ardeola speciosa*). Its head and neck are brown, the back is black, the rest white.

The *asem* tree, or *kaju asem*, is the tamarind tree (*Tamarindus indica*). A tall, stately tree, it was often used to line avenues. The fruits were used to enhance the flavor of various dishes.

Katjang-idju is a kind of bean (*Phaseolus radiatus*) with dirty yellow flowers. The beans are eaten after they have been cooked, and they are also used for chicken feed. The seedlings are a very popular food called *taogé*, known to us as bean sprouts.

34   A *pendopo* is a large, open hall.

Totok was a common word, derived from the Javenese word meaning "genuine," "full-blooded." It came to refer exclusively to full-blooded Europeans, particularly Dutchmen.

35   *Benkulen* is an area on Sumatra's west coast. *Mokko Mokko* is a town in the mountains of that district.

Pedati is a large wooden cart with wooden wheels often pulled by a *karbouw* or water buffalo. It frequently has a canopy of bamboo or leaves. It is also called a *grobak* in Javanese.

36   *Doctor djawa* was the term used for a native physician who, at the time of this novel, had studied at a medical school for the native population in Batavia ("Inlandse artsenschool"). They were licensed to practice medicine and delivered babies and prepared and dispensed medicine. The doctor *djawa* was often the only authorized medical person for a large area. He should not be confused with a *dukun* who was a medicine man who used magic for his cures.

Painan is a coastal town on the west coast of Sumatra, south of Padang.

Sindanglaja is a town in the central mountains of western Java. It is situated just north of the two volcanoes Gunung Gedé and Gunung Pangrango.

Ketjap is a kind of soy sauce. It is made by fermenting the beans of the *Glycine soja* plant.

37   *Si Kriput.* "Si" is often a demonstrative prefix expressing contempt, and it is also often used with personal names. Both meanings are intended here. *Kriput*, also spelled *keriput* means "wrinkled." The cognomen may mean something like "Mr. Wrinkled."

Obat seriawan. *Obat* is Javanese for anything used as an antidote or cure, be it magic or medicine. *Seriawan* is Malay and rēfers to a disease and its antidote. The disease is sprue (from Dutch *spruw*) which is a tropical disease characterized by diarrhea, ulceration of the mucous membrane of the digestive tract, and a shiny tongue. In Malay it can also mean ulcers of the tongue and mouth. The native remedy comes from the bark and leaves of the tree *Symplocos odoratissima*, called *djirak* in Javanese and *Ki sariawan* in Sundanese. These leaves are the main ingredient of the *obat seriawan*.

40   *Padang* is an important city on the west coast of Sumatra, about halfway down that coast.

43   *Betinka(h)* here means "whims" or "having a fit." It derives from *tingka(h)* which, in a figurative sense, means "character," "ways of a person."

44   *"Clicked"* in the sentence "my mother and Aunt Sophie really clicked." In the original, Breton de Nijs uses "getjo-tjokt," which is Dutch usage of the Javanese verb *tjotjok* which means "to bring into agreement," to "conform," "to be fitting."

45   *Nassi tim.* *Nassi* or *nasi* is the common word for rice. *Nassi tim* means rice steamed

in a bain-marie (a container of rice lowered into a larger container of boiling water), so that it remains soft. It was fed particularly to sick people.

48   *Kulit langsep. Kulit* means "skin" and *langsep* refers to a particular color, a pale
      yellow or fawn color. The latter use comes from a Javanese simile, derived from the
      color of the rind of the *langsat* fruit, a variety of *Lansium domesticum.*

49   *Rijswijk Street.* Despite its very Dutch name, this was a shopping street in Batavia
      with a substantial number of French shops.

50   *Kanari tree* is a tall handsome tree (*Canarium commune*) favored in Java to line wide
      streets or avenues. The seeds were eaten raw and taste like walnuts and the oil from
      these seeds was also used. An early photograph of Salemba Avenue lined with
      kanari trees may be found in Nieuwenhuys' book of photographs of old Batavia
      (*Batavia. Koningin van het oosten* [The Hague: Thomas Eras, 1976]).

51   *Krèkot* was the name of a street in Batavia which formed a right angle with the
      Chinese shopping street called *Pasar Baru.*

      Pusaka (also spelled *pesaka*) is usually translated as "heirloom" but can also mean
      "family property" or, in this particular case, refer to valuable personal property.
      The concept of *pusaka*, however, means a great deal more. In many places in
      Indonesia *pusaka* means an object that is holy and can be inherited. Such objects
      are said to contain the spirit of people long dead, and are venerated. One could
      almost translate this common notion of *pusaka* as "fetish." Particularly in Java and
      Celebes (the people from Makassar and the Buginese) regal ornaments that belong
      to a ruler and are inherited from his ancestors are revered. Such objects can be
      weapons (especially krisses), a *sirih*-box, or a sunshade. But in practice a *pusaka*
      may be any object that has some special significance for a region, ruler, or popula-
      tion. See G. A. Wilken, "Het Animisme bij de volken van den Indischen Archi-
      pel," in *De Indische Gids*, 6, pt. 2 (1884): 56–63. Clifford Geertz gives an example
      of stories that are "*pusaka* stories," Javanese folk tales about magical objects. He
      mentions one about a sacred spear and another about a gong that is really a tiger
      (*The Religion of Java* [1960; reprint ed., Chicago: The University of Chicago Press,
      1976], p. 301).

      Geraerdt Knol, the eponymous founder of the De Pauly line, is a fictional creation of
      Nieuwenhuys, although he shams proof from an impeccable source: an actual work
      called *Priangan* by De Haan. In four volumes, it is a great work of scholarship and
      became the basic source for historical information about Java (F. De Haan, *Prian-
      gan. De Preanger-Regentschappen onder het Nederlandsch Bestuur tot 1811*, 4 vols.
      [Batavia: Bataviaasch Genootschap van Kunsten en Wetenschappen, 1910–
      1912]). Nieuwenhuys refers to the first volume. In its second part one will find
      historical profiles of various Dutch officials. As far as I can determine, Geraerdt
      Knol is a composite of several of those figures. (My page references are to the
      section called "Personalia" in this first volume, a section which has a separate
      pagination.)

           The name was borrowed from a Govert Cnoll (pp. 197–200), who advanced
      from sergeant to a high position in the colonies, returning to Holland as a vice
      admiral in 1709. The major traits for Nieuwenhuys' fictional character—includ-
      ing the direct quotes from De Haan—were derived from the life of Pieter Herber-
      tus van Lawick van Pabst (pp. 103–11) who lived from 1780 to 1846. The "au-
      thentic reports" that describe Knol's peculiar behavior are descriptions of Van
      Lawick van Pabst during his stay at the *pasanggrahan* at Gowok (p. 111). Baud's

quote is on p. 110. Van Pabst was indeed a resident of Cheribon. I also suspect that other historical personages make up this composite. Knol's being a "surveyor" may have come from the description of the life of Pieter Tency (who died in 1812) who also worked his way up the colonial ladder and acquired substantial real-estate holdings in Java. The wonderful detail of Knol's sailing across his rice fields comes from Tency's life. On his Tjiluwar estate, the "Tjidané" in the novel, he sailed around a large pond in a "large-sized brig, full rigged and mounting guns." De Haan adds these words, which Nieuwenhuys used verbatim: "zoodat het op een afstand leek alsof hij in de sawah's spelevaarde" (p. 114). Another figure who may have contributed to Knol is Andries de Wilde who lived from 1781 to 1865 (pp. 284-309). De Wilde was involved in some complicated and suspicious land speculations and was an official during the administrations of two governor generals, Daendels and Raffles. As the novel hints about Knol, De Wilde knew them personally. De Wilde married in 1821 (when he was forty) the sixteen-year-old daughter of a sea captain (p. 300). The man named "Engelenburg" in Nieuwenhuys' novel may refer to Nicolaus Engelhard (pp. 77–87). The lives of all these men are linked in one way or another, and all of them were connected in some official capacity to the administrations of the two governor generals mentioned in the novel.

Resident; this was the next highest office in the colonial Indies. At the top was the governor general and directly under him were the residents who governed the thirty-six territories of the Indies. Because this novel deals primarily with Java, a resident was the administrative head of a residency. There were seventeen such residencies in Java and Madura.

The Council of the {East} Indies, in the time of the VOC, ruled the dominions of the Company along with the governor general. The reason for the Council's existence was to curb any autocratic aspirations of a governor general. The number of members of the Council varied and, as one can imagine, there often was friction between the Council and the governor general. In the nineteenth century the Council gradually lost power until it finally became an advisory body.

Raffles, Van Muntinghe, and Daendels. Daendels (1762–1818) was governor general from 1806 to 1811. He attained that high position when, after the French revolution, Holland became a republic, allied itself with France, and was annexed by Napoleon. He was a tough, autocratic governor general, who paid little attention to diplomacy or touchy personalities. Daendels introduced liberal innovations in the colonial system, but was also known for his ruthless suppression of revolts and the use of native labor for public works. He was succeeded by *Raffles* (1781–1826), who was lieutenant-governor of Java and dependencies from 1811 to 1816. This was the British interim administration which occurred during the Napoleonic Wars, when England conquered and took over the Dutch colonies because Holland was part of the French empire. Raffles also introduced liberal innovations, but many were continuations of Daendels's policies. He was vehemently anti-Dutch and sought either to keep the East Indies for Britain or, when this failed, to create a rival to Batavia. He accomplished the latter by negotiating British possession of a small island off the coast of the Malay peninsula that soon flourished as the harbor of Singapore. His substantial *History of Java* (1817) is still of value to students of that island.

Muntinghe (1772–1827) was a high official in the colonial hierarchy whose expertise was acknowledged and used by Daendels, Raffles and Van der Capellen. See H. R. C. Wright, "Muntinghe's Advice to Raffles on the Land Question in Java," *Bijdragen tot de Taal-, Land- en Volkenkunde*, 108 (1952): 220—47.

Pasanggrahan (derived from Javanese) is a resthouse or shelter to accommodate travelers passing through a district. It was maintained by the local population with help from the colonial government.

52   *F. de Haan* was one of the great historians of the colonial Indies. He was born in the capital of Friesland, Leeuwarden, in 1863, and received his secondary education there. In 1884 he obtained a Ph.D. in literature from the University of Utrecht and tried to find employment in the colonial Indies. However, his health was officially judged too fragile and he left for the Indies at his own risk. At first he worked as a private tutor for the children of highly placed officials, but in 1905 he was appointed archivist of the National Archives in Batavia. He retained that position until 1922. In June 1923 he resigned and returned to Holland where he died in Haarlem in 1938. Besides a number of lengthy articles, De Haan will always be known for two monumental works on Java and Batavia. The first is a four-volume history of the Preanger district in Java: *Priangan. De Preanger-Regentschappen onder het Nederlandsch Bestuur tot 1811* (Batavia: Bataviaasch Genootschap van Kunsten en Wetenschappen, 1910–1912); and *Oud Batavia. Gedenkboek uitgegeven door het Bataviaasch Genootschap naar aanleiding van het 300-jarig bestaan der stad in 1919*, 2 vols. (Batavia: Bataviaasch Genootschap van Kunsten en Wetenschappen, 1922–1923), which is a history of the major city of the colonial Indies. Both works contain an immense amount of historical information culled from the archives and secondary literature. Besides the scholarly value of these works, they are also written in a lively and witty style. Neither has ever been surpassed, nor has anyone equaled De Haan's enviable combination of impressive erudition and literary grace. Biographical notices may be found in volume 8 (the third supplement) of the *Encyclopaedie van Nederlandsch-Indië*, and in *Tijdschrift voor Indische Taal-, Land- en Volkenkunde* (1938), 78: ix–xii.

Baud is a reference to Jean Chretien Baud (1789–1859), an important administrator in the Indies, who subsequently became the first minister of colonial affairs. *Medemblik* is a harbor town in the province of North Holland on the coast of what was formerly the Zuider Zee.

53   *Woodbury & Page* were British commercial photographers in Batavia during the final decades of the nineteenth century. There is a picture of them on the first page of Nieuwenhuys' book of photographs: *Batavia. Koningin van het Oosten*.

55   *Tuan tanah* means "landowner" here.

Concordia (also abbreviated as "the Concor") began as a military club in Batavia, but, after it allowed civilian members, increased significantly in size. The building, rebuilt and expanded over the years, was on Waterloo Square in Batavia. It became extremely popular with the Dutch because its main function seems to have been organizing parties. Every two weeks a party was given in the garden with fire works, and every year there was a gala ball. The club was very much part of Dutch social life in the capital.

Aurora and the *Opera Club* were the names of private clubs in Batavia. They were used for amateur theater, for opera performances, or for musical evenings. Because there was relatively little entertainment for Europeans, such clubs became a social "must."

La Navarraise is an opera by the French composer Jules Massenet (1842–1912), which was first performed in London in 1894 and in Paris in 1895. Its heroine is called Anita, the "woman from Navarre" or the "Navarraise."

57   *The crisis of 1883* refers to a decline in the price of sugar. Sugar cane was raised primarily on Java, was controlled by the colonial government, and was mostly administered by the Chinese. After 1870, government monopoly gradually gave way to private enterprise. These private sugar plantations suffered commercial ruin when several nations in Europe actively supported local growing of sugar beets and the regional manufacture of sugar. At the same time, a disease called *sereh* attacked the sugar cane and caused greatly reduced harvests. The combination of the two caused many planters to go bankrupt, forcing them to sell their property.

60   *Djali pits* are the syconia of a grass called *Coix lacryma-jobi* or "Job's Tears." They are tear-shaped, very hard, and look like porcelain. They were used as strings of beads, bracelets or rosaries.

Tjongklak is a game played either with cowrie shells on a boat-shaped board, or with pits from the fruit of a particular tree. The game is played also in Egypt, Syria, and the West Indies; also spelled *tjongkak*.

61   *Donizetti, Hervé* and *Lecocq* were composers. Gaetano Donizetti (1798–1848) was an Italian composer famous for his operas, especially *Lucia di Lammermoor* (1835) and *Don Pasquale* (1843). Florimond Rongé Hervé (1825–1892) was another French composer who, until Offenbach, seems responsible for the genre of the operetta. Alexandre Charles Lecocq (1832–1918) was a French composer who had inordinate success with his opera *La Fille de Madame Angot* (1873) which was performed for 400 consecutive nights and retained its popularity for quite some time.

70   *Sunda region*, the western region of Java. *Priangan* ("residence of the spirits") is the Javanese name for what the Dutch called *Preanger*. This is a large district in southwest Java, bordered on the south by the Indian Ocean, to the north by the former residencies of Batavia and Cheribon, and to the west by the Bantam residency. The Preanger region was about one-sixth of the entire island and of a mountainous terrain that is said to have more active and dormant volcanoes than any other region in the world. Volcanic terrain, old river beds, and an ancient lake bottom provide the Preanger region with fertile soil, which resulted in a dense population. *Buitenzorg* (or *Bogor*) was a cherished spot south of Batavia, the residence of the governor general, and the location of the famous botanical garden. The other names are towns on the road which circles the complex of mountains and volcanoes of Gunung Pangrango and Gunung Gedé. The recurrent prefix *tji* is Sundanese for "water" or "river."

71   *The botanical garden* in Buitenzorg was founded in 1817 by Reinwardt. Its real development as a world famous horticultural center dates from the period between 1837 and 1844 under the direction of Teysmann and Hasskarl. Under the direction of Treub (from 1880 to 1909) the garden increased in significance, while adding experimental stations, laboratoria, and a scientific library.

Mt. Salak is a volcano situated on the border between the former residencies of Batavia and Preanger.

Tonggèret is the name, derived from Sundanese, for a kind of cricket.

72   *Tjibatu* is a village near Buitenzorg.

Peujeum or *peujem* is Sundanese for a leavened Sundanese cake made from moist, grated cassava that has fermented a little and has an odor of alcohol.

73 The interim administration of *Raffles* (1811 to 1816): that period during which Holland was annexed by Napoleon, and when the British, as a result of their war with France, took over the Dutch colonies.

Gamelan, a Javanese and Balinese word, from *bergamel*, which means "to make music." It constitutes the Javanese orchestra used for *wajang* performances (see below), dances, or just for the music itself, although the last is not frequent. Some of the instruments of a *gamelan* orchestra are the *rebab*, a kind of violin with two strings, a *suling* or flute of bamboo, drums, gongs, varieties of an instrument resembling a vibraphone such as the *saron*, the *gambang gangsa*, *gambang kaju* and so forth. The Javanese *gamelan* music and instruments have a complicated history and ritualistic significance. A brief description, in English, may be found in Frits A. Wagner, *The Art of Indonesia* (New York: Greystone Press, 1967), pp. 172–75, and in the first volume of Raffles, *History of Java* (1817; reprint ed., Kuala Lumpur: Oxford University Press, 1978), 1:469–72. The serious student of Indonesian music must refer to J. Kunst, *Music in Java: Its History, Its Theory, and Its Technique*, ed. E. L. Heins, 3d enlarged ed., 2 vols. (The Hague: Martinus Nijhoff, 1973).

Wajang kulit. This is a form of Javanese theater which may be even more complicated than the *gamelan* music that often accompanies such performances. The word *wajang* (or *wayang*) is Javanese (in Malay: *bayang*) for "shadow," hence, by extension, a "shadow play." *Kulit* means "outer skin," "rind," or "peel." Together *wajang kulit* designates a shadow play performed with puppets cut from thin leather. *Wajang kulit* is also called *wajang purwa* because this is the oldest form of Javanese theater. There is also a *wajang golek*, which is a performance with three-dimensional puppets, and a *wajang topeng*, which is performed by actors with masks. The performer of a *wajang kulit* play is called a *dalang*; the person sits behind a screen of white cloth (*kelir*) and moves the puppets across this screen lit by the light of a lamp called a *blenkong*. The *dalang* manipulates the puppets while narrating the texts of the various plays. At first the stories told by the *dalang* were old mythological legends from Java, or episodes from such Sanskrit epics as the *Mahabharata* and the *Ramayana*. Originally, *wajang* was connected with religious or ritualistic ceremonies. A comprehensive discussion of southeast Asian theater (including music and dance) may be found in James R. Brandon: *Theatre in Southeast Asia* (1967; reprint ed., Cambridge, Mass.: Harvard University Press, 1974) which includes a bibliography. A short popular work in English is Amin Sweeney, *Malay Shadow Puppets* (London: Publications of the British Museum, 1972). One text of the *wajang purwa* repertoire was recently translated into Dutch, with an extensive introduction and notes, by J. J. Ras, *De schending van Soebadra. Javaans schimmenspel* (Amsterdam: Meulenhoff, 1976). There is a competent translation of three of these plays (with an introduction and notes) in English. James R. Brandon, *On Thrones of Gold: Three Javanese Shadow Plays* (Cambridge, Mass.: Harvard University Press, 1970).

74 *Niemantsverdriet* literally means "no one's sorrow."

75 *Akar wanggi* (or *wangi*), also called *narawastu* or *larasetu*. These are roots (*akar*) of a type of grass that was once known as *Andropogon muricatus*, but is now called *Vetiveria zizanoides*. The aromatic roots produce an oil (vetiver oil) used in per-

fumes. The British also called it cuscus oil. In British India mats or screens were woven of the fibrous roots and placed in the window openings during the season of hot dry winds. When they were kept wet the wind caused these screens to give off a fragrant vapor that both cooled the room and scented the air.

Ketumbar is the herb *Coriandrum sativum* or coriander.

76 The *sweets* mentioned on this page are cookies (*kwee*), the very common but delicious fried bananas (*pisang goreng*), bananas cooked in water (*pisang rebus*), and roasted corn (*djagung*).

Tuan kandjeng was in Java a form of address to persons of status, formerly reserved for princes.

77 *Elephant plant* (in Dutch: *olifantspoot*) is an herbaceous plant (*Elephantopus scaber*) of the *Compositae* family. This common plant is used for a native medicine, and its young and tender leaves are used as fodder for cattle. In Javanese the plant is called *tapak liman*. *Tapak* means the palm of one's hand or the sole of one's foot, also "footstep." *Liman* means elephant.

Lampu tèmplèk is a little oil lamp with a wick, a chimney, and a polished brass mirror. The mirror is meant to cast the light of the lamp back into the room.

78 The various dishes mentioned on this page are all part of a colonial dinner called a *rijsttafel*. The basic food was rice with (what used to be) some sixty side dishes. *Trassi* is a shrimp paste; *sambal* is a condiment made from hot peppers and a variety of other ingredients; *empal* is roasted meat; *rempejeh* are deep-fried cookies made of rice meal, spices, shrimp, coriander (*ketumbar*), or peanuts; *ketan* refers to a way of cooking rice in which the kernels stay moist and stick together, so that they can be mixed with other ingredients such as grated coconut (*klapper*) or *kintja*, a concoction of coconut milk, sugar, palm sugar, and vanilla.

A *wedana* is a Javanese district official who is below the regent but superior to the chiefs of individual towns or villages.

Tjempaka is a kind of magnolia with fragrant yellow flowers (*Michelia champaca*). *Desa* is the Javanese term for a village in the country (what in Malay is called a *kampong*) and is a common term.

79 *Stephanotis* is the plant *Stephania hernandifolia*. This is an herbaceous climbing plant with tiny flowers. The bulbous roots are sold by native herbalists as *tjintjau minjak*, a remedy against fever and stomach cramps.

Bungur tree is a tall tree—usually over a hundred feet—which is common in the Malay archipelago. The wood is used to build houses and bridges. The tree is also valuable to the native population for its leaves and flowers, which are used as an herbal medicine, for example, to cure hemorrhoids. This *Lagerstroemia speciosa* has the peculiarity that it is without leaves for months while it blooms; its flowers are first white, then pink, and finally purple.

81 *Dezentjé* was Ernest Dezentjé, a very popular painter of mixed blood, who painted tasteless, stereotyped tropical scenes.

83 *Boleh turun*—"[It] can go down." That is, "it can be sent to the servants' quarters."

86 *Dukun* is Javanese for an herbalist, sorcerer, or one who presides over certain ceremonies and rituals. *Dukuns* can, among other things, be specialists at harvest and circumcision ceremonies and at finding lost objects, interpreting dreams, or acting as mediums. Female *dukuns* can be midwives, helpers at wedding ceremonies,

or masseuses. *Dukuns* are still very important for daily Javanese life. See Clifford Geertz, *The Religion of Java*, pp. 86–111.

Priok is an abbreviation of Tandjung Priok, the harbor of Batavia, some five miles north of the city. It was built toward the last quarter of the nineteenth century after the Suez Canal was opened in 1869. The building of the harbor started in 1877, and by 1886 it was in use. It is connected to Batavia by a canal, a railroad, and a highway.

Petit Trouville was a bathing resort near Priok.

87   *Selamatan* is, in Java, a communal feast of a religious nature. A *selamatan* can be given for the most varied of reasons—births, deaths, harvest, bad dreams, and so on—and is held in the evening, only attended by males. The food is prescribed according to the occasion, incense is burned, the host gives a formal speech to present the reason for the gathering, and a prayer is chanted with each pause punctuated by the *amien* ("Amen") of the participants. Then the food is distributed according to a certain procedure, and each person eats a small portion of it. Most of the uneaten food is taken home. For the role of the *selamatan* in contemporary Javanese life, see Clifford Geertz, *The Religion of Java*, pp. 11–85.

Hadji is a Mohammedan who has been on a pilgrimage to Mecca. From the Arabic *haj*. The word is also used as a prefix of respect for anyone who is making or has made such a pilgrimage. From the Malay archipelago such pilgrims usually went by boat, often decrepit freighters with little to recommend them. The moral issue of Joseph Conrad's *Lord Jim* centers around such a ship and such a crowd of *hadjis*.

Kain plekat refers to a material that had a plaid pattern woven into the cloth, rather than being superimposed as with batik. The Javanese word *plekat* comes from *Palikat*, the name of a town in India from where this cloth originally came.

Kopiah is a man's cap made of black velvet. It may be described as a fez without a tassel.

Tawar is the verb in Malay for haggling, an activity that is mandatory if one wants to buy something either in a shop or in an open market.

Tikar is a floormat for people to sit on.

Amien, usually spelled *amin*, is Arabic for "amen," meaning "so be it." In Arabic it also means "trustworthy" and is a proper name.

88   *Slendang* is a cloth that forms a sling. Worn across the chest, over one shoulder, and across the back, at hip height, women use it, usually, to carry an infant or young child.

The *Buginese* are a remarkable people from southwest Celebes. They are a maritime people who displaced the Javanese and Malay as the marine traders in the archipelago. The heart of their land is the region called Boni (or Bone) in Celebes on the Gulf of Boni.

A *balé-balé* is a low bench made of bamboo either to recline or sleep on.

89   *Lower town* refers to what in Dutch is called the "Benedenstad" of Batavia, meaning the old seventeenth- and eighteenth-century city of Batavia. Europeans no longer lived there after 1870.

Djamu is Javanese for a medicine, usually one administered by a *dukun*.

90   *Molenvliet* was the canal dug to connect the old city of Batavia with its newer "suburbs," such as Weltevreden. By 1656 it was used as a means of transportation.

It was once famous for the estates that bordered on it and its busy atmosphere of commerce, as well as for the Javanese women who did their laundry in the canal or bathed in it. It can also refer to the road that ran alongside the canal.

Gang Kenanga was the name for a street in old Batavia. *Gang* is Malay for "passageway" derived from the Dutch *gang*.

Guling called a *rolkussen* in Dutch, was a long kind of bolster, used in bed. It has been called a "Dutch wife," though the *Oxford English Dictionary* defines "Dutch wife" as "an open frame of ratan or cane used in the Dutch East Indies, etc. to rest the limbs upon in bed."

Njonja kumis can be translated as "Madam Mustache." *Kumis* means "mustache" and *njonja* means "madam" or "lady," indicating a woman of position.

Menjan is incense, properly speaking benzoin or gum-benjamin, an aromatic resin from the *Styrax benzoin* plant. The term "benzoin" comes from Arabic *luban-Jawi*, which meant "frankincense from Java," although Java here meant Sumatra, which is where most of this resin was once found.

91 *Malam djumahat* refers to the period from dusk on Thursday evening until sunrise Friday morning. *Malam* means "night." Orientals often count a week by nights, because they figure the day to begin at sunset, hence *malam ahad* is Sunday night for them but Saturday night to us.

The holy cannon mentioned here is a fertility fetish, although cannons were also regal *pusakas* (see above). When Cornelis Speelman besieged Macassar for the second time in 1668, the fort of the sultan did not really fall until the Dutch captured the holy cannon, called *Anak Macassar*. For the history of this famous cannon see K. C. Crucq, "De geschiedenis van het heilig kanon van Makassar," *Tijdschrift voor Indische Taal-, Land- en Volkenkunde* 81 (1841):74–95.

In Surakarta in Java, one will also find such a cannon, associated with the royal family. It is called "Satomi" because it is believed that the spirit of a woman by that name passed into the cannon. It is kept in the *kraton* (royal compound) and is reputed to warn the monarch of impending dangers. The spirit of Njai Satomi's husband is said to have passed into another cannon in Batavia, having traveled on its own from Surakarta to Batavia. It is this cannon that is believed to promote fertility in women because it has a knob toward the back of the piece, which the Javanese see as a phallic symbol. Barren women court its favor with offerings of rice and flowers and then straddle the cannon, lowering themselves down onto the knob. See G. A. Wilken, "Het animisme bij de volken van den Indischen Archipel," *De Indische Gids*, 6, pt. 2 (1884), pp. 60–61. The cannon was called "Si Djagur" and "Kjai Setama," was over twelve feet long, and was still there when Aldous Huxley visited Batavia in the twenties. He describes it as follows: "The Malays may call themselves Moslems; but they are still, at heart and by nature, animists. Nor is it to the spirits alone that they pay their devotions. There is no God but God and Mohammed is his prophet. No doubt. But a cannon is cylindrical and, long before they became Moslems, the Javanese were worshippers of the reproductive principle in nature. An immemorial phallism has crystallised round the old gun, transforming it from a mere brass tube into a potent deity, to be propitiated with flowers and little lanterns, to be asked favours of with smoking incense. Men come and, standing before the sacred symbol, silently implore assistance. Women desirous of offspring sit on the prostrate god, rub themselves against his verdigrised sides and pray to him for increase. Even white ladies, it is said, may be seen at evening alighting inconspicuously from their motor cars at the Penang Gate. They hurry across the grass to where the God is lying. They drop a few gardenias and a supplication, they touch the God's unresponsive muzzle; then hurry back again through the twilight, fearful of being recognised, of being caught in the flagrant act of worshipping at the shrine of a God, who was being adored a thousand generations before Adam was ever thought of and beside whom the Gods of Zoroaster and the Vedas, of Moses and Christ and Mohammed are the merest upstarts and parvenus." Aldous Huxley, *Jesting Pilate. An Intellectual Holiday* (New York: George H. Doran Co., 1926), pp. 207–8.

93   *Bandjermasin* was a district in southeast Borneo, opposite the island Laut. This former sultanate became involved with the Dutch when the latter came to trade for pepper and forest products. From about the middle of the nineteenth century the colonial government was constantly embroiled with native guerilla warfare, until the first decade of this century. *Blauwhoedenveem* was a company, originally from Amsterdam, which cared for the storage and transportation of various goods and products.

95   *Rembrandt.* The S. S. *Rembrandt* was built in 1906, and sold as scrap in 1928. The liners that sailed between Holland and the colonial Indies evoke, perhaps more than anything else, a sense of nostalgia in the minds of Dutch colonialists. Three recent books evoke this vanished era of ocean liners and boat-trains: Rudy Kousbroek, *Een passage naar Indië* (Amsterdam: De Harmonie, 1978); A. Alberts, *Per Mailboat naar de Oost* (Bussum: De Boer Maritiem, 1979); *Selamat djalan* (Amsterdam: Kosmos, 1980). *Selamat djalan* is Malay for "have a good trip."

After the Suez Canal was opened on November 16, 1869, it became feasible to establish a regular service between Holland and its colonies. In 1870 the shipping company, N. V. Stoomvaart Maatschappij Nederland (Royal Netherlands Mail Line), was established in Amsterdam, and in 1875 the Rotterdamsche Lloyd was established in Rotterdam. In 1883, these two companies agreed to consolidate their services so that from 1889 there was a biweekly sailing from Holland to the Indies. The S. S. *Rembrandt* belonged to the N. V. Stoomvaart Maatschappij Nederland. That company had a boat-train (from 1926), which started in The Hague and went via Cologne, Basel, and Milan to Genoa; the Rotterdam Lloyd also had such a train, also departing from The Hague, but going via Paris to Marseille. Passengers boarded the ship either in Genoa or in Marseille, and followed a route that seldom varied, through the Suez Canal with Port Said as a foretaste of the tropics. Passengers could disembark there and go shopping, especially in the famous Simon Arzt department store, which was founded by a family of German Jews. It became almost a ritual to buy Simon Arzt Egyptian cigarettes as proof that one had been in Port Said. These were flat, oval-shaped cigarettes, sold in either tins or flat boxes, and were usually smoked by women. If one did not leave the ship, passengers could buy souvenirs, such as pouffes or handbags, from the bumboats that bobbed up and down far below the promenade deck. The next memorable part of the journey was crossing the Red Sea, probably the hottest part of the trip. This was followed by a brief stay in Colombo, the large harbor of the island Ceylon (now Sri Lanka). From Colombo it was only three days to Sabang and the first encounter with the Indies. Sabang is a harbor on the little island of Pulau Weh, right off the northernmost tip of Sumatra. After Belawan (a harbor on the east coast of Sumatra, halfway between Sabang and Singapore) and Singapore, the ship would proceed to its major port, Tandjong Priok, the harbor of Batavia. It would then steam along the northern coast of Java, to Semarang and Surabaja. The return trip reversed the itinerary, calling on the same ports.

Life on board these ships, and on the boat-trains as well, was luxurious. Those who had never been to the Indies had their first encounter with the exotic in the person of the (usually) Javanese waiter, called a *djongos*, in his white jacket and batiked headcloth. This mode of traveling reached its heyday between 1920 and 1940.

96   *Djokja* (Djokjakarta) is the name both of the capital and of the district on the southern coast of Java.

Bloot means "nude" in Dutch; when this man introduces himself he is saying "I'm naked."

97   *Vieux Doelen* is a hotel in The Hague. Most of the streets mentioned in the subsequent pages were part of a section of The Hague where retired personnel from the colonies settled. Around 1940 some 60,000 of them lived in a city of about half a million inhabitants. A nineteenth-century account of such people living in The Hague can be found in the novel *Indische mensen in Holland* by P. A. Daum, first published serially in Batavia in 1888, and as a book in 1890; a modern reprint is P. A. Daum, *Indische mensen in Holland* (Amsterdam: Querido, 1980).

Bau banké means "the smell of a corpse." *Bau* means a "scent" or "odor," either pleasant or unpleasant, and *banké* or *bangkai* is a carcass of an animal or, contemptuously, a human corpse.

98   *Country of origin* here used as a phrase, is meant to provide the reader with the allusion to a celebrated novel (a fictionalized autobiography) *Het land van herkomst* (*Country of Origin*) by E. Du Perron (1899–1940), published in 1935. This book, along with Multatuli's *Max Havelaar* are the two most celebrated texts of Dutch colonial literature. *Het land van herkomst* was published in a French translation as *Le pays d'origine* (Paris: Gallimard, 1980), and its first English translation is forthcoming in this series.

Rambutan is the fruit of the *rambutan* tree (*Nephelium lappaceum*). This red fruit with a spiny rind is very popular in the Malay archipelago. The fruit flesh is eaten either raw or cooked, and has a tart taste.

99   *Malu* is a Malay term for experiencing, either in a good or a bad sense, a feeling of shame. Hence: "to be modest," "to be shy," but also "to be shameless," "to be disgraced," "to be embarrassed," or "to be dishonored." In a mystical sense *malu* means "humility before God," and *bibir-bibir kemaluan* is Malay for the pudenda, *bibir* meaning lip (i.e., lips of modesty).

Amok means here merely "angry," but this word, which has become part of our language, usually meant a furious attack by a native who would kill indiscriminately until he is put out of commission. It may well be interpreted as a form of suicide. That this was not rare may be deduced from the fact that in Java there was a special implement in the guardhouse (*gerdu*) to subdue a man running *amok*. This was a large fork with teeth or thorns, called *tjanggah* in Javanese. Yule in his marvelous dictionary *Hobson-Jobson*, ed. W. Crooke (1886, 1903; reprint ed., New Delhi: Munshiram Manoharlal Publishers, 1979) has a long entry on this word (pp. 18–23), arguing that its origin may well come from India. He notes that it was first used in English in 1672 by Andrew Marvell. One may compare it to what in Scandinavian lore is called "berserk." Multatuli once defined running *amok* as "committing suicide in the company of others."

102 *Ethical policy of the government.* Generally assumed to have begun in 1900, this policy legislated a revised relationship between the kingdom of the Netherlands and its colonies. The government in The Hague was no longer to rule the Indies for the sake of the Dutch nation, but was to prepare the colonies for self-government, which included investing large sums in the nascent future of an independent nation. The financial expenditure was justified by Van Deventer (1857–1915) in 1899 as a "debt of honor." Fransen van de Putte (1822–1902), who was a minister of the colonies, stated in 1900 that Holland's colonial rule should be done with "clean hands" and that extensive reforms should be instituted "for conscience's sake." These liberal precepts were turned into practical reality during the first two decades of this century. Holland extended its rule over most of the archipelago, although up until that time it had restricted itself to Java and certain selected regions of what were called the "outer possessions." By extending its control the colonial government aimed at rehabilitating the life of the entire native population by improving the educational system, medical services (especially inoculation programs against epidemic diseases), agrarian reforms, and by offering financial assistance to the small farmer. The government wrote into law the decentralization act of 1903, which divided the nearly absolute power of Batavia among more localized administrations meant to include native representation.

In 1918 a People's Council was created to provide increased legislative power to the inhabitants of the Indies, and in 1922 the constitution was revised so that it would no longer regard the colonies as part of the kingdom but as equal territorial regions. The program of liberalization was executed by such governor generals as Idenburg who served from 1909 to 1916, Van Limburg Stirum (1916–1921), and De Graeff (1926–1931).

Perhaps the major irony of this process of democratization was that it also provided the impetus for a burgeoning nationalistic movement, which culminated with Indonesia's declaration of independence in 1945.

The governor general referred to in the text is probably Van Limburg Stirum. A brief discussion of this policy may be found in R. Nieuwenhuys, *Tussen twee vaderlanden* (Amsterdam: Van Oorschot, 1967), pp. 13–16.

103 *J. P. Coen* was a liner of the Royal Netherlands Mail Line, built in 1915. The Dutch sunk it in 1940 in Holland to block the entry to the harbor of IJmuiden.

104 *Udjan kapok* is a Malay descriptive phrase for "snow." *Udjan* means "rain," and *kapok* is Javanese for "tree cotton," the silky down that is found in the seeds of the silk-cotton tree (*Ceiba pentandra*). Hence snow is "a shower of white down."

107 *Bèot*, the *babu* mentioned in this novel is based on Nieuwenhuys' *babu* in the Indies. To this day there are retired colonialists in Holland who still go through the house purifying it by burning *menjan*.

108 *Buntut djangkrik* means in Javanese literally "the tail of a cricket." *Buntut* means a "person's behind," "the stern of a ship," or a "tail," and *djangrik* refers to a Javanese cricket. Hence it means here a hair curl that looks like a little tail.

111 The author furnished the information that *Sudarpo* was modeled upon a Javanese called Setijadjit who took part in the Communist uprising in 1948. The uprising took place in the fall of that year in the southern region of middle Java, in the city

of Surakarta—which lies west of the volcano Gunung Lawu—and the city of Madiun, east of the same mountain. That region was held by the republican forces of Indonesia which was then ruled by Sukarno and Hatta. The political background is complex but a summary of the events follows.

Surakarta was saved from leftist forces in September, but the PKI (the Indonesian Communist Party) took over the city Madiun and a number of smaller towns about mid-September of that year. However, the popular uprising they had counted on did not materialize and Sukarno publicly expressed his disapproval of the takeover. The republican government took military action, not only because it was anti-Communist but also because it feared Dutch intervention if it appeared that Indonesia would turn Communist. In less than two weeks the Indonesian army defeated the Communist sympathizers and managed to kill or capture most of the leaders. The republican forces took revenge and executed some 8,000 people. See Jan Pluvier, *Indonesië, kolonialisme, onafhankelijkheid, neo-kolonialisme. Een politieke geschiedenis van 1940 tot heden* (Nijmegen: Sun, 1978), pp. 91-98. *Magelang* is another city in central Java, east of the mountain Gunung Merbabu. *Doctor djawa* is a native physician (see above, note for p. 36).

Alun-alun is, here, a general term for a village square, or a square in a city. Originally, however, it referred in Java to a large quadrangle, covered with grass, surrounded by waringin trees, with one or two trees in its center, in front of a royal palace.

114 *Rozenburg plates* refers to Dutch pottery manufactured by the Rozenburg works in The Hague. It is now expensive and not easily found because of its limited production. The pottery is famous for its delicate art nouveau patterns and its eggshell porcelain. The decorative plates and vases were made between 1899 and 1914.

115 *Sajur lodeh, babi ketjap, sambelans*, and *serundeng* are all Indonesian dishes. *Sajur lodeh* is a kind of vegetable dish with soup meat, cabbage, bamboo sprouts, string beans, various spices, and coconut milk; *babi ketjap* is a pork dish with soy sauce and various spices; *sambelans* or *sambals* refers to the many varieties of a condiment made from hot peppers and other ingredients; *serundeng* is grated coconut mixed with peanuts and coriander (*ketumbar*) and toasted.

Jack Smith was a British baritone, very popular at the time, who sang almost in a whisper.

Kurhaus was and is an entertainment complex in the fashionable resort town north of The Hague, called Scheveningen.

The Ramblers were a very popular seven-member Dutch dance band with an amazing longevity. First organized in 1926 it lasted for thirty-eight years, until 1964. From about 1933 the band was also very popular on radio and, during the war, they were heard via the BBC. They played a kind of music that mixed jazz and popular music, and had as guests various notable jazz artists such as Coleman Hawkins and Benny Carter. By coincidence the leader of the band, Theo Uden Masman, was born in 1901 in Cheribon in Java. He died in 1965.

127 *Klontong* also spelled *kelontong*, is Malay and Javanese for a Chinese peddler who used to announce his arrival with a kind of rattle, which was also called a *kelontong*. Here the term is meant to be derogatory. *Budjang* is the word for "bachelor," but also has connotations of "servant" or "worker." Hence it means here something like an "office drudge" or "office slave."

130 The negative aspect of the *dream* here is suggested by the color purple. *Owls* are also

a negative symbol because the native population feared them, and their cry was considered a bad omen.

131 *Tabeh tuan muda* means literally: "Greetings young master." *Tabeh* is the common word for "hello," *tuan* is the common Malay word for "master" or "lord" and was the customary form when addressing male Europeans. *Muda* means "young," "unripe," or "of a pale coloring," also used in the sense of "junior."

134 *Mandi room* is the room where one took a bath. *Mandi* means "bathing," "to bathe in a river," and *siram* meant to pour water over one's body. The *mandi* room usually had a square container of cement or stone, fairly large, which held fresh water. There was a bucket called *gajung* (like a New England sap bucket) with a wooden grip placed between the two sides and just below the rim. This was dipped into the water and then lifted to pour over one's body. One never bathed *in* the water.
Klipsteen means literally in Dutch "a piece of stone broken off a rock or cliff." In the Indies it also meant a coral rock and was a derogatory term for an "Indo" or Eurasian.

135 *Djamu* was a herbal concoction drunk as medicine, and "to *pidjit*" meant to give a massage; this was usually done by the female servant of the lady of the house. It is a kind of massage where the flesh is kneaded and slightly pounded, not rubbed.
Petéh (also *pete* or *petai*) is Javanese for the beans in the pod of a tree (*Parkia speciosa*), which stink but are considered good to eat, and are also used in *sambals*.
Raden Saleh and *Pasar Baru* were streets in Batavia.
Sapi-Ie was a shoe store in colonial Batavia that was owned by an Indonesian. This was rare, and the store was one of the first with native ownership (author's information).

136 *Panàs* means "hot," *kipas* is a "fan" and the phrase *Allah tobat, panas* means "Good God, it's hot."

137 *Siram* means here "to take a bath" by pouring water over one's body.
Koppie tubruk is a kind of black coffee drunk in Indonesia. It is made in a cup by pouring hot water over the coffee and letting it brew there.
Orang udik means a person who lives in the country, as opposed to a city dweller.

138 *Kulit bulé* means "a very white skin." *Kulit* is "skin" and *bulé* is Javanese for "albino."

140 *Gerzon* was a fashionable woman's shop.

142 *Licht, Luft und Sonne* and *Deutsche Jungen und Maedel*—German phrases meaning "light, air, and sun," and "German boys and girls."

144 *Rumah sial* means an unlucky house. *Rumah* means "house," and *sial*, "bringing bad luck" or "ill-omened."

147 *Lembang* was a city in the Preanger region in the southern foothills of the volcano Tangkuban Prahu, north of Bandung. The city had a high elevation and, therefore, enjoyed a good climate, for which reason a sanitorium was built there. Lembang was also the city where the great naturalist, Junghuhn, spent the last years of his life; he died there in 1864. Because he was developing methods to grow cinchona trees in Java, the city became the center of quinine research. Junghuhn is included in the anthology of this series.

148 *Sados* and *deelemans* were similar carriages. A deeleman was small, had two wheels, with a canopy over the seat of the passenger who entered by a small door in the back of the carriage. It was pulled by a single horse. It was called after its designer Charles Theodore Deeleman (1823–1893), an engineer. The carriage was some-

what fragile and was, perhaps, not designed for heavy Dutchmen but for the more slender Javanese. See the article: H. J. de Graaf, "Charles Theodore Deeleman," in *Moesson* 25, no. 1 (July 1980): 6–8.

151 The *kembodja* tree is the *Plumiera acutifolia*, known for its white and yellow flowers, for a white sap which oozes from the trunk at even the slightest cut, and the distinctive pattern of its branches. It is particularly associated with cemeteries because it was often planted in graveyards, and in this is similar to our cypresses. *Kembodja* or *kambodja* is Javanese, although in Malay the tree is also called *bunga kubur* or *tjempaka biru*, i.e., "the blue tjempaka." Perhaps it is better known to us as frangipani.

Gado-gado is an Indonesian salad of various vegetables such as cabbage, French beans, beansprouts, usually in a sharp sauce.

Glossary

Unless otherwise noted, the words are Malay. If the word or phrase is not listed in the glossary, consult the notes.

adu (or *adoh*): a common interjection expressing disbelief or astonishment.

alun-alun: a general term for a village square.

amok: here merely "angry," but more often referring to that furious state of mind in which one will kill indiscriminately.

baadje: is the Dutch diminutive of the Malay word *kabaja* (see below), a kind of jacket.

babu: Javanese for a female servant with various functions.

badju kaos: undershirt.

bébé: a long loose house dress, like a shift or muumuu.

besaran: large house; from *besar*, meaning "big" or "important."

betinka: derived from *tingkah*, it here means "to have a fit" or "whims."

desa: Javanese for "village."

djait: seamstress.

djamu: Javanese for a medicine, usually administered by a *dukun*.

djas tutup: a man's jacket, buttoned down the front and with a closed, standing collar.

djeruk: the generic term in Javanese for citrus fruit.

djongos: Javanese for houseboy, servant. It may be a corruption of Dutch *jongens* meaning "boys."

es puter: ice cream. *Es* is a corruption of the Dutch word for ice: *ijs*.

gendih: water jug of unglazed earthenware.

gudang: a storage room, warehouse, shed.

hadji: a Mohammedan who has made a pilgrimage to Mecca.

hidung pesek: a flat nose. *Hidung* means "nose."

hormat: a show of honor or respect due to a social superior.

kabaja: a loose jacket worn by women, which reaches just below the hips. Its front is open and it has no buttons. To close it one uses the *kerosang*, three brooches connected by a small silver chain. It has long, narrow sleeves. A *kabaja tjina* was worn by men, especially the Dutch, and was a loose cotton jacket with an upright collar.

kakeh or *kakek*: Javanese for "grandfather," "an old person."

kali: Javanese for river.

kampong is Malay for a village. In Javanese it can also mean a neighborhood or section of a city, or a compound (a single house). Javanese uses the term *desa* for an independent hamlet. The Dutch used *kampong* most frequently. In this novel it is also a metonymy for "going native."

kasar: rough, coarse; here applied to people, and meaning therefore, "unmannerly," "boorish."

kassian: literally "to feel pity, sympathy, mercy." It was a very common expression used by Dutch colonialists for anything that one felt sorry for. Comparable to the Spanish *pobrecito*.

kebon: a "garden"; it can also be an abbreviation of *tukang kebon*, the gardener.

kebonan: enclosed garden, an estate.

kepala batu: literally "head of stone," what we call "pigheaded."

kètjap: soy sauce.

kipas: fan, used by women to cool themselves.

klambu: gauze curtain hung over a bed to keep mosquitoes out.

klewang: a single-edged sword, similar to a machete.

klontong: street vendor, usually Chinese. The word derives from the rattle he used to announce his arrival.

kondé: a woman's hair style in which the hair is combed back and pulled tight to form a bun at the nape of the neck.

kramas: Javanese for "to wash," here also to clean a floor by scrubbing it with soap. The Javanese didn't use soap but used ashes from burned rice stalks.

krossie males: popular variation of *kursi malas*, from Arabic for "chair" and Malay for "idle," "lazy." This was what the British called a "long chair"; it often had a curved back and armrests that could be extended to the front to rest one's legs on.

kulit langsep: a Javanese simile for an admired fawn-colored complexion. *Kulit* (skin) *bule* means a skin as white as that of an albino.

lampu: lamp or light; i.e., *lampu abang*, red stoplight.

lengang: refers to a swaying motion. In Javanese romances, heroes had such a walk, a mild swagger. However, it is meant here to indicate a sinuous swaying of the hips while walking.

lepas: literally "freed," "loose," "open." Here it means "to let go," i.e., "to be dismissed."

malu: to be shy, ashamed, or embarrassed.

mandi room: the room where one takes a bath, not a room with a toilet.

mandur: an overseer, foreman. Probably derived from Portugese *mandador*. In Sundanese it could also refer to the head of a village.

melatti (or *melati*): a variety of jasmine.

menjan: incense; properly benzoin or gumbenjamin.

nassi (or *nasi*): rice, in the sense of the staple food of the Indies, or as cooked in a particular way, such as *nassi tim*, which is rice steamed in a "bain-marie."

nonna: Javanese for an unmarried European woman; "miss" or "young lady." This is not to be confused with *njonja*, which indicates a married woman of certain social rank.

njonja besar: the "great lady," the wife of a wealthy or socially prominent man.

obat seriawan: *obat* means anything used as an antidote for a disease, and *seriawan* refers to the disease called "sprue" and the leaves and bark of the *Symplocos odoratissima* tree. Hence: a medicine to cure sprue.

orang blanda: Dutchman or, in general, a European.

orang udik: a person who lives in the country, rather than in an urban environment.

pajong: umbrella. It can also mean a parasol that was held over the head of royalty or nobility to indicate rank.

panas: hot, warm, heat (especially solar heat).

papaja (in English "papaya"): a large, yellow fruit, similar to a melon (*Carica papaya*).

pasanggrahan: a word derived from Javanese, meaning a resthouse or shelter for travelers.

pasar: market.

pedis (also spelled *pedes* or *pedas*): hot, peppery, sharp taste.

perkara: from Sanskrit for "matter," "affair," or "concern." Here it means "family affairs." *Perkara ketjil* means "a small matter or concern."

pisang: banana; either the tree or the fruit.

pondok: a shelter for the night; a lean-to, hut, or shanty.

pusaka: revered heirlooms (a fuller discussion is given in the notes to chapter 3).

rambutan: a red fruit with spiny rind and a tart taste (*Nephelium lappaceum*).

rantang: a hamper; a stout basket made of rattan, bamboo, or the like, to carry provisions.

rèpot: Javanese for being difficult or causing trouble.

rèwèl: to be quarrelsome, hard to get along with; *tukang rèwèl* means to have a "difficult boss."

rijsttafel: the Dutch word (both a noun and a verb) to indicate the main meal eaten by the Dutch in colonial Indies. Its main ingredient was plain rice, but it had a large variety of side dishes.

rudjak: a fruit salad with a hot sauce.

sado: a small carriage with two wheels, a canopy over the part where the passenger sits, pulled by a small horse. From French *dos-à-dos*.

sambal: a condiment eaten with *rijsttafel*, made from hot peppers and a large variety of other ingredients.

sampiran: a term from Batavia, derived from Sundanese, meaning a clothes tree that was covered by mosquito netting, also *sampiran kain*.

sarong: the skirt worn by both men and women. Usually batiked.

sawa (or *sawah*): irrigated rice field.

sèbèl: Javanese for "to be unlucky."

sial: means "bad luck" or an ill omen.

sobat: a word from around Batavia, from the Arabic *sahabat* (a term used in Malay), meaning a friend, a companion.

susa: trouble or worry.

tawar: Malay verb for haggling. A person never paid whatever price was first mentioned in either an open market or a store.

tikar: floormat to sit on.

tinka or *tingkah*: its most common meaning was "whim" (as of a spoiled child), or "having a fit."

tjebok: the meaning here is that after one has relieved oneself, instead of wiping with toilet paper one washes by pouring water from a bottle or can.

tjempaka: a magnolia variety.

toko: a Javanese word for "shop" in general, and a Chinese shop in particular. Chinese *tokos* were famous among the colonial Europeans for containing the most amazing variety of goods in a small space.

totok: term from Javanese ("genuine," "full-blooded") that came to mean a full-blooded European, especially a Dutchman.

trassi (or *trasi* or *terasi*): a general word for a condiment used with *rijsttafel*. The best-known variety is *trasi udang*, a paste made from shrimp, which have been left to dry in the sun, then pounded to a paste, and left to ferment. The strong smell of *trasi* is unmistakable.

tuan besar: literally "the big boss"; *tuan* means "Mr." or "Sir," even "lord," and *besar* means "big" or "important."

tukang kebon: a gardener. Strictly speaking a *tukang* is a man trained in handicrafts. *Kebon* (or *kebun*) is a garden, hence someone well versed in tending a garden.

udik: here "the country," as in "living in the country." It also means "upstream."